Every Life Treasured

Jennifer Q. Hunt,
Hannah Hood Lucero,
and
Aubrey Reiss Taylor

Edited by Sarah Everest
Cover by Kelsey Gietl
ISBN 979-8-9991324-0-6

A Mother's Tender Hand

by Jennifer Q. Hunt

Note: The condition called "Mongolism" in this book is now known as Down Syndrome. The word "retarded" is also used. These older terms are used for historical accuracy; they are offensive and should be avoided in modern usage.

Chapter 1

Wednesday, September 19, 1934

Alice Vogel stood before a mill cottage in need of fresh white paint and a new tin roof. It would get neither, she knew, for the inhabitants hadn't enough to eat. And that was why she was here.

She checked her Manila folder. The Tanner family. Father and Mother, both aged 44. He'd lost an arm in the Great War but had been working in Lindale's textile mill until an injury last month. Nine children, six still at home. The youngest, Bobby, aged three, was listed as retarded.

She walked up the concrete steps from the street into the front yard. An old tire had been made into a swing that hung from a towering oak, and two gray rockers on the porch gently swayed in the breeze of the autumn day. The sounds of children playing and a rooster crowing came from the backyard. Alice marched up the brick porch steps and rapped on the screen door.

The woman who answered her knock was predictable, exactly what Alice had anticipated. Graying brown hair. A missing tooth. Frumpy flour-sack dress over a gaunt and sagging figure. The smile, however? That was unexpected.

"May I help you, miss?" Kindness colored her tone, rather than suspicion, though her voice carried fatigue. A little boy rested on her hip. He looked too big to be lugged about, but

Alice guessed he was the youngest child. His eyes suggested Mongolism.

"I'm hoping I can help you, actually. My name is Alice Vogel, and I'm from the Floyd County Charitable Fund."

"Is this government help?"

"No, ma'am. It's a group of churches and businesses in the county who are trying to help those in need."

"Lotta folks worse off than we are," the woman answered cheerfully. "Did Seth ask you to come?"

"Seth?"

"My oldest boy."

"Oh. No, ma'am. One of the teachers at your children's school became concerned when the kids mentioned being hungry all the time."

The woman bit her bottom lip, and tears came to her eyes, which she quickly blinked away. "Reckon you ought to come in then."

The house felt stuffy. Mrs. Tanner waved at a kitchen chair and took the one across from her. A stained lace tablecloth covered the table, and a painted kerosene lamp sat in the middle of it. Alice detected a faint scent of Ivory Soap Flakes and woodsmoke. She guessed that the stove was wood-burning.

"My Ezra is laid up pretty bad," the woman volunteered, "but the doctor thinks he'll recover. We was doing all right when we had his income too. He's a supervisor over at the mill, ya know. Or was. I dunno if they'll give him his old position back." She bit her lip again.

"You said, 'his income too.' Is there another source of income for the household, then?"

"Well, Seth, of course. He's working twelve-hour shifts at the mill six days a week and taking on extra jobs as he can. That's how his daddy was hurt, though. Fell from a thirty-foot pine tree he was taking down, trying to earn a little extra. I hate Seth's doing the same and sometimes fixing automobiles late into the night, getting hardly any sleep. We need the money, but I don't need the worry."

"Any other source of income?"

"I can sew but just get mending occasionally. Most folks take care of it themselves."

"What would you estimate the monthly income to be?" Alice pulled the paperwork out of the folder and her Shaeffer pen from her purse and prepared to fill in the form.

"Miss Vogel, I don't mean to sound unthankful, but we ain't never accepted charity . . ."

This remained the most common objection Alice heard. While there were those who would lie and connive to collect greater benefits, the vast majority of once lower-middle-class hard-working people remained loath to take any sort of organized assistance, no matter how dire their situation.

"I understand," she recited, "but please do consider for your children's sake."

At this point, the child on Mrs. Tanner's lap began babbling the same two sounds over and over in a sing-song voice. She gave the boy a small wooden animal, which he proceeded to put in his mouth, then tried to hit her with. Alice pursed her lips in frustration—the child's annoying behavior distracting her from the task at hand—though his mother seemed not to notice.

"Mrs. Tanner, what do you have for supper tonight?"

The woman's face reddened. "I planned to cook up some grits in last night's bacon grease, and there's some okra and tomatoes left in the garden."

"Do you have food canned for the winter?"

"The garden didn't do well this year. I've been feeling poorly and then caring for Ez and Bobby. Seemed we had to eat everything that grew—"

"Are you aware that diseases such as pellagra, beriberi, and rickets are caused by lack of adequate nutrition? You are putting your family at great risk."

The woman sighed and blinked back tears again. "What do I need to do to get the food assistance?" she asked quietly.

"I'll just need you to verify the names and ages of everyone in the family and the monthly income, and we can get you some relief."

Mrs. Tanner looked over Alice's list of her family members. "Yes, that's right. My oldest two girls are married and Jimmy joined the Army a couple months ago. I miss that rascal." A fond smile brightened her careworn face.

Alice wondered how the woman could miss one out of such a crowd, especially when his absence gave some measure of relief to the dire situation. She bit back this thought and instead, glancing over the form without looking up, said, "And I assume you are not pregnant?"

When no answer was forthcoming, Alice paused, pen in hand, and met the woman's tired blue eyes.

"Actually, I am," she murmured.

Alice exhaled, hoping her shock didn't show on her face. Of all the stupid and irresponsible things! But she had no right to preach on that score. She had come to help this woman.

She nodded and made a note. Mrs. Tanner set Bobby on the floor. He said something that sounded like more senseless babble to Alice, but his mother said, "Yes, you may see Daddy."

On legs unsteady for his age, the child tottered off to the back of the house, and faintly from another room, she heard a man's enthusiastic greeting, "Hi-ho, there, Bobby-boy. Come and see me." Like Mrs. Tanner's smile, it was unexpected. Out of place for the desperation of this family.

"I'll be back tomorrow with a box of groceries to help," Alice said when the form was completed. She rose and smoothed her dress. "If I could find you a job, are you able to work?"

"I can't leave Bobby," Mrs. Tanner said. "It has to be work I can do here."

"I'll see what I can find," Alice promised. "Have you ever considered State Hospital for Bobby?"

Again, Mrs. Tanner worried her bottom lip. "I'm sure it doesn't make sense to you—or make sense on paper—but I'll starve before I'll send him away."

She spoke so matter-of-factly that Alice realized this was not a figurative or dramatic declaration, rather information on the priorities of this home. Mrs. Tanner was right. It didn't make sense. With the retarded child out of the way, the woman could take on work at the mill and have enough money for the family to meet their needs. How long had it been since she hadn't worried over the next meal? Since she had been to a doctor for herself? Since she had a decent garment? The woman would slowly die herself, inside and out, to keep a child with no future.

Alice disagreed with these priorities. Vehemently. But she must take her time. She'd gotten the woman to agree to food assistance. That was a start. There would be time to work on the rest later, especially if she brought a food box here each week.

"Let's go out the back door, and you can see the other children," Mrs. Tanner said as she also rose. The back door was opposite the front, and as they walked down the long hallway between, Alice peeked into the other rooms. The home was reasonably clean and tidy, though not perfectly so. The stench of diapers wafted through a utility room Alice assumed to be where the woman did her washing. Framed photos on a back wall showed babies and growing children. Alice paused before a photograph of a young couple that looked as if it had been taken in the early 1900s. It took her a moment to recognize Mrs. Tanner in the girlish face. The smile was the same.

Mrs. Tanner caught her gaze. "That was a long time ago," she said softly. "'Bout a year after Ezra and I were married. That girl didn't know how hard or how good it would be."

Alice wondered what the woman considered good from her life, but as she stepped out into the early evening, she sucked in her breath. A tall young man threw a baseball back and forth with several younger children. "Ah, Seth's home." Mrs. Tanner smiled again. She called to her son, and he came over.

"Miss Vogel, this is my oldest, Seth. Seth, Miss Vogel's here from one of the local charity groups to help us with some food."

"Miss." Seth touched his cap. She had hardly had time to take in his pleasant features and lean but muscular frame when he jumped in front of her, then staggered backward a step, as his younger brother sent a baseball flying their direction. Unable to catch it in time, Seth took it square in the chest.

"Watch your aim, Zeke," he called. "You about knocked out Jean Arthur here."

Alice flushed at his comparing her to the Hollywood star.

Turning back to her, Seth drawled, "You all right, Miss Vogel?"

"Yes," she stammered, still stunned, "but I'm surprised that ball didn't knock the wind out of you."

He shrugged and winked. "I'm hardier than I look." Zeke trotted over to retrieve the ball and muttered an apology before running off again.

"I got a job fixing the Coopers' Model T tonight," Seth told his mother.

"Come on in, then, and rest a minute while I fix you some grits and eggs," Mrs. Tanner replied with obvious affection. Seth nodded, then looked back at Alice.

"Miss Vogel, you didn't walk here, I hope?"

"I parked my automobile down the street at the train depot."

"It's getting dusky. Let me walk you there."

She started to protest that he didn't need to worry about it but changed her mind. She wanted him to. Perhaps she could convince him to persuade his parents to make the changes necessary to improve their family's life.

He walked on the outside of the broken sidewalk as they headed down the few short blocks to the depot.

"Do you like your work at the mill?" she asked when he didn't initiate any conversation.

"It's work. Doesn't pay to be choosy in this economy."

"True."

"Do you like your job?"

"I like helping people. Sometimes it's frustrating when I can't. Or when they won't make the changes they need to."

"They need to or you think they ought?"

She looked up at him sharply. He reached out a hand to steady her as she stumbled over the uneven concrete. His grip was firm without being forceful.

He glanced at her. "Careful there." He released her arm. "I'm sorry, Miss Vogel—"

"Alice. Please call me Alice."

"Sure. And I'm Seth. Anyway, my comment wasn't fair to you. I'm jaded, I guess, because people judge. About Bobby. They don't know how great he's been for our family."

"Great?"

"Yeah. I was about eleven when my dad went to the war. He was gone over a year and came back with one arm. But he was a different person. I don't know if it was his injury or the things he saw there. His temperament changed."

"He became abusive?" she asked, thinking of many stories of veterans she'd heard over the years.

"Oh, no. Nothin' like that. Just withdrawn. Bobby—when the doctor said Bobby wouldn't be right in his mind and we should put him in an institution—I saw in Dad things I hadn't seen in years. It was as if he had something to fight for again.

"Bobby's special. He's unfailingly loving. It's not always easy having him with us, and folks don't understand. But he's drawn my whole family together and healed something that was hurt in Dad."

Alice set aside the carefully reasoned speech she'd planned to try on Seth. "Here's my car," she said, her cheeks flushing a bit at the ostentatious black and gold Packard 8 Coupé. A gift from her parents for her college graduation to express how proud they were for her choice to "do good in the community." They had no idea it would always be penance and not passion driving her efforts.

He whistled. "That's the cat's meow. You be safe going home, ya hear?" He opened the door for her.

She murmured her thanks. "It was a pleasure to meet you, Seth."

"Likewise, Alice." His gaze lingered a beat longer than necessary, then he tipped his cap and began the walk home, whistling, "Brother, Can You Spare a Dime?" and casting a long shadow in the setting sun.

Chapter 2

Wednesday, September 19, 1934

Milly Tanner cracked eggs into the bowl and listened to her children squabbling in the next room. She'd settle them in a minute. Seth needed food before heading to another job.

"Lord, it hurts me to see him working all the time, with no time for rest or fun of any kind. Or courting."

She hadn't missed the way Seth's eyes had lit up at the lovely Miss Vogel. Her oldest boy was older than she and Ezra had been when they'd wed. Nothing hurt her like the way he'd had to give up all his savings for his own future to pay for Ez's surgery and medical bills after the accident. And he hadn't complained about it once, hadn't even asked her. Just done it. Because that was Seth.

Zeke had started eighth grade this year. He could get a job at the mill next fall and surely by then Ezra would be well enough to work again. She'd have a new baby though, and Bobby still needed a lot more care than her other children had at this age. She hadn't missed the shock on Miss Vogel's face when she'd admitted to the pregnancy.

The girl reminded her of a much younger version of herself. Idealistic. Put together. Confident. Pretty. No doubt it astonished her that any man would still be interested in a middle-aged matron. It surprised Milly herself the way Ezra could still find in her tired, aging body his blushing bride.

When Seth came back in, she set a plate of hot grits and eggs before him. The smell of the eggs turned her stomach and she nibbled on a cracker. She'd forgotten to get the tomatoes and okra in all the fuss about Miss Vogel.

"This is a lot, Momma. You got enough for you and Daddy?"

He didn't ask about the other kids. He knew she'd feed them. But he was on to her with her "Oh, I'm not hungry tonight." With Ezra confined to bed, she could sometimes skip meals without him finding out. Seth knew and would raise Cain if she didn't eat.

"I've got more. I thought the grits had to last all week, but that Miss Vogel said she would come back tomorrow with a food box, and they'll have one every week till your daddy's back on his feet."

"That's good, Momma. I know we don't like to take charity, but we gotta eat, and these are extreme circumstances, what with Daddy laid up and all."

"I know. She was friendly for a social worker, though I suspect she was judging us."

"I didn't think she put on airs."

"Maybe not. Prob'ly I'm overly sensitive about it."

He rose, the plate already empty, and brought it to the sink. How she wished she had a slice of bacon or ham to put with the meager meal. He must always be hungry.

Seth bent down and kissed the top of her head. "You're pretty perfect, I think. It'll be OK. If we get this food help for a bit, maybe we can pay to get the power turned back on before winter." Whistling "Can the Circle Be Unbroken," he headed down the hall to go to his next job, but she heard him stopping in the bedroom to talk to his father and wrestle Bobby, making him squeal with laughter.

"Lord, he's such a good young man. Please, let him have a future," she whispered, heart heavy. Then she called the others to the table and said the blessing. The conversation grew lively, and she helped Bobby with his food and listened to the kids chatter about a game at school and who'd been cast as a Pilgrim and who as an Indian for the Thanksgiving program. Ruby and Beth would be wanting costumes, and she hoped she could manage something. She'd already had to tell Beth no to attending a birthday party earlier in the month because they didn't have anything suitable for a gift.

While the kids cleaned up the kitchen by lamplight, she took a plate in to Ezra, and the two of them ate their meal by the soft light of another lantern while she told him about the day. The shadows concealed the worry lines on his face, and she hid her anxiety in a cheerful tone as she told about the funny things the kids had said, and the gossip from their next door neighbor, and at last about Alice Vogel and the food boxes.

"I'm sorry, Milly," Ezra said. "So sorry. Mighty foolish for a one-armed man to have been climbing a tree to start with."

"Ez Tanner, you're the bravest, stubbornest man I know. Now this help is just for a short time, and it won't hurt us none to be humble enough to accept it. Tell me what you read about today."

"You won't find it interesting," he assured her, but she didn't miss the way his eyes softened, and he hid his slow smile at her compliment. "More legal stuff. I've been thinking about a career change. Something less physically taxing. Maybe I could work in a county office or something."

"Of course you could. You'd be the best thing that ever happened to them."

Beth brought Bobby in, and she changed him for bed and sat in the old rocker, snuggling him. At the top of the hour, she switched on their farm radio. After Ezra's injury, Seth had helped her move it in here. He'd drilled the hole in the floor to run the wire down to the jar of sulfuric acid in the cellar, the 32-volt battery that powered this magical box. The radio had given Ez some relief and distraction from the misery of his recovery.

Now the news announcer led off with the story of the arrest of Bruno Hauptmann in connection with the kidnapping of the Lindberg baby. Milly shivered a little. She'd hated hearing all the details of the brutal tragedy two years ago. Brushing hair off the forehead of the sleeping Bobby, she wondered for the thousandth time who could hurt a baby.

She hadn't told Ezra about her pregnancy yet. He didn't need another thing to fret over, another thing to make their situation seem impossible. She laid Bobby in his little cot beside their bed. He'd wake two or three times in the night, most likely, and crawl into their bed by morning. She thought back to Miss Vogel's words.

Yes, she had considered State Hospital. How would she teach him to communicate clearly? The doctor had said his hearing wasn't good. When he was a little older, he'd need glasses. Eating and sleeping still presented challenges for him that she didn't know if he'd outgrow. She couldn't afford the best care for him now, and his needs would only increase.

But to give him to professionals who did not love him? Who would see him as a job and not a person? Who wouldn't melt at his infectious giggle or understand his babbling words? He held a special place in her heart—and Ezra's. He embodied loving when it didn't exactly make sense.

And thinking of that, Milly felt a little sorry for Miss Alice Vogel in her heels and smart suit and hat and pink lipstick and perfectly curled hair. Because maybe she'd never loved or been loved when it didn't make sense, and that was something no charity institution could deliver.

Chapter 3

Thursday, September 20, 1934

Alice went home that night and baked a cake. She would add it to the Tanners' box of food items the next day. She should go there first thing in the morning, she supposed, but if she timed it right, toward evening, Seth would be there. Did he like chocolate cake? How long since the family had had a treat? Would he smile to see it?

Seth. He hadn't seemed intimidated by her money. Which of course wasn't really hers, but her parents'. She had an easy life compared to the people she worked to aid; she didn't *have* to work at all, for one thing. Her father's income provided for a lifestyle that included vacations, new clothes, and an automobile for each of them. Mother had a housekeeper who saw to the laundry and most of the cleaning and cooking. Alice had gone to high school and then Berry College, her alma mater and Miss Berry's example both fueling her desire to live a useful, purposeful life.

Only she didn't feel useful. In a world beset by crushing need, her efforts to fight poverty felt insignificant, fleeting. Perhaps as Ralph's wife, she would have been able to—no use dwelling on that now. Or ever.

The cake sat on her desk most of the next day at the Presbyterian church in Rome where the Charitable Fund had been granted a small office space. It's rich chocolate scent teased her, and she wished she had made two, so she'd have one to come home to. Thankfully, most of the morning she spent away from her office, helping to prepare and then serve a hearty soup to the needy in the area. Alice put leftover soup into two large glass jars and added them to the groceries for the Tanners.

The city clocktower read after four o'clock before she headed out to the mill town of Lindale on the outskirts of Rome. This time, she parked on the street near the front yard stairs, not wanting to tote the heavy crate far.

Kids came running out of the house to greet her. She entrusted the cake to twelve-year-old Beth, and enlisted fourteen-year-old Zeke to carry in the heavy crate. She didn't think she'd ever in her life been as excited over groceries as the children before her. She grabbed the two glass jars of soup and followed them into the house. Mrs. Tanner met her at the door.

"Lord bless you, honey," she said. "It's like Christmas come early."

She smiled. "Glad to be of service," she murmured.

"We'd be much obliged if you'd stay and eat with us." Mrs. Tanner looked about as if assessing her home. "If you don't mind a little mess and noise."

Alice felt it would be counter-productive to eat the much-needed food she'd brought them. On the other hand, she didn't know how she could refuse such a gracious offer without looking like she thought herself better than them. "I'd love to," she accepted.

Mrs. Tanner began making biscuits with the flour and milk Alice had brought, and the youngest girl, Ruby, began jumping up and down in delight. "Now Ruby, you help Miss Vogel set the table," Mrs. Tanner instructed.

"Please call me Alice."

Ruby looked up at her and wrinkled her brow. "Are you a mama or a daughter?"

"I'm a daughter, like every other girl," Alice answered, slightly confused.

"But do you have children?" Ruby chewed on the end of one of her golden-brown braids.

"No. I'm not married yet."

"My sister Ellen got married in June, and she wore a pretty dress, and we had cake, and now she lives in Cartersville, and we don't see her much." The girl prattled on, but the question had left Alice cold and the follow-up even more.

"Do you like children? Do you want lotsa babies?"

"I—I don't know," she stammered. Not ten of them. She knew that. And maybe not any.

"Seth's home!" shouted Jane from a perch by the window, her announcement followed by the squeak and slam of the screen door. The children swarmed their brother, even little Bobby. Seth swung the boy over his shoulder and tickled him, then stepped into the kitchen and set his canteen and lunch pail on the worktable. Alice noted that he was the only one of the kids not to have Mrs. Tanner's light brown hair, and she wondered if he looked more like Mr. Tanner, whom she'd not seen yet.

Seth kissed his mother on the cheek, then smiled at her. "Hi, Alice. I heard a rumor there's cake?"

"Indeed."

"Swell. Momma, you go in and eat with Daddy. I'll mind the kiddos out here."

"Bobby needs help," she began, but Seth waved her away.

"Guess I know how to do a thing or two. You sit with Daddy and have a minute."

Alice tried to keep her mouth from dropping open. This man had put in a twelve-hour work shift, walked home, and he stepped into the house and got busy helping his mother? She'd never in her life seen or heard of such a thing.

"Let's say grace," he instructed when all seven plates were fixed and fourteen hands washed. All the kids bowed their heads, though several squirmed as they waited to eat.

"Lord, we are so thankful for this food You've provided and for Miss Alice who brought it. For Christ's sake, Amen."

"Amen!" shouted the kids, who were soon inhaling their soup and biscuits. Alice watched Seth alternate between eating his own food and helping Bobby, who sat in a wooden high chair, with his. Seth asked the kids about their school day and everyone seemed to talk at once. Alice sat taking it all in and eating the simple soup that for many of those she'd served today would be their only decent meal for the day—or week.

The room grew dim as they ate, and a rumble of thunder outside startled them. The children scattered to the front porch to check for an approaching storm.

"You might need to stay a bit longer." Seth turned to her. "Hate for you to drive home in a thunderstorm."

"Yes," she agreed. "Let's wash up the dishes and then have some cake."

He gave her a once over. "You don't strike me as the dishwashing type, what with those white hands and painted fingernails."

She scowled at him. "I made the cake and washed up most of the dishes afterward, thank you very much."

His lips twitched, but he said nothing and instead whistled a jaunty bit of "Sweet Georgia Brown" as he heated water on the wood-burning stove. She did put one of Mrs. Tanner's flour-sack aprons on over her own silk tunic blouse and straight cotton skirt.

"How much to get the power back on?" she asked, noting the light fixtures.

"I'm working on it."

"I just thought, with the days getting shorter and cold weather around the corner—"

"Yep. I'm working on it."

"I didn't figure you for as stubborn as your mother."

He laughed out loud. "Oh, honey, I come by it honestly from both my parents. Only reason Dad's still kicking is 'cause he's too stubborn to die."

He rolled up the sleeves of his flannel shirt, revealing muscular forearms, and began shaving soap into the hot water.

"What exactly do you do at the mill?" she asked.

"Maintenance, mostly. I'm a mechanic. I went to high school at Berry. I woulda gone on to the junior college, but I needed to work. Planned to be an auto mechanic, but the position at the mill was too good to pass up. It's decent money, and the company takes care of its folks. There's just a lot of mouths to feed and a lot of medical bills here."

He didn't sound defensive, despite the fact that she'd been more or less interrogating him. A deafening crack of thunder was followed by the heavens opening, and they had to talk louder over the pounding rain on the tin roof.

"I went to Berry, too. My father wanted me to go to Agnes Scot, but I wanted something more practical. Do you think I'm very stuck up?"

"I've met worse." His lips twitched again. "You're an OK dish dryer, anyway, despite my misgivings."

Their eyes met, and they shared a smile.

When the dishes were done, he helped her put them away. Then they moved to the living room and played charades based off book characters with the kids. Mrs. Tanner came back to get Bobby and put him to bed, and they tried to hold back their laughter to a reasonable level as Ruby pretended to be Brer Rabbit and Jane gave an overly-dramatic silent rendition of *Anne of Green Gables*.

"Wish Dad could get out here," Zeke remarked.

Alice wondered if the man could use a wheelchair to get around the house. Surely being able to join his family for meals or go to the bathroom would be an improvement for his situation. Remembering Seth's matter-of-fact response about the electricity, she didn't ask, but an idea took root.

They ate half the cake, and seeing Seth's eyes light up and hearing his exclamation of pleasure around a mouthful made it worth the effort and more. About eight-thirty, the rain slacked off, and Alice gathered her things to go. Outside, Seth walked her down the two sets of steps to her car.

"If I asked you out for a Coca-Cola, would you say yes?"

She was pleasantly surprised by his boldness. If he wasn't going to let the difference in their economic levels discourage him, why should she? She liked him.

She smiled up at him. "I think I would. Why don't you ask?"

"Can't this week, but next Saturday night, about seven?"

"OK."

"I'll pick you up at your house?"

She hesitated. What would her father say? Mother and Father were always pushing her to date, but their suggestions were consistently people better connected and with more money than their own family.

"My father may grill you a bit."

"I expect so. I'm not a coward."

"All right." She smiled shyly again and told him the address. "I'll see you then."

She smiled all the drive home.

Chapter 4

Thursday, September 20—Wednesday, September 26, 1934

"Momma," Seth said, coming in from walking Miss Vogel to her automobile. "I'm taking Alice out next Saturday night."

Milly worried her bottom lip. The boy hadn't been anywhere or done anything fun in longer than she could remember. If he wanted to go on a date, she'd not stop him. But *Alice*? The stylish and sophisticated Miss Vogel? That girl would break his heart.

"We're just going for a Coca-Cola and to talk," he said before she could voice her rising objections. "I'm not proposing marriage."

"I know. She's kinda—wealthy."

"Guess I won't hold that against her if she doesn't hold against me that I'm not."

"I'll make sure your suit's clean and pressed. I'm glad you're going to have fun."

He smiled and hugged her and went whistling down the hall to take care of his final evening chores.

"Ah, Lord, please protect my sweet boy and bring him a wife worthy of his good heart," she prayed. She didn't think Seth likely to be turned merely by a pretty face. There must be more that drew him to this young lady.

The following Wednesday she knelt on the floor changing Bobby's diaper when she felt a sharp cramp in her side. It's suddenness caused her to stick her thumb with a diaper pin, and she hissed in pain. Easing up onto the couch, she mentally calculated how far she might be in this pregnancy. Ten weeks? Twelve? What she wouldn't give for a nap, but if she took her eyes off Bobby for a minute, he could run out of the house into the street or get ahold of something dangerous and get hurt. He loved to climb and seemed absolutely fearless. Maybe she could get him to lie down on the sofa with her for a bit.

A knock sounded at the back door. Biting back a groan, she got up, took hold of Bobby, and padded down the hall.

It was Alice and with her . . . a wheelchair? In the seat of it sat their weekly food box.

"Hello, Mrs. Tanner." She spoke faster than usual, though from nerves or excitement, Milly couldn't guess. "Some folks at Harbin Hospital heard about the situation, and they offered for y'all to borrow this wheelchair until Mr. Tanner doesn't need it anymore."

"When I talked to the nurse there after Ez's surgery, she said we had to rent a chair," Milly replied, hoping she didn't sound suspicious. She straightened her wrinkled calico dress, noting Alice's stylish short-sleeved sweater and pleated wool skirt which fell a little below the knee. Milly smoothed her faded brown hair back into its bun as she looked at Alice's shoulder-length curls, the bright, buoyant tresses a match for the girl's personality.

"See, I went through the county health department, and they asked if our charity could borrow a wheelchair, and the hospital agreed to permanently donate it for us. You use it as long as you need it, and when you're done, our organization will keep it for whoever else might need it in the future."

Milly reminded herself that God could provide through many different means. She'd have preferred for Him to send them a thousand dollars anonymously in the mail or make Ezra all better and give him a job that amply paid the bills, but His ways were not hers. She'd figured that out long ago.

"Thank you, Alice," she said. "Do you mind to bring it in? I'm having some pains in my side."

"Have you seen the doctor about your pregnancy?" asked Alice, pushing the chair through the front door. It carried the scent of the hospital, which in Milly's mind was a mixture of disinfectant and desperation. She recalled sitting on a waiting room bench, Seth next to her, while they waited for word of Ezra's surgery.

"No. I—" She lowered her voice and looked at the bedroom door, not wanting this to be the way her husband found out.

"Let me find out when the Healthmobile will be around next." Alice took the cue and lowered her own voice. "Or if it's not too far away, I can drive you to it."

"I can't leave Ezra and Bobby and—"

"I can watch Bobby if needed. Would Ezra be OK for a few hours?"

"Probably. I wouldn't bother, except I want to make sure the baby's all right."

"They will give you a booklet and maybe a blanket and infant clothes too." Alice took the heaviest items out of the crate and carried them into the kitchen, then brought in the crate itself. Then she began rolling the wheelchair down the hall, the wheels squeaking a bit. Seth could put a bit of oil on them.

"Me-righ! Me-righ!" Bobby yelled, prancing about the contraption.

"All right, Bobby, you climb in, and Miss Alice will push you right on in to see Daddy."

Alice stopped and Milly helped Bobby into the rattan chair. He rested his arms on the wooden arm rests, his feet dangling far above the wooden foot rests, and rode proudly as Alice pushed the chair. Milly led the way to the open door of the bedroom. Ezra sat in bed, studying, resting against the pillows that cushioned him from the cast iron headboard. Classical music played softly on the radio.

"Well, praise the Lord," he exclaimed when he saw the chair. "This is an answer to prayer."

"Alice, this is my husband, Ezra Tanner. Ez, this is Alice, whom all the kids have been going on about." She gave him a look. Surely he remembered this was the girl Seth wanted to step out with.

"Pleased to meet you, my dear, after all the good things I've heard—and the chocolate cake I devoured."

"Bobby, you sit here with daddy while I see Miss Alice to the door," Milly said. By the back door, out of earshot of the bedroom, she said, "Thank you. And I guess I will take you up on going to the Healthmobile if they don't get here to us soon. I've had a bit of spotting and now the cramping. Would like to know that all is well."

"That's good, Mrs. Tanner. I'll find out the information and let you know."

Alice offered her pretty smile and promised to see her in a week with another food box, if not before. Milly stepped back inside, equal parts relieved and anxious. The

Healthmobile was run by the state, and government people made her nervous, as did doctors. Both of those groups had urged them to put Bobby away, to give up on him.

His behavior right now didn't differ much from any toddler's, though most folks judged a three-and-a-half year old still in diapers or grew frustrated trying to communicate with his limited and slurred vocabulary. She knew these were the first of many ways where Bobby would be "behind" other children his age, and she grieved that others would look down on her sweet boy, would miss the amazing person hidden under the differences.

But she also worried. When she grew old and had a son who had grown physically but not mentally, how would she manage his needs, especially if Ezra remained weak?

"Lord," she whispered. "Forgive me. I'm not just borrowing tomorrow's trouble but years and years ahead."

When the children came home to find their father at the kitchen table, they were ecstatic. That night's meal of beans and bread felt like a holiday with all of them sitting together again. Ezra told jokes and listened to their little tales about their day. Only Seth thought to ask where the miracle chair had come from. He didn't say anything when Milly told him, but his satisfied smile told her all she needed to know. He already had feelings for this girl. Milly looked at the food and the chair and the smiles around the table and hoped they weren't coming at the cost of her dear son's heart.

Chapter 5

Saturday, September 29, 1934

Seth came at seven on Saturday night to pick up Alice for their date. She hid in the coat closet to eavesdrop on Father's interrogation. Father began by offering him a sherry, which Seth declined.

"And how did you meet my Alice?" Father asked.

"Through her work," Seth answered smoothly.

"And your employment?"

"I'm a mechanic. I fix and maintain the equipment for the Pepperell Manufacturing Company in Lindale."

"Your education?"

"High school at Berry."

"Hmm."

Alice felt her stomach tighten. Father's *hmm* usually indicated his displeasure. She started to go bouncing into the room, but paused again at the sound of Seth's easy drawl.

"I'd just like the chance to talk to Alice and get to know her," he said. "If you'd prefer us to stay right here in this living room, that's fine."

Alice did not think it the least bit fine and let out a sigh of relief when Father replied, "No, that's not necessary. Have her home by ten, and keep your hands to yourself."

She wondered if Father had ever given Ralph such a warning and what Father would think to know how little it had been heeded. She slipped out of the coat closet and into the living room, greeting Seth brightly and bidding Father a good evening. She noted that he looked handsome in a suit and fedora, and though his garments were a bit worn, they fit him well.

Seth squinted at her as they stepped outside into the brisk evening.

"What is it?"

"Your dad told me to keep my hands to myself, but I'm pretty sure there's a spiderweb in your hair, and I wanted to brush it out for you."

She laughed. "Yes, please do. I was hiding in the coat closet to eavesdrop, and Rhoda never cleans in there."

So lightly she hardly felt his touch, he removed the offending web. "You look swell." He walked over to a Model T and opened the door for her.

"I didn't realize you had an automobile," she said when he'd seated himself behind the wheel.

"I don't. This is the one I repaired the other night. They paid what they could and said I could borrow it anytime."

He drove downtown and parked on Broad Street near a diner. They stepped into the tantalizing aroma of fresh coffee and Bing Crosby crooning "Love in Bloom" on the radio. Seth picked an out-of-the-way table and glanced at the menu board.

"I know I said Coca-Cola, but I'm going to get coffee and cherry pie. What would you like?"

"Sounds good. I'll have the peach."

The buttery, sweet pastry melted in her mouth, and the conversation was easier than Alice had expected. Movies, songs, books—an avid library patron, Seth was better read than she, though when he found time to read, she could not imagine. They chatted and laughed. He had one dimple high on his cheek, and his teeth were white and straight, giving him a pleasing smile.

"Do you go to church?" he asked at a lull in the conversation.

"My mother is a member at First Presbyterian, and I was christened there. I go with her occasionally."

He nodded in acknowledgement. "We go to First Baptist."

She thought there wasn't much more to say on the topic, but his expression turned pensive, his blue eyes almost misty. "What does it mean to you?" he asked.

"Church?"

"Church, Christ, the gospel."

"I'm trying to help people, like Christ taught." She hoped her answer would suffice.

"And doing a good job at it," he answered with a smile. "I guess what I'm wondering is—is He more than an inspiration to you?"

"Well, He's the Savior, of course. What does it all mean to you?" she hedged, still not sure what answer he sought.

He exhaled. "Everything. It means everything to me."

She had no idea how to answer. He was probably too religious to overlook what she'd done, but he didn't have to know.

"You remind me of my mother's relatives. My aunts and grandparents. Mother's cousin Adam in Atlanta is a famous doctor, and whenever he comes to the family reunion, he prays as if he must talk to God all the time about everything."

"I try to do the same. It's—"

"Alice!"

She involuntarily turned at the last voice she wanted to hear and saw the last person she wanted to see. Ralph strode toward their corner table. His eyes narrowed, taking in the two of them, their empty plates and cups, and her pink ruffled chiffon dress that had been one of his favorites because it flattered her figure and coloring.

His gaze leveled on Seth, before swinging back to her as he put his hand on her shoulder. "It's wonderful to see you, Allie."

She ground her teeth and shook off his hand.

"Hello, Ralph. Seth, this is Ralph Comstock, a friend from my college days. Ralph, this is Seth Tanner, a friend from the present epoch of my life."

Ralph snorted at this explanation. Seth extended his hand, and Ralph reluctantly shook it. Then Ralph began talking. His new Rolls Royce. His new job. He was going to run for state representative. He made sure to flash his Cartier wristwatch multiple times. Alice felt nauseated seeing the contrast between the two men. She tried to interrupt Ralph's self-important soliloquy, but he talked over her polite attempts to end the unwanted interruption to her date. Finally, Seth stood.

"It was nice to meet you, Mr. Comstock, but I need to be getting Miss Vogel home now."

"I can take her home, if you need to go." Ralph's hand wrapped around Alice's upper arm.

She met his gray eyes. It was all there. He would use their past against her in a heartbeat. She would have to let Ralph take her home or his big, fat mouth would start talking about her. Them. Tears filled her eyes, and she gave an unintentional gasp for air.

To her surprise, Seth stepped forward, took hold of Ralph's arm, and removed it from Alice's. His voice remained level, no nonsense.

"I told Mr. Vogel I would have his daughter home by ten, and that's what I'm going to do. If you would like an audience with Miss Vogel, you can come see her on your own night."

Ralph tried to stare Seth down, but when he didn't flinch, he said only, "I'll be telephoning you, Alice," and strode off. Alice exhaled and picked up her pocketbook. They left the diner and walked back to the Model T in the now cool, dark evening. She shivered and thought she ought to have grabbed something besides overheard information from the coat closet. After he opened her car door, Seth removed his suit coat and handed it to her with a smile.

"Thank you." She pulled it around herself, breathing in his sandalwood scented aftershave mixed with hints of woodsmoke and gasoline.

Neither of them spoke for the ten minute drive back to her family's house on Fourth Street. "I'm sorry about Ralph," Alice said at last as Seth pulled the flivver into the driveway. "I was having a nice time with you."

"I assume you two dated?"

"Yes. For almost two years. He broke it off. About a year ago."

"Do you want him back?"

"He—no. But he—I thought he wanted a future together. And then he didn't. Yet how he acted back there. So controlling. And I—I'm utterly confused by him."

Seth shifted the Model T to park and turned to face her. "Let me not add to your confusion, then, Alice. I like you. I'd like to continue getting to know you. And I didn't care for the way he ogled you and grabbed you."

She flushed. If he knew where Ralph's familiarity stemmed from, there would be a lot more he didn't care for.

Seth continued. "I don't have a car, let alone a Packard or a Rolls. I don't own a fancy watch, and this is the only suit I've ever had. I'm a hard worker, and I aim to provide for my family now and in the future, but it won't be—grand. I'm not really interested in prestige. I want a home built on faith, with children and laughter and loyalty. When I pledge myself to my future wife, I won't be looking back or looking around."

Her eyes filled with traitorous tears. He had wealth in character, in which Ralph was impoverished. If only she hadn't—but she had. And now Ralph owned her, and Seth would never want her. She must not needlessly torture this good man or herself by letting this attraction go further.

"I wish—I can't. I'm sorry," she choked out. She opened the door. "Please don't walk me to the door. I—I enjoyed the time with you. Truly. I—good night." She practically jumped out of the car and ran up the walk to the front door, fumbling in her purse for the key. He remained parked in the driveway to see her safely in the house, then slowly backed out and left.

He let her go. Because he wasn't Ralph. Seth gave her freedom to choose and respected her choice.

With all her heart, she wished she'd made the right choice when she still had the chance.

Chapter 6

Saturday, September 29—Thursday, October 4, 1934

Milly waited up till Seth got back Saturday night. For one thing, the power was back on, and she suspected it was his doing. When he came in the back door about eleven, he wasn't whistling. Maybe he just didn't want to wake the little ones, she told herself. But in her heart, she knew. Her suspicions were confirmed by one look at his face as he came over to where she sat in her favorite chair, mending overalls by the electric lamp light.

"This your doing, about the power?"

He shrugged and lowered his long, lanky frame onto the sofa. "We all worked hard to make it happen. What we've saved on food helped."

"Thank you. It makes a heap of difference to have these lights, not to mention the washing machine and refrigerator can be used properly again."

"Yes." With the toe of his shoe, he traced the pattern in the worn rug on the floor.

"Didn't go well?"

"It went fine, till her old boyfriend showed up and started going on about all his nice things and big plans." Seth kicked at the rug.

"She wants more than you can give?"

"I dunno. She said she was confused. Then I was confused by her answer."

"What exactly happened?"

He repeated the evening's conversation.

"Did she look like she still has feelings for this Ralph?"

"Not really. She looked almost scared of him. I didn't like his demeanor with her. Too—possessive."

"Hmm." She snipped off a thread. "I'll be spending some time with her next week, I reckon. She's going to take me to the Healthmobile."

"What for, Momma? You sick?"

"No." She sighed. "I told your daddy tonight, so I might as well tell you. I'm expecting again, and there's been a few things concerning."

"Oh. It'll be sweet to have another baby around. I'm glad you're going to see the nurse. And I'll try to help out more—"

"Seth Tanner, you are doing all a man can and more. I'll be fine. It's a hard season for us all. I'm glad you went out for fun tonight, and I'm sorry it didn't go the way you wanted."

He shrugged again, but she knew he didn't brush things off quickly. Instead of offering him platitudes, she rose and kissed the top of his head. "Let's get some rest," she advised, and he murmured a goodnight as she padded down the hall.

*****

On Wednesday morning, soon after the kids had left for school, Bobby pulled the tablecloth off the kitchen table. A deafening crash announced a shower of dishes and the half-full milk jug hitting the wooden floor.

"Uh-oh, uh-oh," said the boy from where he stood surrounded by the crumbs of breakfast and broken glass.

Grimly, Milly picked him up and took him in to Ezra, explaining what had happened. Carrying the sturdy three-year-old gave her a hitch in her side and cramps in her middle. Tears of frustration pooled in her eyes as she gathered up the broom, dustpan, and mop. Maybe there was no use crying over spilt milk, but when you already had to water it down to make it last for a small army of growing children . . .

She had to get down on her hands and knees to get the littlest slivers of glass, and when she stood, a wave of dizziness almost knocked her over. She took a seat, but the feeling was slow to pass. Just when she thought maybe she could finish cleaning up, she heard a knock at the front door.

As she guessed, Alice stood there with the weekly food crate.

"Mrs. Tanner, are you all right? You look quite pale."

"I'm not sure. Bobby made a great mess of the table, and I think I overdid a bit—"

Alice hurried in, put down the crate, and set to work. "You sit down," she ordered. "I can do this."

Milly looked on, humiliated at having this fancy girl in her smart heeled shoes and manicured fingernails cleaning up such a mess. But Alice did a thorough job, saying nothing as she mopped the sticky floor and threw the broken glass into the garbage.

"Thank you," Milly whispered when the younger woman finished.

"I think you need to see a nurse," Alice said.

"Maybe so. Did you find out anything about the Healthmobile?"

"It will be in Rome tomorrow. Are you OK to wait till then?"

"Yes, I'm feeling better now that I set for a spell."

Alice's brow knit in concern, but she said, "Don't get up to show me to the door. I'll be here tomorrow morning to drive you to the Healthmobile."

"Thank you, Alice. For all of your help."

Alice shifted a little, opened her mouth as if she were going to say something, then shut it again. Milly supposed she might think they bore her ill will after the unpleasantness on the date with Seth, and she added kindly, "We all think highly of you and appreciate what you've done for us."

"I, uh, yes, well, I, uh, am glad to help." She turned and left quietly, and Milly looked after her for a long time, not daring to give words to the questions swirling in her head. She heard Bobby getting louder in the bedroom and hauled herself upright to go see to him before something else got broken or he got hurt. The boy could get into mischief faster than a minnow could swim a dipper.

The next morning, Milly put on her church dress and readied Bobby in his best clothes with a fresh diaper. She explained her errand to Ezra and made sure he had some lunch set out for when he grew hungry.

The fine automobile made Milly want to weep at the late '20s style of her best dress and its worn seams. The Packard's seats were gray striped upholstery, as plush as first class on any railroad car. The gleaming wood dash with its instrument panels overwhelmed her, but Alice chatted a bit as she drove effortlessly. Bobby made sing-song noises Milly knew were his version of "Old Macdonald Had a Farm." She sang a few verses with him.

She was surprised when Alice parked on Third Avenue at the Presbyterian church. Wasn't this where she worked? Had she managed to get the Healthmobile here special? Milly didn't want to ask. She felt queasy after the car ride and took a few deep breaths of cool air as she opened the door and slid out.

Alice came around next to her and nodded toward a children's swing set. "Would you mind if I watch Bobby outside rather than make him sit in the car?"

"That's a wonderful idea, if you don't mind." Milly looked at the imposing clinic on wheels and twisted and untwisted the straps of her pocketbook. She took another deep breath and observed the simple beauty of the purple and yellow pansies in a concrete planter outside the church.

"I—don't know anything at all about children," Alice admitted. "What does he need me to do exactly?"

"Mainly watch that he doesn't get hurt or put something in his mouth. He likes to hear poems and songs and to have you point out birds and squirrels and things."

Milly looked at Bobby. "Bobby-boy, you be a friend to Miss Alice and mind her, while Momma goes inside this wagon. I'll be back soon." She kissed his forehead and handed him to Alice, then resolutely picked up her pocketbook and walked to the Healthmobile, ignoring Bobby's wails. He would be fine. Surely.

Wild thoughts of Alice kidnapping him and taking him to State Hospital assailed her. If she hadn't been having dizzy spells and spotting again this morning, she wouldn't have bothered with seeing a nurse. It wasn't as if she didn't know about pregnancy.

At the door, she glanced back. Alice still stood beside the car, but Bobby had plopped down on the gravel and refused to get up. She watched as Alice crouched beside him, pointing to the nearby swings.

Clutching the straps of her purse, Milly pushed open the door of the traveling clinic. She had to think about this new little one. For whatever reason, God had chosen to entrust them with another life, and she would love and care for this child, too, whatever the cost.

Chapter 7

Thursday, October 4, 1934

Alice, an only child, had not been joking when she'd said she knew nothing about children. Never had she been as keenly aware of her lack as right this moment, kneeling in a parking lot trying to reason with a stubborn, crying toddler that his mother would come back. She didn't even know if he understood her with his condition.

She started to pick him up and return to the car when she remembered what Mrs. Tanner had said about him liking songs. She began to sing, "Old Macdonald." Gradually, Bobby calmed, hiccuped, and looked at her. When the song ended, he clapped his hands together.

"Mo, mo."

More?

"I'll sing more if you come with me over to that grassy place." She rose and held out her hand. He took it and walked unsteadily beside her. A bird flew past, low, and he stopped.

"Bud, bud!" he exclaimed. His big smile lit up his whole face. Tow-headed, in miniature denim overalls, he didn't look significantly different from any other cute and precocious toddler. She wished she'd been less judgmental of this family wanting to keep their own child.

"Do you like birds? Let's see if we can find some more."

They hunted around the church grounds for birds to spot and identify, listening for chirps and calls. Then she pushed him on a swing, slowly as he remained unsteady. When she caught him right before he landed face first in the dirt, she decided they'd better do something else. Bobby took off chasing another bird, but was soon distracted by a pile of dirt. He plopped down in the middle of it and began grabbing it by the handful.

Alice didn't know what to do but kneel beside him. She smoothed the red clay soil out flat and began tracing letters in it: A for Alice, B for Bobby, over and over.

"You can't teach a kid like him." She looked up to see Ralph towering over her, and her heart rate began to accelerate.

"Look at his eyes, Alice. He's retarded. That kid'll never learn. He should be in an institution."

"What do you want, Ralph? Why are you here?" She brushed the powdery clay off her hands and stood.

"I came here looking for you. I thought you worked in an office in the church."

"Sometimes. Sometimes I'm hands-on helping people." She crossed her arms.

"Why did you refuse my telephone call on Sunday?"

"There's nothing I need to say to you or hear from you. And you ruined my date Saturday."

"That wet blanket? He's not good enough for you. Why are you determined not to give me a second chance? I love you, Alice. I was a fool to let you go, and I know that now."

Oh, he was smooth. She looked at him in his immaculate three-piece suit, with his perfectly slicked hair, smelling of too much aftershave and not enough honest sweat, and she wanted to vomit all over his impeccably shined shoes.

"Let me go?" She sneered. "I remember it as abandoning me when I needed you most."

"What can I do to prove myself to you? It can't be too late. Tell me what to do to make things right, and I'll do it."

"You think you can buy me, don't you? A gold bracelet, tickets to a concert, what? I'm not for sale, Ralph."

He stepped closer and seized her arm. She jerked away from him and took a step back, positioning herself between Ralph and little Bobby.

"But you were, weren't you?" He spoke into her ear in a menacing undertone. "Don't forget, I can ruin you."

"And I you," she hissed back. Sudden coughing from Bobby jerked her attention back to the child. Dirt coated his mouth, and he was gagging.

"Oh no, Bobby, don't eat," she cried, wondering where she could get some water. She looked around desperately for help to see Ralph striding away. Was he going to get water? No, he got in his Rolls Royce and drove off. She picked up Bobby and hurried inside the church building, finally locating the drinking fountain. She held the handle and tried to lift him for a drink at the same time, succeeding in getting both of them extremely wet.

The wind felt cool against her damp clothes, so she carried Bobby back to the car. The sun had warmed it inside, and she settled him on the passenger's seat and sang every children's song she could think of. She had paused to think when Bobby looked up and said, "Wuv oo."

She blinked and blinked again. Ralph had just said, "I love you, Alice," and the profanity of his profession next to the purity of Bobby's stood in such stark contrast she couldn't even speak. She hadn't done anything for this child to care for her. She'd not even thought his family ought to keep him.

She recalled Seth saying that Bobby had helped to heal hurts in their family. She was mulling on this when Mrs. Tanner came back, shoulders sagging, carrying a little paper bag. Bobby squealed in delight. His mother got into the front seat, and he launched himself at her and held her tight.

The older woman had obviously been crying. "Are you OK?" Alice asked. "What's wrong?"

Mrs. Tanner shook her head. "Don't mind me. It wasn't a cheery visit, but we'll be all right."

"What do you mean?"

"They want me on bedrest, said otherwise I'll lose the baby. I don't know how I'll manage. They said I'm too old for another pregnancy, and the child will likely have something wrong like Bobby does. It—it was just a lot to take in. I should've been more careful about timing things with my cycle. I was so tired—and now I'm more exhausted than I've ever been in my life."

It *was* a lot to take in. Alice tried to wrap her own mind around it. "Do you *want* to have another baby?"

When Mrs. Tanner didn't answer right away, Alice continued. "There's a place I know about. It's clean and safe. You would simply go to sleep and wake up and there wouldn't be any more pregnancy."

"An abortion, you mean?"

Alice swallowed and nodded, hating the word.

"No, I couldn't do that. I—truth be told, I don't want to be pregnant, don't need another baby. But I know I'll love him or her fiercely once I meet them and not even be able to imagine my life without them."

"But how can you take care of Bobby and the children you already have when . . ." Alice let the question hang. She wouldn't pressure the woman, but she didn't understand.

"God will provide. He always does."

Alice said no more. She put the car in gear and began driving them back to Lindale. When the two tall mill stacks came into view, she thought of Seth working there. Seth, the antithesis of Ralph, inside and out.

Bobby fell asleep on the ride home, and both women were silent. It wasn't until Alice put the car into park outside of the Tanners' home that Milly finally spoke.

"I want to tell you a story, Alice," she said quietly. "If you have a few minutes."

Alice turned to look at her and nodded slightly. Tears shone in Milly's eyes, but her face didn't bear the distress it had when she'd walked out of the clinic. A softness made her plain face pleasant as she began, "When I was seventeen . . ."

Chapter 8

Events from 1907

"When I was seventeen," Milly began, praying silently that God would give her the words. "I fell in love. Crazy, head-over-heels, heart-pounding in love. We spoke of marriage and planned a future together. Jack took me for long buggy rides in the country, and alone and passionate, we began to let down our guard. I became pregnant.

"My parents were furious. My father called me all kinds of names and demanded that Jack and I wed immediately. But this man who'd professed his love over and over left town. Left me. Left our child."

She rubbed a hand over Bobby's soft hair. Thumb in his mouth, cuddling in her lap, his face looked angelic in slumber.

Milly could still remember the emptiness she'd felt, the terror. Her body was changing daily. Nausea. Swelling. Aches and pains and soreness. A tiny round bump, easy to hide for now, but she knew it couldn't stay hidden forever. And the only person who could make it all OK had betrayed her.

One morning, Mother told her to pack a bag, that she must go away. They took the train across Georgia and into South Carolina. While Milly sat queasy and heartsick, Mother never spoke to her. Not one word. She left a space between them, as if Milly were contaminated by a disease.

Milly had no idea what to expect when they finally disembarked in the town of Anderson and walked several blocks to stand before a three-story Victorian mansion which bore a sign "Home for Fallen Women." At the door, they were greeted by a matron in a long, old-fashioned black dress who took them to an office and began going over the rules.

No mail. No visitors. No contact with the outside world at all. A minister came to the home each Sunday, for they were not permitted to go to church. The very sight of them would scandalize the innocent good girls of the community.

No going outside, except at designated times, to walk around the fenced yard.

Study and chores would occupy all waking hours of the day.

She would give birth in the home with a doctor to attend her who would take the baby to an orphanage as soon as it was born.

Mother looked pleased with this. "You will see to it that she doesn't form an attachment with the child, then? I looked into the Florence Crittenton homes, and while they have good Christian teaching, they encourage the girls to keep their babies. We'll have none of that."

The matron nodded. "Absolutely. The girls may not know the gender of the child or even see it. It will be as if it never happened. We keep each girl here until all puerperium signs have disappeared."

"But what will happen to my baby?" Milly couldn't abandon this innocent child the way her parents and Jack were abandoning her. *She* deserved it, but her little one didn't.

"What does it matter?" Mother demanded. "It's a bastard."

And then she left. No goodbye, no embrace, no reassurance of her love. She simply turned and walked out. The matron took everything Milly had brought and put it away, then made her change into a long, dowdy gray wool dress and get busy scrubbing laundry.

She soon discovered there were other rules. Lots of them. The girls were forbidden to talk at meals or at their work. Though there were a dozen of them there, Milly remained lonely, never allowed to speak freely or have an unsupervised conversation with another young woman. The matron seemed determined to make the time there as much like prison as possible in order to impress upon them the evil of their ways. With the help of a girl who had delivered her baby and was leaving, Milly sent a letter to Jack, begging him to come rescue her and their child.

Every Sunday, a different minister came, and they had to sit in hard straight-backed chairs perfectly still for an hour and listen to what most often was a message berating them for their wanton ways and extolling the virtues of chastity. They were reminded that the pains of childbirth were God's judgment for their sin and that they should accept them with humble contrition.

Indeed, nothing was done to relieve or even comfort the laboring women, and the birthing room lay so near the bedrooms that several nights Milly lay awake listening to moans and screams of misery, a laboring girl crying for her mother or for mercy. Etta Jones died in labor, and the minister who came the next Sunday chose as his text "except ye repent, ye shall all likewise perish."

Milly was eight months pregnant when a visiting minister came whom they'd never seen before. When the matron wasn't looking, he handed her a small folded letter and murmured, "Read this and write an answer to send back with me."

Astonished, she opened the note and carefully hid it under guise of reading her Bible. But she heard not one word of the sermon. Though her initial hope had been that Jack had replied, the letter was not from him but from a quiet, boring classmate she'd never thought of much.

My dear Milly,

When you disappeared and were not at school anymore, I began trying to find you. I heard the rumors about what happened and finally found Jack. He said you are carrying a child, but it is not his. I know that's a lie, and I gave him a black eye and busted lip to help him remember the truth. He did tell me where you are, which enabled me to work out this plan with my cousin, Sam Thompson, who lives not too far from there.

I've loved you for years. I want to marry you and adopt the baby and raise him or her as ours. I know you don't feel the same about me as I do about you, so if you aren't interested, I understand. I just thought you ought to have a choice and not be forced to give your baby away. I was adopted out of an orphanage when I was five, and I guess that's why I really want to see kids grow up in families that love them.

Pastor Thompson will get word back to me, and if you want to go forward with marriage, he will help us make the arrangements.

With kind regards,
Ezra Tanner

Though the growing baby pressing against her from all directions sometimes made it hard to breathe, her breathlessness during that sermon had nothing to do with her pregnancy and everything to do with the choice before her. She racked her brain for everything—anything—she could remember about Ezra Tanner, but precious little came to mind. He'd been in love with her for years? How had she missed this in their tiny high school of 25 students?

Marry a man she didn't love and keep her child? Or give up her baby so she could go on to choose her own life? Jack didn't want her, and her parents despised her. She'd been told repeatedly by them, and by the matron here, that she was a disgrace who had no hope of finding a good husband now. Ezra was the only person who cared about her. He must have gone to considerable trouble to get this note to her.

With the only writing utensil she could find—a short, stubby pencil—she wrote:

Thank you, Ezra. I am honored by your proposal and wholeheartedly accept. I pray I can be a good wife to you and make you happy. —Milly

The kind minister took her reply, read it, and nodded. "He will come for you at the end of this week," he promised in an undertone.

Later, lying in her narrow metal cot, unable to find a comfortable position on the thin mattress, she wondered if it was all a dream. How could Ezra really love her, especially now? How could he love this baby? Much as she hated this place and wanted out, the thought of leaving also scared her. Could she entrust her whole future to a near stranger?

Tossing and turning, she began to pray, for the first time in longer than she could remember. God wouldn't really listen to a sinner like her—yet where could she go but to God? Desperately, in the wee hours of the morning, she poured out her hurt, her loneliness, her desperation. She cried out for forgiveness and cleansing for Christ's sake. Somehow she knew He was listening, and peace stole into her heart that this opportunity before her with Ezra was part of His plan. That God would be with them in the vast unknown future.

Several days later, she went outside for her hour of exercise and fresh air. As the days grew warmer, the girls had been tasked with preparing the garden beds. Ezra himself stood there, on the other side of the fence, waiting for her. Solid and strong, he was not handsome, but he smiled, and his eyes lit at the sight of her.

"One of the other girls has the matron distracted," he said. "Do you still want to go with me, Milly?"

"Yes," she gasped and burst into tears. "I can't believe you came. That you would do this."

"We have to hurry," he said simply, but he took her hands through the bars of the iron fence and squeezed.

"There's a ladder in the shed." Milly went to get it and awkwardly carried it over to the fence. Once she was balanced precariously at the top, Ezra reached up and grabbed her around her now thick waist and lowered her to the ground. He took her hand, and they hurried to the train station.

"We'll go to the justice of the peace," he explained. "But not here, in case someone comes looking for you."

Ezra kept hold of her hand for the length of the train trip, speaking gentle reassurances that all would be well. They stopped at Abbeville and went to the courthouse, where she stood in the hideous gray institution dress, swollen from pregnancy but scrawny from lack of food, so scared she was shaking, and pledged her life to Ezra Tanner forever.

It had been the best decision she'd ever made, save finally turning her broken heart to the Lord. Ezra and his parents had never looked at her as defiled or disgusting. Her mother-in-law had been with her for the delivery of her baby. And Ezra had sat with her too. The pain had been intense, but the sweet atmosphere of grace and love had made it bearable. And then the doctor had laid a baby boy in her arms.

Tears streamed down her face as she looked into his sweet face and realized that this moment would have been denied her without this man's incredible, selfless love.

"Will you name him?" she asked Ezra.

Milly's story came to an abrupt end as Alice gasped, face drained of color. "It was Seth, wasn't it?"

"Yes. I almost lost my son. If it hadn't been for Ezra, if God hadn't given me the courage to leave and start a new life—I would have missed so much. I can't even imagine my life without Seth. There were many who didn't understand. My parents never welcomed me to their home again. But my foolish mistake wasn't greater than the sovereignty and redemption of God."

Alice's hands were shaking as she gripped the steering wheel.

"I need to go," she whispered.

"All right," Milly nodded. "All right. I just thought maybe it would help you."

Alice looked up, stricken.

"To see why I could never destroy this child." She rested a hand on her slightly rounded middle.

"Yes, I see," Alice whispered. "I need to go."

Milly shook Bobby gently awake and climbed out of the car. She turned and smiled at Alice. "Thank you for all your care," she told the girl with a smile. She took Bobby's hand and walked up the concrete yard steps. She looked back once to see Alice still staring straight ahead, face awash of tears.

Chapter 9

Thursday, October 4, 1934

Alice went back to her office and began making telephone calls. By the time she left to go home, the arrangements were made. Mrs. Tanner would have help. She could rest, and someone would come every day to take care of Bobby and the household chores. It would all work out, and she could keep her baby safely growing inside. Such a brave, good mother, she would love this child. The whole family would.

Alice wanted nothing more than to go home and lose herself in the latest Agatha Christie mystery, *Murder on the Orient Express*. To try to forget this day and the emotions it had stirred up. But when she got back to her parents' house, there stood Ralph again, as pressed and polished as earlier in the day. And Mother had invited him to have dinner with them.

"You look a fright, Alice. Go upstairs and freshen up," Mother said in an undertone. Woodenly, Alice nodded, resolved to take as long as possible. She was sitting on her bed, one stocking on, one off, staring into space when Mother tapped on the door.

"Alice Vogel, what is wrong with you?" Mother hissed. "Ralph wants to spend time with you, seems interested in renewing your courtship. Surely you're not going to throw away a chance like this over some country yokel?"

Alice stared up at her mother. She would have said the same thing herself only weeks before. Before she'd met the

Tanners and had begun looking for answers to questions she'd never even known to ask.

"I don't feel well," she attempted, not having the energy or time to explain now the things she should have told her mother months ago.

"Put on some fresh make-up and come down and see if a bit of dinner doesn't revive you. You've been working too many hours helping your indigent people, Alice. It's noble work, and your father and I are proud of you. But if you wear yourself out, you'll be no good to anyone."

Mother stepped over, hugged her, and kissed the top of her head. Alice pushed down the emotions threatening to spill over and rose to put on the make-up. She may have looked put together by the time she stepped downstairs, with her hair freshly curled and a dab of *Joy* behind her ears, but her mind was swirling with Milly's story—which was Seth's story too.

Thankfully, Father remained ever eager to discuss politics with Ralph, and they kept up a steady stream of conversation over who would replace Speaker Rainey, who had died in August, and if the Democrats would keep control of the House of Representatives after the midterm elections. Alice picked at her roast beef and scalloped potatoes in silence, mind far from the political machinations that fascinated her father and former beau. At last, the meal ended, and she and Ralph went to sit in the library. She chose an armchair by the fireplace rather than the sofa, so he'd have to sit away from her. Instead, he stood with one arm leaning against the mantel and stared down at her.

"Let's have it out, Allie," he said, and she bristled at his nickname.

"You abandoned me when I needed you most, Ralph. I was scared and alone, and you weren't there for me."

"I gave you the money, didn't I? You had the best in doctors and accommodations. You were never at risk. I've told you before, I had to distance myself from you for a while. In case something got out. It was for us. For our future."

"It was for yourself. Just as it was for yourself that you dated other women while we 'had' to be apart." She rolled her eyes. "I can see exactly what a future with you will look like."

"What's that supposed to mean?"

"Oh, you'll give me nice clothes and jewelry and lavish vacations. We'll get along well enough. My social work will help build your political career. And then something unplanned and difficult will happen—because it always does—and you'll find comfort in an affair or two, but expect me to keep quiet about it because you take good care of me and we're a great team, and public reputation, and all that baloney. And through it all, the good and the bad, I'll still be alone."

He shook his head and lit a cigarette, blowing the pungent smoke nearly into her face. "I don't know what you want from me."

She thought of Ezra traveling over fifty miles to rescue a hugely pregnant girl who didn't love him, then marrying her, and adopting and raising another man's child as his own. That sort of love she'd never seen on the silver screen or read in a novel. Yet in a mill town in Georgia, in a cottage bursting with a lot of children and not much else, there lived a couple who loved each other through unplanned pregnancies and battle scars, through the better and all the worse.

"Go away, Ralph. I want you to leave and not come back."

"You don't want to do this, Alice. I can put it out that—"

"Go ahead." She narrowed her eyes. "The truth is, you've already cost me the one thing I want. There's nothing left you can take from me now."

"If you throw me out now, I won't come back begging."

"Maybe you think that's a threat, but it would be a relief. Please, if you ever cared for me at all, please leave."

"Sure, Allie. I'll leave. And no one else will take you but the unwashed scum you think you're going to elevate. They'll drag you down to their level. You'll wake up one morning with five kids, wearing a flour-sack dress, hoping the soup line is open, 'cause your husband went off to ride the rails." He threw the cigarette into the cold fireplace.

She rose defiantly. "Misery isn't exclusive to poverty, Ralph. You produce a particular kind of misery that all your money and influence can't ease. *Get out.*"

He stepped forward and grabbed her, pulling her close and running his hands over her as if he meant to kiss her—or more. She pushed him away as hard as she could, and he pushed her back so that she stumbled and almost fell. She cried out, and he stormed away; a moment later she heard the front door slam shut.

She sank back into the arm chair, too depleted to stand. She barely looked up when her parents came into the room.

"Did you quarrel?" asked Mother.

"Did he hurt you?" Father demanded.

"He shoved me, but—"

Father made for the door.

"Please don't go after him," Alice pleaded. "Please let it be over between him and me. Please. I don't want . . . I can't build a life with him. Please."

"All right, darling," Mother soothed. "Of course, we won't force you. We just thought—you were so distressed before when things ended between you two."

"He broke my heart, and I can't ever trust him again. I—" She longed to tell them everything, and yet the truth would crush them. They were proud of her, for her social work, and her degree, and for the wholesome young woman they believed her to be. She couldn't face their devastation if they knew the truth.

"I'm tired," she whispered. "I'm going up to bed."

Within a few minutes, she had crawled under her downy comforter, but it was hours before a troubled sleep came.

Chapter 10

Friday, October 5—Wednesday, October 17, 1934

Someone knocked on the front door at seven o'clock the next morning. Milly walked slowly to open it, leaving the kids eating their breakfast oatmeal. Thankfully, Bobby still slept and might continue to for another hour. Beth would be staying home from school to take over the household duties, so Milly could rest and try to keep from losing the baby.

A woman about her own age in a modest brown day dress greeted her.

"Mrs. Tanner?"

"Yes."

"I'm Ida Greene. Alice Vogel over at the Floyd County Charitable Fund asked me to take on Tuesdays and Thursdays."

"Take on?"

"See to the household while you get the needed bedrest."

"Oh. I—I don't have funds for—"

"Everything's been taken care of," she said cheerfully.

"But my daughter can stay out of school for a while . . ."

"There's no need. I'm to be here to see to anything you need me to do until the children get home from school."

Milly gulped and couldn't find words. She stepped aside and let the woman in.

"You settle yourself in that chair," Ida suggested with a friendly smile and a nod at the living room rocker. "I've five children of my own, and I know what to do."

"Thank you," Milly managed and padded weakly to sit down. She hardly knew what to think. She didn't want help—again. Surely the charity organization wasn't doing all this on top of everything else. There were others with greater needs. She could manage.

Ezra came wheeling out, and she explained the situation to him.

"Honey, look at it this way. If you can sit, you can grow the baby and work on some of that new mending pile to earn money. It's as good as getting a job."

She swallowed. "Maybe you're right. But I have a terrible feeling Alice is paying for this out of her own pocket."

"We don't know that. And even if she is, she's doing it because she wants to."

"I think she feels guilty. I told you what she offered. There's only one reason she would know about something like that—"

"Milly, love, suppose that's true. Maybe helping you's part of her finding healing. To save a life where she took another."

Milly shook her head. Her heart ached for Alice. The look in her eyes when Milly had told her own story had been haunted. Something deep and painful lay under Alice's competent and charming exterior.

"Maybe," said Ezra thoughtfully, "Maybe God brought her into our lives for her as much as for us."

She nodded. "You're a wise man," she murmured. "I'll let it be. For now."

She rested all that week and into the next. It felt strange and disconcerting having someone else do her laundry, wash her dishes, and keep an eye on Bobby when he grew tired of sitting beside her looking at their same dilapidated picture books. But she began to feel better. Her spotting stopped and her blood pressure lowered.

On Wednesday the 17th, instead of one of the ladies in Alice's rotation, Alice herself arrived, with their grocery box.

"Sue couldn't come today, and I know it's past time for me to visit and make sure all is going well," she said simply, looking about the house with a small smile.

"It's been wonderful," Milly exhaled. She started to say more but sensed Alice's hesitation. She looked less sure of herself than Milly had ever seen her. So Milly sat back down and continued working on Mrs. Gorham's mending pile, which would bring in $1.50. Soon Alice pulled out a stack of children's books from the library.

"Bobby, look, I've got new books," she offered. "Have you heard *The Little Engine that Could* or *The Story About Ping?*"

Bobby eagerly sat down next to her and mostly listened while Alice read. Milly dozed in her chair as Alice's pleasant tones told the story of *The Velveteen Rabbit.* She awoke to a sharp pain in her middle.

She went to the bathroom and discovered she was bleeding. After a long while, she walked resolutely out to the living room where Bobby had fallen asleep against Alice's side.

"I'm going to lie down for a bit," she murmured. "It appears I'm losing the baby after all."

"What?" Alice looked up in alarm. "If we went to the hospital—"

"No, honey. I've had a miscarriage before. They can't stop it."

"There has to be something we can do."

"Just keep Bobby cared for, and it will ease my mind considerably," Milly assured her. "It's OK, Alice. I'll be all right. It's a sad thing, but this child must be intended to be a treasure waiting for us in Heaven."

Alice nodded, looking ready to cry, and Milly went into the bedroom to tell Ezra. He sat beside her on the bed, his one arm comfortingly around her. So, so much they'd been through together. Her mind flitted back to the story she'd told Alice last week.

"It was when you held Seth, you know," she murmured now.

"What was?"

"The first time I loved you. I didn't say it then, but I knew. The child my mother had despised and no one thought I could raise, you accepted. And I knew in that moment, I wanted to live my life right alongside you."

"I'm sorry most of it has been hard," he answered. "I've always wanted to give you more."

"You've given me unconditional love. Nine children to love on earth and now three to meet in Heaven. And yes, I do think of you as giving me Seth, because without you, I never would have been able to know him and love him and raise him.

A dozen more souls to love Jesus, Ezra, because you showed the love of Christ to me."

He pulled her closer and she rested her head on his chest. The pains came again, stronger, some with an intensity that took her breath away. Ezra couldn't ease them, but he stayed with her while the loss became final, sharing this tender moment when life and death intertwined and Heaven took back what it so briefly had bestowed.

In the evening, long after the children had come home from school and Seth from work, Milly emerged from the bedroom in her worn but warm wrapper and slippers. The kids were playing a game at the kitchen table, and Seth and Alice were finishing up the dishes.

"Momma, are you OK?" Seth hurried over to her, drying his hands on a towel and giving her a gentle hug.

She nodded. "I'll be fine, son." She cleared her throat and blinked, looking at the two of them. "I know folks don't normally speak of such things, but you've both been part of caring for me these past weeks, and I—I thought y'all might want to see the miracle of God's creation in this little girl."

She opened her hand. She'd gently wiped the blood away from the tiny being, only as long as her palm, with perfectly formed tiny hands and feet and translucent skin revealing miniature organs inside. A tiny nose, closed eyelids, even the beginning of downy hair made the being recognizable to her at once as one of their children. Already, she had the look of a Tanner sibling.

A crash startled Milly. Alice had dropped the plate she was drying, and it shattered on the floor. The girl's hand flew to her mouth, and tears pooled in her eyes. Without a word, she ran out of the house, the screen door slamming and echoing in her wake.

And Seth followed her.

Chapter 11

Wednesday, October 17, 1934

Alice couldn't get to her car fast enough. Seth came hurrying out behind her.

"Alice?"

"Please, let me leave."

"I'm not stopping you, only, I'm not sure you ought to be driving right now. Do you want me to take you home?"

She didn't want that. But she couldn't stop crying to see. Couldn't stop shaking to hold the wheel. She sat down on the concrete steps, head in her hands, trying to make the world stop spinning.

"Let me get your things," he said quietly, and went back into the house, returning with her bag, filled with the library books she'd read to Bobby, her purse, and a novel she'd planned to loan Mrs. Tanner.

He opened the passenger door to the Packard and helped her in, then went around to the driver's side. She wanted to ask him how he would get home. She wanted to apologize for causing further trouble in the midst of their loss. But she couldn't speak. Could scarcely move. Every time she closed her eyes, she saw Milly's baby, and she knew.

The doctor had told her the thing inside her would *become* a baby if they didn't remove it. That no one would ever know, that it would be as if it had never happened. He'd promised she wouldn't even remember it any more than she remembered any particular month of her menstrual cycle. He'd assured her she was doing the right thing as a daughter to protect her parents' reputations and feelings.

And she had believed him because she'd wanted everything he'd said to be true, even as she'd ignored a quiet warning in her conscience that maybe she couldn't undo the consequences of her actions so easily. That she might look back with regret someday—

That day had come sooner than she'd expected, and the full realization and weight of what she'd done to her baby crippled her.

The silence in the car grew unbearable as tears trekked down her cheeks and her chest heaved with silent sobs. Seth stole glances at her occasionally. Once, he reached over and briefly squeezed her shoulder after he shifted gears.

Then he began to sing. It was a hymn she'd heard once or twice. Something about praise to God. "With healing balm my soul is filled . . ." How could there ever be healing for what she had done? Then:

> The Lord is never far away,
> but through all grief distressing,
> an ever present help and stay,
> our peace and joy and blessing.
> As with a mother's tender hand,
> God gently leads the chosen band:
> To God all praise and glory.

As with a mother's tender hand. Now her hands gripped the edges of the gray striped upholstery, remembering a day about a year ago when she'd grasped a pen and signed her approval to ending her baby's life.

Seth's voice sounded as smooth as Bing Crosby's and made the anthem a lullaby. When he finished the song, he murmured, "Momma used to sing that to us whenever we were sad or upset."

"You are blessed to have such a mother," she whispered, and he hmm'd his agreement, while still looking at her with concern.

Finally back at Fourth Street, Seth pulled the Packard into the driveway and shut off the engine.

"How will you get home?" she whispered.

"I'm fine. What about you?"

She looked at him for a long moment. The post light and a distant street light dimly illuminated his profile, but the darkness around them helped cloak the darkness of her confession.

"I—killed my baby. I had an abortion. It was Ralph's child, and he said it would be a big scandal and mess up our future, so he gave me the money and told me where to go. And I did it because I wanted him back. I killed my baby for a man who didn't even love me!"

Seth reached for her hand and held it in both of his. "He should have married you. He should have protected you and his child."

"Yes," she whispered, barely able to get out audible words around her sobs. "But I should have stood up to him. Should have stood up for my baby. Like your mother did for you, for Bobby, for the child she lost today. I knew it was wrong, even if I didn't fully understand it was already a person."

After a long time, Seth spoke again. "It was wrong, Alice, but it wasn't unforgivable."

"No? It should be. Why do you think I do all this social work? It's not because I'm a good person. It's because I've been looking for some kind of atonement I'll never find. Because I gave myself outside of marriage, and then I took the life of my child."

She jerked her hand away and pulled her bag to her chest. "Goodbye, Seth," she whispered.

"I'll be praying for you, Alice. That you understand the forgiveness we have in Jesus. I'm here if you ever want to talk." His compassionate voice broke her a little more. When she gave no reply, he squeezed her hand, then left the car and walked into the dusk, humming the tune of the hymn he'd sung.

At last, Alice gathered up the strength to get out of the car. She took in the comfortable two-story brick home where she'd grown up. Her parents had given her so much, a life most of her peers envied. She'd been the sole focus of their attention and affection. If she could find in them or in her upbringing a valid excuse for what she'd done, it might be a bit of salve on her raw conscience. But no relief of blame came.

Mother and Father rose as she stepped into the living room.

"Alice, thank goodness you're home," Mother exclaimed, hovering, the cloying scent of her bath powder nearly making Alice gag. "The most terrible rumor—but you must know."

"Know?" she asked stupidly.

"About—what they're saying," Mother stammered. "From the look on your face, you must have heard it too.

Ralph's cousin is spreading a vicious lie. She said the reason he ended things when you were in college is because you were of easy virtue and tried to get him to take responsibility for another man's child—"

She looked up at their faces, both of them desperate for her to deny the accusations now being spread abroad.

I can ruin you, you know.

He had. Utterly. She'd lost the relationship she thought she had with him and any future relationship with a worthy young man. Now, apparently, she'd lost the respect of her parents and the community. And as bad as all this loss was, it didn't compare to the worst. She closed her eyes and moaned, for she saw again that tiny human in Milly's palm. She'd lost her child by her own choice.

"I had an abortion last year," she said flatly. "Ralph paid for it. It was his child."

Leaving them gawking, she went upstairs, fell across her bed, and wept.

Chapter 12

Sunday, October 21—Thursday, November 8, 1934

Several days later, Milly finally had a chance to talk to Seth. The others had all gone to bed after a full and pleasant Sunday together, but he sat by the living room lamp, staring into space. His uncharacteristic idleness and solemness jarred her.

"What's the matter, son?" she asked gently. "Is it about Alice?"

He moved to stir the embers of the dying fire. A lingering odor of woodsmoke permeated the room from the first blaze of the season on this chilly night.

"She told me she had an abortion," he said without meeting her eyes. "When she saw your baby, it made it all real to her. That it was a child, you know, a life. She thinks she can't be forgiven. I want to help her see that she can. But she wasn't really in the right frame of mind to listen anyway."

"Probably not. She'll grieve now though, which is healing."

"Momma, I . . ." his voice trailed off, but finally he met her eyes. "Would you think I was crazy if I said I still love her? I know she did an awful thing, having the abortion. And of course she wasn't chaste to get into such a situation. But I want to take care of her. That Ralph took advantage of her. If he would've manned up as he should have, she never would have been left feeling she had no other way."

"I wouldn't think you were crazy. No more crazy than your father coming after me when I was carrying you."

He nodded, thoughtfully. "I guess all this with Alice has made me understand your and Daddy's story a little better. How scared you musta been. How you didn't know how it would all turn out."

"I don't want to see you get hurt if Alice rejects you again," Milly said.

"It's OK if she rejects me, if she'll only accept the forgiveness she has in Jesus," Seth answered. "That's why I gotta talk to her. She thinks she's unlovable, but maybe if she knows *I* still love her, she'll be able to accept that Christ does, and much more than I ever could."

Milly cleared her throat and blinked her eyes. She was terribly proud of this young man's character, even though she felt it wasn't due to her at all.

"I'll be praying, son," she promised. "For both of your hearts. You tell Alice I've been praying for her every day."

*****

A knock on her bedroom door woke Alice from partial slumber. She blinked and looked around the dim room, wondering what time it was and what day. When she'd gone to work the day after the rumors began, she'd been fired on the spot, for the charity could not employ a young woman of questionable character. Mother had talked about going away, taking a trip to Atlanta or Charleston or even Florida. As if a trip could fix this.

72

The knock again. Mother opened the door. "Alice," she said, determination in her tone, "that young man is here again."

"What young man? Again?"

"The mechanic. Seth, is it?"

"Yes. Seth Tanner. He's been here before?"

"He's come twice in the past two weeks, but I told him you weren't receiving guests. But you have to leave this room sometime, and he seems most concerned for you."

She nodded. "I'll come down in a minute," she said.

Her clothes were rumpled from sleeping in them. She changed to a fresh dress and ran a brush through her hair. Her eyes were red and puffy, and she looked pale from too many days indoors, but she didn't bother with cosmetics. Seth knew the ugliest thing about her, so what if he saw her looking ugly too?

He wasn't wearing his church suit this time, but a simple flannel shirt, dungarees, and suspenders. He smiled gently when she stepped into the front hall.

"Hullo, Alice."

She nodded, not finding any words for the myriad of emotions swirling in her. He'd come. None of her college friends had come to see her, none of her childhood playmates. Her parents seemed to be holding her at arms' length, unsure what to do with her. Only Seth was here, and wonder of wonders, looking pleased to see her.

"What if we sit outside? It's a nice day, and you look like you could use some sunshine."

"OK."

She followed him to her backyard where they sat down on a wooden bench. Except for some brave pansies and late roses, the flowers were gone, but the oaks and elms arching overhead made the yard a wonder of crimson and gold. How many perfect autumn days had she missed holed up in her bedroom?

Seth took her hands. "I went by the charity to talk to you, and they told me what happened. I'm really sorry your personal business has been made public."

"It's nothing I don't deserve after what I did. I've been half expecting a police officer to come and haul me off to jail. I broke the law, besides it being morally wrong."

"There's something I want to say to you, and I'd like you to hear me out."

"I'll listen," she promised, looking into the distance to avoid his unflinching gaze. His scent was a combination of woodsmoke and something like motor oil, manly to the core, and his very otherness compelled her to listen to him as much as his determination to come and talk to her.

"Alice, Scripture tells us Christ bore our sins in His body on the tree. Jesus became sin for us that we might become the righteousness of God in Him. That's the Gospel. None of us deserves forgiveness, and none of us can earn it. That's what *grace* means."

He paused, and his feet crunched some leaves below. He put his arm around her, and she buried her head against his chest.

"Father's an atheist," she began, "but Mother took me to church and told me about Jesus all my life. I always thought it a nice story. But lately, I've been reading the Bible, because I feel so—desperate. Desperate to know if God could still love me."

"So much that He already made a way for your forgiveness before you ever sinned."

"Mother says I'm fixating on it too much. She says having the abortion was the best way to fix my mistake. She's only upset people found out. But I saw your tiny sister. She was a person. And my baby was too."

"And your baby's life—and death—was not in vain if it leads you to Christ. If it gives you a new perspective on life and a new appreciation for the value of every one."

"I don't understand why God would let your little sister die. Your mother wanted her. She's a good mother."

"I don't know why. But her life won't be in vain, either, if it also helps you understand and appreciate your own baby. Momma named her, you know."

She met his eyes then, their soft blue looking back at her with such tenderness.

"What name?" she whispered.

"Alice. Because you came into our lives about the same time and helped us through a difficult season."

Alice couldn't speak around the lump in her throat. Maybe they thought her a godsend, but in reality, *they* had changed *her* life.

"I'm thinking about going away," she blurted out.

He smoothed her hair. "If you need to. We all miss you. Just 'cause you don't work at the charity anymore doesn't mean you can't come visit us as a friend. Bobby asks about 'Miz A-wice and books' everyday."

She smiled for the first time in weeks. "I would like that," she said softly.

He met her eyes again. "I would too, Alice. I would like to see you again very much." He squeezed her shoulders briefly before rising and adjusting his newsboy cap on his dark hair. He looked back at her and smiled, and even though he didn't say the words, she knew he loved her more selflessly than anyone ever had. Long after he let himself out through the gate, she sat recalling their conversation.

She didn't deserve Seth Tanner. And she didn't deserve Christ's forgiveness and redemption either. Somehow she'd been offered both.

And now she knew her baby's name.

Grace.

Epilogue

Alice climbed the concrete steps and then the porch steps to the Tanners' front door and rapped hesitantly. She twisted and untwisted her cold metal coat buttons till Milly opened the door.

"Alice!" the older woman cried and enveloped her in a warm embrace. Alice felt tears sting her eyes. How she had missed this place and this family!

"Now you come on in." Milly began bustling. "Let's get you some tea and some pie. Jane, you put on the kettle. Beth, you go see what Bobby's calling me for. Alice, how are you here all the way from Atlanta? And look at you, so pretty and stylish, but of course you always are."

The interior of the house had been painted recently, Alice noted, and a new bookshelf adorned the living room, the radio beside it. Milly herself had on a pleasant floral house dress, which looked as if it might have come from the Sears Roebuck catalog and not flour sacks.

"Is it going all right, Mr. Tanner back at the mill?" she asked as Milly sliced wedges of buttermilk pie.

"Oh, he's not at the mill, honey. He went back to work there, and they were glad to have him, but after studying all that law stuff while he was down recovering, he got a job at the county courthouse. He's making more money than he ever

77

has, and it's not as taxing on him physically. He don't do any odd jobs after work anymore, just comes home and spends time with the kids and me. Did you ever hear of anything so wonderful?"

"I'm delighted for you." Alice removed her beret and gloves, wishing she'd taken time to change into something less fancy than the clothes she'd worn on the train from Atlanta to Rome. "Seth didn't write me about that."

"He hasn't been around much himself, Seth hasn't. He still works every waking minute."

"That's so he could buy a house and marry you, Miss Alice," cried Jane, hands clasped in dreamy wonder.

"Jane, girl, that's your brother's to tell, not yours," chided her mother.

"Truth be told, his letters have been sporadic of late, and I began to fear he'd changed his mind," Alice admitted. "Cousin Adam used to tease me that Seth and I were single handedly responsible for keeping the United States Postal Service in business, but over the past six weeks . . ." She let the sentence trail off like their correspondence had and hoped her face didn't display her misery for Milly to read.

Milly shook her head. "You need to talk to Seth before we all go giving away all his news. Now, he'll be by here about six o'clock to collect his mail and hoping I'll ask him to stay for supper. You sit and visit with us, Alice, till then."

But during her year in Atlanta, Alice had grown used to working alongside another woman. She'd lived with her great aunt and uncle, who had a cottage on the Wisteria House property where their son lived and operated a diabetic clinic. Aunt Carrie, as down to earth as Milly Tanner, had included

Alice in the housework as naturally as if she were her own daughter.

Now, Alice chatted with Milly while she peeled vegetables, telling all about the Florence Crittenton Home for unwed mothers where she'd worked this past year. She loved making each young woman's first moments there welcoming and reassuring. Loved organizing the paperwork and had even discovered she had a knack for fundraising through making connections with the wealthy and influential women at the Atlanta Woman's Club. She could move easily from one social class to the next, and that made her good at her work.

Her Atlanta relatives, even learning why she had fled from home, had accepted her and shown her something she'd never known before—what it meant to not only believe the Gospel, but to walk with Jesus day by day. The love they'd poured into her, she'd been able to pour into the hurting women at the unwed mother's home. And the model of Christian marriage she'd seen with Uncle Joseph and Aunt Carrie and the younger relatives near them had given her a longing for a home like theirs. A love built on the greatest love of all.

She would go back there, after this Thanksgiving break, unless . . . unless an opportunity presented itself that meant even more to her.

At five-thirty, Mr. Tanner arrived home to rambunctious hugs from the children. He greeted Alice as happily as if she were one of them. She continued to converse with Mr. and Mrs. Tanner, but all the time, her ears were straining for the first sounds of Seth's arrival. A quarter after six, the children finally began clamoring about him, and then she heard him noisily making his way down the hall, teasing and carrying on with each of them.

When Seth stepped into the kitchen and saw her, he stopped short and froze.

"Hello, darling," she murmured.

Seth stood by her side in two great strides.

"Aren't you a sight better than mail?" he said, cupping her face, and looking as if he meant to kiss her, then realized their rapt and suddenly silent audience. He hugged her instead, and she breathed in the scents of Ivory soap and his leather jacket. "Good thing I went home and got cleaned up before coming here."

"Y'all run along," Milly said. "I'm sure you've got a heap of catching up to do."

"Are you gonna ask—" Ruby began loudly, but Beth clamped a hand over her mouth, resulting in a tussle.

"You wanna take a walk and see my new house?" he asked.

"Of course."

"Me go! Me go!" Bobby cried.

"Not this time, Bobby boy," Seth said, but the child looked so crestfallen that Alice interceded on his behalf.

"Let him come, Seth. He can be our chaperone."

"Ha! All right, whatever you want. You know he'll expect me to carry him on my shoulders half the way."

The walk took a full ten minutes. Seth took her hand and asked about her trip up and how much time she had off for the holiday, but their conversation felt stilted, the twittering birds filling in the silent spaces. Alice blinked back tears, and twisted and untwisted her coat buttons again, wondering why his letters had changed in frequency and tone. Had he found someone else? Changed his mind about their future? But if that were the case, why had he looked thrilled to see her?

She felt Seth watching her as they turned down a quiet tree-lined street, and he stopped before a sweet little bungalow.

"Oh," she breathed.

"It's, uh, small, I know, compared to—"

"It's perfect."

"Do you want to see inside?"

"Definitely."

He unlocked the front door and set Bobby down. The boy scampered to a corner of the living room, where Seth had set up wooden blocks and a toy train set.

"Oh, Seth, how thoughtful of you," she murmured.

They walked through the rooms together. Living room, kitchen, dining room, and green-and-white tiled bathroom. Two small bedrooms.

"Is it too small?" he asked again when they were back in the main room.

"You're the only one living here. You tell me."

"Alice—are you just back for Thanksgiving?"

She traced the toe of her square heel pump along the woodgrain on the hardwood floor. "I—your letters changed. I worried you might have . . . second thoughts."

"No. I bought this house for us, and I planned to come visit you in Atlanta to see if you would be willing . . . but first I went to talk to your father."

She sucked in a breath. "What did he say?"

"He laughed. Told me all the ways he'd provided for you financially and asked did I really think you'd leave all your important work in the capital city to come be a grease monkey's wife?"

"He didn't speak for me, Seth."

"I know. But I began to wonder if I'd been crazy all this time to think you'd choose this life. When you could have and do so much more. I thought I must be a fool to even hope for it." Seth exhaled and looked at her. "I don't want you to have any regrets about how marrying me might limit your life."

She rested her hand against his cheek. "I once let fear of my life being limited lead me to the worst decision I ever made. You and your family taught me that sometimes we are freer within a limited sphere than when we think we can do anything we want. I would be honored to do *this* life with you, Seth—if you're still asking."

"Oh, I'm asking." He stepped over to the mantel, opened a decorative wooden box, and fished a small diamond ring out of the inside. "Alice Vogel, I love you. Will you marry me?"

"Yes," she whispered as Seth lowered his mouth to hers and pulled her close, kissing her with the ardor of a man who knew what he wanted. She clasped the back of his neck and melted into his arms and his gentle, generous affection.

Their moment was interrupted by small hands pulling at their clothes.

"Me 'ug 'oo! Me 'ug 'oo!"

"A hug for you, too, huh?" Seth smiled down at his little brother. "Come here then. First, I have to tickle you."

Bobby shrieked with laughter, and soon Seth was chasing him around the little house. She smiled, watching them.

"And what are you thinking about, Miss Vogel?" Seth asked, returning to her and pulling her into his arms again.

"That I can't wait to marry you and get started making this house too small."

The End

Author's Note

The pro-life issue is one that has been important to me throughout my life, but that took on a more personal meaning in 2013, when I was pregnant with my second child. After a routine ultrasound at 18 weeks, I was sent to a specialist who gave us a lot of confusing information about our baby's condition. We found out that he had two "markers" for Down Syndrome, and a lot of tears, anxiety, and soul searching followed that visit. I began to realize that there was a difference in being against abortion as a practice and in being truly *pro-life*—recognizing the value and worth of every person as fearfully and wonderfully created by a Sovereign God.

During those difficult weeks, I remember reading one mother's testimony that your baby is not a diagnosis but a person, a person whom you will love. That gave me peace as we waited for further information about our son's condition. It turned out that the markers in his heart and kidney resolved. He did not have Downs, and, in fact, after an initial 20 hours in the NICU at birth, he grew to be my kid with a freakishly strong immune system. While I am thankful for his health, I also recognize that that was not the only way our story could have ended happily. I have been blessed to know many families with a beautiful and beloved extra-chromosome child.

(By the way, Trisomy 21 was not named "Down Syndrome" until the 1960s, after Dr. John Langdon Down. The offensive terms "Mongolism" and "retarded," would have been used before that time.)

The setting for this story—Rome and its suburb of Lindale in northwest Georgia—is home to me now, and it was fun to incorporate it into the story. I live in one of the century-old mill houses like the one described as the Tanners' house, complete with concrete steps from the road into the front yard. The Lindale Mill employed the town and operated a highly successful manufacturing plant for several decades as well as building a close knit community. Berry College's beautiful campus is one of the gems of North Georgia, and the story of Martha Berry and her work to bring an education to the poor children of her community is truly remarkable.

The Floyd County Charitable Fund is entirely of my own imagination, but the Healthmobile was a real initiative to help women and children in rural parts of the state get the health care they needed.

The home for "fallen women" described by Milly is fictitious and would have been a severe example of an unwed mothers' home in any era. While there were homes that were unwelcoming and pressured the young mothers to give up their babies, other maternity homes were run by loving Christian women who desired to serve the Lord and help the women in their charge. The Florence Crittenton Homes of the late 1800s and early 1900s were located in cities across the nation. With a strong evangelical emphasis, they trained women for motherhood and honorable employment and encouraged them to keep and raise their children. As the government began to get more involved and societal attitudes shifted, the homes facilitated more adoptions, and the atmosphere and services changed, eventually losing the Christian focus of their founder. The Atlanta Florence Crittenton Home opened in 1892 and operated until 1981.

My long-term readers may recognize "Cousin Adam" and "Uncle Joseph" and "Aunt Carrie" from my Wisteria House Series. A future novel may include other members of Alice's extended family. You can keep up with my stories by signing up for my newsletter at www.jenniferqhunt.com or by following me at Jennifer.Q.Hunt.Author on Instagram.

Many thanks to my writing partners Hannah and Aubrey—it was a delight to work with y'all on this special book. And I was thrilled that my own cover designer, Kelsey Gietl, was chosen to create our beautiful cover. Getting to work with my friend and fellow author Sarah Everest as our editor was another joy in this project. And thank you to Sarah Hanks, founder of Brave Authors, for giving me this opportunity and organizing the whole project.

For those struggling with guilt or pain over a past abortion, the resources available at https://deeperstill.org have been created for your unique needs and come highly recommended.

The Missionary and the Marine

by Hannah Hood Lucero

Chapter 1

12 Months and Three Days Ago
New Orleans, LA

" . . . Happy birthday, dear Walt. Happy birthday to you!" DuWayne Walters beamed at his makeshift family as they concluded the obligatory serenade. His facial muscles strained to maintain the expression when his friends and girlfriend transitioned into an off-key rendition of *For He's a Jolly Good Fellow.* They meant well, but the reminder of his involuntary medical retirement from Marine special operations took a sizable chunk out of the enjoyment of being the center of attention.

Iris Jones had one hand resting on her swollen abdomen, fork hovering in her other as if she might stab the cake before it was even cut. Her husband, Barrett Jones, Esquire, draped his arm around her shoulders, restraining her and gently prompting her to lower the fork. They were like night and day, and not just because she was the scrappy street rat while he was from more refined stock.

Walt cleared his throat, pulse ticking up when his girlfriend of three years, Nadia Hamdan, slid her hand into his. He automatically met her dark brown eyes which were glinting at him in the candlelit private room of the swanky French Quarter restaurant. Her bright red lips parted, but she didn't get a word out before Iris spoke loudly across the table.

"You gonna blow that candle out before the whole top of the cake is coated with wax, birthday boy?"

Walt extinguished the candle in question and turned back to Nadia, glancing over her shoulder to meet the mirthful gaze of her brother. Tarif nodded encouragingly. There was no backing out. Not after the conversations they'd had over the course of the last month. And there wasn't any more time to procrastinate. For starters, Walt wasn't getting any younger than the three decade mark he'd hit yesterday, and he needed to move on to the next chapter of his life. More importantly, Tarif and Nadia had a red-eye out of New Orleans, and Walt wanted time to celebrate one more milestone with his friends—assuming Nadia didn't shoot him down entirely.

"What's wrong, *Albi*?" Nadia squeezed his hand as she used the Arabic pet name, reminding him that if she could so readily call him "my heart," she wasn't likely to shatter it with a rejection. How had he gotten so lucky? Not only did Nadia love him, but she had embraced the two most important people in his life—his mom and little sister. Occasionally, he questioned if it was really him she wanted to spend time with, or if the thick-as-thieves trio had been running a long con under his nose.

Mom had been dropping hints about him settling down since the day he'd told her his pen pal was officially his girlfriend. And Ashley never missed an opportunity to point out how lucky and undeserving Walt was, and how he better not screw it up.

He pushed his chair back, wincing as he shifted his semi-bum left leg into position and knelt down to the floor on the good knee. With Nadia's hand still in his, he swallowed his rising emotions. Her eyes brimmed with tears and a collective gasp came from everyone except Tarif.

"Nadia Saada Hamdan. I have loved you since the moment I laid eyes on you."

"You mean when you pointed a gun at me?"

"Okay, you got me. I have loved you since the second time I saw you, crouched behind that dumpster off Saint Claude Avenue with shrapnel and burning debris raining down on us."

She shook her head, laughing under her breath and muttering, "Liar."

"You changed everything when you responded to my first email. You kept me sane in the midst of chaos for months, giving me something to live for and a reason to come back home. That first dance in the middle of Jackson Square . . . I knew then that I'd never look at another woman again." He grew serious, tears filling his eyes to match the ones now trickling down her perfectly flushed, tawny cheeks. The silent understanding in her gaze wiped out the residual doubt in his mind.

Of course she'd say yes. Hadn't they talked about the future, kids, and building the kind of legacy that neither of their fathers had given them? They were meant for each other, stronger together, and uniquely equipped to understand the scars life had inflicted on both their souls.

"I know this isn't how things were supposed to go. I'm jumping the gun by at least a year. But I don't want to wait any longer for the next chapter. Now, only one of us is going on *missions*."

She snorted softly at his pun. What more could a guy ask for than a woman who understood his humor and laughed at the worst of his jokes? Nadia sharing the gospel of Jesus Christ was a far cry from anything he'd ever been tasked with in the Corps.

"Will you let me be the home you come back to when you take a breather from that Great Commission?" He cupped her face with his hand and brushed some of her tears away. "Will you marry me . . . sometime soonish?"

Nadia took a deep breath, pulling her hand from his to frame his face firmly as she leaned closer.

"DuWayne Kent Walters, you are the last thing I expected for myself." A grin tugged at the right side of her mouth. "Thankfully, God knows so much better. I have loved you since that first email . . . even if I refused to let you know it for a while."

"I had my suspicions."

"Yes," she whispered where only he could hear.

"Yes?" he said a bit louder.

She nodded, leaning forward until their lips met. The loud cheers of their audience barely registered in his mind as it raced with elated thoughts of how he was kissing the woman he would spend the rest of his life with. The one who would give him children and a home and a renewed sense of purpose. His little sister was right, Nadia was way too good for him, but he wasn't about to remind her of that fact.

"To the happy couple!" Iris rasped emotionally. She raised her glass of sweet tea when the newly engaged duo refocused their attention to the table.

Not a dry eye.

"Love gives us hope." Barrett lifted his glass as well, saying, "My hope for the two of you is endless joy, lots of mini-Walts—"

"Hey, now." Iris shoved Barrett's shoulder. "Careful what you wish for."

Walt shrugged. "She has a point."

"I'll amend that to say, may you have children as beautiful as Dee and as level headed as their Uncle T, with just enough Walt to keep us smiling." Barrett waited for a response.

"Here, here!" Tarif raised his glass in agreement.

Everyone toasted and laughed together, tossing around suggestions for the perfect wedding date and location.

"This is getting out of hand." Nadia laughed after Iris suggested they rent out the Audubon Aquarium, but only if their NFL buddy, Silas Landry, could be in the mermaid tank for the ceremony. "Will you guys do me a favor?"

"Name it." Walt kissed her cheek. "The bride gets everything she wants."

"That's the thing." She sat up straighter. "I don't want to fall into old thinking. I . . . don't need the temptation of things I already put behind me. It would start with a flower arrangement here and a tablecloth there, and before you know it, I could turn into a complete monster."

"What are you saying?" Some of Walt's anxiety returned. "You don't want a wedding?"

"I'm not saying that." She intertwined her fingers with his. "All I need is you, *Albi*. What I really want is for you to get the wedding of your dreams, whatever that looks like. I'll be happy with the courthouse, a church, or even behind that old dumpster on Saint Claude. So long as you're standing next to me. You plan everything. Or work with Iris, Maggie, and Ash. You understand, right?”

The way she swallowed hard and blinked up at him put a lump in his throat. She was scared of the spoiled rich girl she used to be.

“Yeah, baby.” He squeezed her hand gently. “I get it. Don’t give it another thought.”

As if someone had pinched her, Iris yelled, “Hey! Where’s the ring?”

Walt slapped his hand to his forehead before digging into his right pocket.

“I knew I was forgetting something.”

Tarif chuckled from the other side of Nadia. “I would have reminded you if Iris hadn’t.”

Walt opened the small black box. He’d debated buying a new ring, but Tarif had assured him that *this* one would mean so much more to Nadia. Her hand flew to cover her crimson lips as she stared at the small solitaire diamond set on a simple gold band.

“Our mother’s ring,” she finally said, darting a look at her brother. “Tarif, are you sure? It was meant to be yours . . . for your wife.”

“Who’s to say I’ll ever marry?”

“Bite your tongue,” Nadia chided. “I want nieces and nephews. But I will accept the ring, of course.”

“Of course,” Tarif said in a serious tone, but winked at Walt when Nadia returned her gaze to the jewelry in question.

Walt took the small ring from the safety of the velvet and placed it on Nadia’s finger. A perfect fit.

"Oh, Dee. What a treasure." Iris sobbed into her slice of cake, no doubt wishing she had something of her mother's. When she'd been orphaned, she'd also been robbed of anything that belonged to her parents, thrown into the foster system, and been all but forgotten by the outside world.

Walt's heart grew light in his chest as the conversation ebbed and flowed, and they all ate too much of the decadent cake from Sucré bakery. If this was the future God had planned for him, surrounded by friends who were more like family, he was beyond blessed. Once his leg fully healed, he'd be able to find a new career and build the little homestead he'd always dreamed about.

By the time Barrett picked up the check—despite protests from Tarif and Walt—it was nearing nine o'clock. They'd stayed too long for Walt to ask for a dance in Jackson Square.

"Six months isn't long," Nadia chimed as she slid into the seat next to Tarif.

"It's a date. Six months from now, a dance *and* a kiss this time."

"Fine. If you insist."

She still teased him about how forward he'd been, trying to kiss her before he'd taken her on a proper date. Thank God they were beyond all the guessing games now. Maybe he'd marry her right before their dance in the heart of the French Quarter.

The closer they got to the airport, the harder it became to breathe. Something felt different this time. Was it because they were engaged? It's not like that factor made him love or worry about her any more than he had before. Was it a projection of his own PTSD because Nadia and Tarif would be in a country that bordered Saudi Arabia, where he'd nearly died? Oman was the fourth safest country in the world—supposedly. If he voiced his concerns, Nadia and Tarif would repeat the same reassurances they always did.

Nadia must've sensed his worry from where she sat sandwiched in the middle of his Silverado's bench seat.

"*Albi*," she purred, laying her head on his shoulder and squeezing his bicep with the hand that had the new-to-her heirloom engagement ring. "Are you thinking too much again?"

"Maybe." He let out a long sigh.

"We'll be—" Tarif began.

"Completely safe." Walt finished for him. "So I've been told. And it still doesn't make me feel any better."

The Hamdans exchanged a look that Walt registered in his periphery.

"If I had a visa . . . and less of a limp . . ." Walt rambled, trying to think of ways around the obstacles.

"Next time," Nadia said with a note of promise in her voice.

"I'd be a garbage missionary," he argued against himself. "We all know it."

Tarif let out a hearty laugh. "God uses all types, Brother. Or have you forgotten the mountain of cards stacked against the two of us."

"Good point."

Walt may have spent his entire adulthood in nearly constant battle with the very people the Hamdans hoped to convert, but Tarif and Nadia had grown up completely immersed and sold out to Islam, raised by a father so radical he had spiraled into full blown terrorism. Abdula Hamdan had risen to the highest echelon of ISIS before being sentenced to life in prison for material support to a foreign terrorist organization. The first miracle had been Tarif and Nadia's conversion to Christianity after how they'd been raised.

Ironically, Walt, Iris, and Barrett, had all been involved in the operation that took Abdula Hamdan down for good. The second miracle was that the ragtag team had cultivated unbreakable bonds with Tarif and Nadia—though, that had a lot more to do with their conversion than any other factor.

Walt pulled his truck up to the drop-off curb for departures at Louis Armstrong International Airport, dreading the thought that he was about to kiss Nadia goodbye for six long months. Tarif opened the passenger door and sent a pointed look back across the cab.

"Five minutes," he said before shutting the door and moving toward the tailgate to offload luggage.

"Will you wait for me, Walt?" Nadia smirked.

He tried to muster a smart remark to play along, but only managed to stare at her dark eyes for a beat too long.

"Uh-oh." She bit down on the bottom lip that was significantly less red after all the eating and kissing they'd indulged in over the course of the evening.

"You know I will." His chest ached, desperate for the mission trip to pass quickly so he could be right back at this airport, picking her up. "I'm all in. No matter what."

"Me too," she whispered. "I love you so much."

"I love you, baby." He wrapped her in his arms, pulling her close and kissing her temple. Breathing in a lungful of her unique fragrance—cinnamon, jasmine, and vanilla—he exhaled the words, "I don't want you to go."

Nadia was silent for a long moment. Finally, she shifted in his arms to look up at him. Her finger trailed along his jaw, her eyes roaming over his face as if committing every centimeter to memory.

"My purpose is to finish my course." She reminded him of her mantra derived from Acts 20:24.

Walt had memorized the entire verse before they'd ever started dating. She'd had the same automatically generated signature on the bottom of every email correspondence she'd sent him over the course of the five years they'd known each other. In the beginning, he'd read it each and every time because he liked the parallel it set between them. Both were on a path of total surrender to their cause. Nadia valued her calling to testify about God's grace over her own life, just as Walt was willing to die in service to his country.

Somewhere along the way, the verse had stopped reminding him of what they had in common and had become something he hated. The more he grew to love Nadia, the harder it was to accept her willingness to wage war on forces much more dangerous than men with guns. The target on her back was otherworldly, but so was the shield protecting her. And that was the real issue. Walt wasn't her protector—God was. It should bring him comfort, but it drove him insane. He couldn't kill the fleshly need to be the one to keep her safe.

"Walt, come on." Nadia tugged on the back of his neck until his forehead rested on hers. "You're overthinking it."

"I'm a weak man, Nadia."

"I know that's not true."

"My faith is lacking," he insisted.

After a deep breath, she nodded. "Okay. You need to do something about it. Workout your faith as much as you workout those biceps."

He forced his worry down and his lips up, reminding himself that the worst feeling to carry into a deployment was a heavy goodbye.

"You're right."

"I usually am." She placed a quick, feather-light kiss on his lips.

"I can't wait to marry you." He took advantage of the little time they had left, kissing the beautiful woman so thoroughly he hoped she still felt the love lingering on her lips well into next week.

After the five minutes Tarif had allotted, a tap on the passenger window drew Nadia's attention away from Walt's kiss. She waved at her brother and slipped the engagement ring off her left hand.

"Whoa, whoa, whoa," Walt protested. "What's happening?"

She chuckled and held the ring out toward him. "Keep it safe for me, *Albi*. Please."

"You're not going to wear it?"

"I don't want to lose it." She pressed the ring into his palm. "The mission field is no place for something so precious."

An idea popped into his head as he pulled the velvety box out of his pocket and tucked the ring safely back into it.

"I need one more minute." He leaned over Nadia and retrieved a pair of pliers out of his glove compartment. "I'm not letting you leave here with a bare finger."

"I'm intrigued." Nadia studied his every move as he fished his dog tags out of his shirt and slid them over his head. He wrapped the ball chain necklace around her finger and guesstimated the best spot to cut the chain, then snapped it into a ring that he slid onto her finger.

"Why do I get the feeling you've done that before?" Nadia tilted her head.

"I have."

A look of betrayal flashed in her eyes.

"A Marine buddy—Langston was his name—fancied himself in love with a sweet little cocktail waitress in Las Ve—" Walt stopped talking when Nadia's left eyebrow shot up. "You know . . . the details aren't really important."

"Hmmm." She kept the judgmental expression plastered on her face, but her eyes betrayed the laugh she held inside. "Did Langston take the waitress to a Vegas chapel?"

"Nope." Walt diverted his gaze to the dash. "We spent the night in a drunk tank and never saw her again. Then narrowly escaped the wrath of Captain Crosson when we got back to base."

"Too bad." Nadia shook her head. "Poor Langston."

"Yeah." Walt would mess up the goodbye with his big mouth, but he hated open-ended stories. "Langston died a few months after that."

"ISIS?" Nadia's voice wavered. She always assumed her father was to blame when Walt opened up about fallen

Marines. And though she tried to hide it, he saw how she carried a guilt that didn't belong to her.

"Babe. No." He shook his head, lying through his teeth. "A training accident."

Maybe he should get an FBI badge like Iris's. He could fabricate a story as well as the most seasoned Fed.

A second, more forceful knock accompanied Tarif's muffled Arabic.

"What did he say?" Even in the dark, Walt could see the blush fill Nadia's cheeks.

"Roughly translated, 'The sooner we leave, the sooner we get back.'"

"You're lying," he accused.

"You're lying about how Langston died." She gave him a sad smile. "And I only left out the part that I'm going to smack Tarif for insinuating."

"Ha!" Walt could imagine. "I heard *tifl*. He's talking about us making a baby, isn't he?"

"Keep working on your Arabic, so you don't have to wonder about these things," she whispered, leaning toward him.

"Love you, Dee." He kissed her one last time.

"I love you, *fiancé*." She slid away from him and opened the passenger door. Then she tacked on, "Eternally."

Chapter 2

Present Day
Yemen

Nadia Hamdan attempted to open her eyes as hands gripped her shoulders, shaking her gently. Between debilitating fatigue and swelling from the backhand she'd taken yesterday, she couldn't make out the face of her rescuer. It had to be Walt. Hadn't she heard his voice moments ago?

"I missed our dance, *Albi*. And your birthday." She mumbled. "I'm so sorry."

"Nadia." The heavy French accent of her fellow captive robbed her of the hope that had once again formed in her hours of unconsciousness. Why did her dreams have to be so vivid? "Nadia, they are coming."

"Walt." His name escaped her chapped lips a moment before the door to their prison burst open.

Tears burned her eyes when the harsh and familiar voices of their captors assaulted her ears.

God, will you ever save us?

Nadia wept, ignoring the threats of more violence. What did it matter anymore?

"Take me, worthless dogs." Josephine Bain demanded in Arabic, drawing the attention away from Nadia after a boot kicked the pallet beneath her.

Jo didn't fear them, and she didn't need to ask for their attention to get it. Taking Jo today had been their plan all along, and both the women knew it. It was her turn.

It would be evening before they brought Jo back. Through the thin wall, Nadia heard the quiet song of their neighbor, Noah. Had he slept later than usual, or had the men come for Jo early? Most days, the three prisoners shared a moment of peace before Hell opened for business. Every morning, Noah sang the same hymn in his native tongue. It was the only German Nadia knew. Jo had translated it every time Noah had sung until the words were familiar and written on Nadia's heart along with all the scripture she'd memorized over the first five years she'd been a Christian. She hadn't held her Bible in ten long months, but she'd recited every word she could recall at least a dozen times to Jo. Noah had shared others he'd memorized as a child.

Her favorite part of the song drew her full attention.

The Lord is never far away, but through all grief distressing, an ever present help and stay, our peace and joy and blessing. As with a mother's tender hand, God gently leads the chosen band: To God all praise and glory.

Nadia prayed in desperation, "God forgive my weakness. I know you are good. You see us and you have a plan." She sucked in a ragged breath, reminding herself that no matter what happened to Jo's body today, no one could take her soul. God held that in his hand. "Please . . . give me perseverance like my mother. I'm begging you to send rescue or bring us all home to you, Lord. Anything but more of this . . ."

When Noah's song faded and Nadia's tears began to dry, she shifted on the filthy pallet where she lay. Struggling to draw a satisfying breath, she focused on remembering the faces of her loved ones. Her mother was the most difficult to remember. All Nadia ever truly had was a faded picture and the vague memory of how it felt to be loved unconditionally. Saada Hamdan had died while her children hid in a closet and witnessed the horrifying murder.

Nadia missed the feel of her brother's strong arm around her shoulders more than almost anything. He'd always been there to shield her from their father and other dangers—now he was with Jesus. She'd watched in horror as Tarif was cut down by the bullets of the men who'd taken her. For twenty minutes she'd stared at her brother's unmoving body before she was forced into the trunk of a car and carried across Oman's border, into what Jo had confirmed was her birthplace—Yemen.

Nadia swallowed the lump in her dry throat when her fiancé's face filtered into her thoughts. It was better for everyone that Walt could not see her in this state. He loved her, she had no doubt, but she couldn't stand the thought of looking into his eyes when he realized all that had happened. Everything he'd feared and more.

Every inch of her malnourished body ached when she crawled to the corner of the cell to retrieve her hidden engagement ring. The simple chain was all she had left of her old life, and she'd long since convinced herself that the tiny piece of Walt gave her strength. It hurt, sliding the ring over broken skin, but she'd wear it while she had the chance.

At least the pain in her abdomen wasn't from a beating. The terrorists didn't punch her in the stomach anymore, not since she'd started to show. She must be six months along by now. Maybe seven. It was hard to keep track. Her first pregnancy had lasted less than two months. In that time, she'd truly come to know herself. At first, she'd feared what was growing in her womb. After a time, the fear had faded and she'd believed herself indifferent. It was when the bleeding began that she saw the truth in her heart. She was a mother, and her first child was dying.

It had been the one and only time she'd begged her captors for mercy. Their leader callously responded, "Next time, tell us as soon as you know of your condition. We will take more care. A grandson of Abdula Hamdan will make a fine soldier for Allah. If it is a girl, we'll make use of her too." He'd motioned for the men to remove Nadia from his presence without explaining his threat, but Nadia knew what would happen to any daughter born to the monsters. Some things were worse than death.

Her stomach revolted at the thought of her father. He knew she was there—had somehow orchestrated killing Tarif and damning Nadia to this fate. The men reminded her often that it was her own betrayal and infidelity to Islam that had led her here. They weren't trying to convert her back. In the eyes of her father and his minions, she wasn't worth it. Her fate was to suffer until Abdula Hamdan gave the order to kill her—or when the potted desert verbena plant in the corner of her cell withered away. There was just enough sunlight to keep it alive. It was a twisted game, and a constant reminder of how sadistic her father was. He'd taken the only good memory from her childhood and made it her worst nightmare. How was he able to maintain such power from an American prison?

"God, if you don't save me in this life . . . save my baby from the torment of these evil men. Let us die together."

With a surge of outright rebellion, she rubbed the ring on her finger and determined not to take it off again. If there was one thing she knew how to do, it was enraging Muslim men to the point of murder. They would finish her off when they realized that she'd kept something so significant right under their noses all this time. It was from a military dog tag, worn by a Marine who had killed many of their brothers, and she'd make sure they knew it. The thought actually put a smile on her face. Walt would be devastated to learn of her death, but she would die knowing he'd inspired her final act of defiance.

Nadia waited and prayed for the entirety of the day, but Jo was not brought back when the sun disappeared. She slept, woke, and prayed again, hearing Noah's song before he was taken away, and an eerie silence pressed down on her. Neither of her friends returned, and she knew what that most likely meant. She was utterly alone amongst the demons of the false god she had once worshipped. If she were the only one left, it wouldn't last much longer.

Death would be God's mercy for her.

*****

New Orleans, LA

FBI Field Office

"Shut the door." Iris didn't bother to greet Walt as he burst into her office. Her boss, Conor Flynn, stood behind her desk chair, eyeing something on Iris's computer.

"Look at this." Conor motioned for Walt to stand next to him.

His heart raced, confusion and nausea overtaking him when he saw the familiar scene on the video Iris started. Two terrorists spoke Arabic—likely propaganda for their cause. A woman knelt between them. Her black hair sent a jolt of panic through him at first glance, but her skin was too pale and her eyes too light to be Nadia's.

"Who is she? When was this? Where—"

"Josephine Bain." Iris cut him off. "French DGES confirms she was one of theirs."

Was.

"A French spy?" Walt gulped, knowing what the rest of the video would show. He didn't understand the words she managed to speak over the Arabic. The woman didn't relent, not even when one of the men punched her in the jaw. She spit blood on his shoe and spoke over him again. It was a miracle they didn't have her gagged. Probably, they didn't want to muffle her screams when they got to the point. "What is she saying?"

Iris paused the video and clicked to another screen. Walt followed along as she read the translation aloud. The first points were intel about the compound: where it was located in Yemen, how many fighters manned it on any given day, and the best times to strike—one for maximum kills and one for an easier target. The information took an abrupt turn after that.

"The missionary is here. Her name means 'Hope' and 'The one who praises Allah.' But she serves Christ …"

Nadia.

"It's her," Walt croaked. "When do we leave?"

"Declan's team is already loading gear onto a private plane." Conor gripped Walt's shoulder. His brother, Declan

Flynn, was no stranger to rescuing victims of human trafficking.

"I'm going with them." Walt stood to his full height, barely feeling the tug in his left leg. He was strong enough. God would make him able—for Nadia.

"They're leaving out of Charlotte." Conor shook his head. "Can't delay to get you there."

"I'll meet them in country."

"You're not going," Iris said firmly. He opened his mouth to fight her when she gave him a pained look that made his heart stop in his chest.

"Why?" He swallowed his panic. "No one would risk sending a team if they thought Nadia was already dead. Why would you bench me on the rescue?"

"You're all but on a no-fly list as it is, Walt. You've threatened one too many bureaucrats." Iris shook her head. "And your leg—"

"My leg is fine," he growled. "I'm fit enough for the private security job you set up. This isn't any different."

"You're too emotional," she spoke over him. "We can't pretend the intention isn't to wipe them out if you're on that bird."

"Why pretend at all?"

"You know why," Conor interjected. "Trust me when I say, my brother won't hold back. But if it looks premeditated, you know federal prison is on the table for anyone who participates."

"Walt." Iris closed her eyes, looking like she might vomit. "There's more."

"What?" He looked back to the computer as Iris scrolled. There was one more line of dialogue before the words: *asset terminated*. Walt blinked at the words as they shifted in and out of focus. His blood pressure spiked in an instant, and if he could get his hands on the nuclear football, there wouldn't be anything left of Yemen by the time he finished unleashing his wrath.

He read the final words over and over, praying they would change.

She is with child and fading fast. Hurry.

Chapter 3

Yemen

Warm fingers brushed against Nadia's neck, her wrist, her forehead. Hands shifted her, and suddenly she was floating. Was it finally Jesus?

The touch was too kind and gentle to be one of her tormentors. She drifted into darkness only to be disturbed again by the sound of men yelling. Smoke filled her lungs as someone carried and jostled her as if they were running at full speed with her cradled in their arms. A loud engine roared to life, and the familiar smell of exhaust overpowered the smoke in the air.

"What do you think, Doc?" A man spoke in English as the strong arms brought Nadia to rest on a new surface.

She tried to open her eyes—tried with all her might to speak.

"Bruised, malnourished, dehydrated . . . but alive," the man beside her—a doctor or medic—answered. Something cold touched her stomach as several other voices bombarded the space.

"Is the baby alive?" one of the newcomers breathlessly asked, and someone banged on a hard surface three times right before the vehicle they were in strained into motion and traveled over the rough earth, jostling Nadia more than the running man had.

"For now." The cold object disappeared and a warm hand grasped hers. "We've got you, Dee."

"Walt," she managed to rasp out.

"He's waiting on the other side," the man answered. "Mad as a hornet the feds wouldn't let him come with us."

Her eyes fluttered open at that. The man was barely visible in the dim light, but his face was familiar. An old friend. Had she worked with him when she'd crossed paths with Doctors Without Borders?

"I know you." Her voice was barely a whisper. The vehicle swerved, causing the man to brace himself so he didn't topple onto her.

"You know my brother." He took her hand again, squeezing it tight. "My name is Declan Flynn, and I'm taking you home."

The darkness pulled too hard for Nadia to hold her eyelids open. Everything began to fade as the hum of rescue carried her far away from her living nightmare.

Thank you, Jesus.

*****

Washington, D.C.

"Dec said it will be a hard recovery." Conor paced the Inova Fairfax Hospital helipad, making Walt's anxiety spike higher.

"You said that already, boss." Iris gripped Walt's forearm. "And it's no more helpful now than it was the first time."

Walt had never been more grateful for his friend and her connections in D.C., even if they didn't afford him the right to join the mission. If he'd been cleared to go to Yemen, Nadia would already be in his arms. At least she was finally in American airspace. And between Conor's friendship with the Assistant Director of the FBI and Nadia's story catching the attention of the newly elected Vice President—a fellow Marine—they had the best medical team in the country waiting and ready to fix whatever the Yemeni terrorists had done to her.

God, please.

It was all he had. There were no words to form a real prayer. All he'd been able to feel for three days was unquenchable hate and crippling fear—both of which were better than how he'd slowly been losing his mind for a solid ten months, not knowing where Nadia was or if she was still alive. He'd had a fleeting moment of relief when Declan Flynn had called to tell them Nadia was stable enough for the nearly seventeen hour flight home. But she hadn't been conscious to talk to him, and the picture Declan had sent moments after hanging up was horrifying.

The terrorists had clearly starved her. It was a wonder she was able to carry a baby at all. Bitter bile coated Walt's throat at the thought. He paced in the opposite direction of Conor and Iris until he heard the helicopter come into range. Time moved in slow motion until the flight nurse, who'd gone to meet the plane, jumped out of the chopper, followed by a man who could be Conor's twin and a few other guys who must've been on the mission with him. They didn't slow down as they rushed Nadia past the waiting trio.

"She spiked a fever. The baby is in distress," Declan yelled as they all began to chase after the team.

Walt ignored the dull pain in his knee and pushed through, keeping Nadia in his line of sight the entire way. He was able to grab her hand for the brief moment the team paused at a set of double doors. That's when he felt the ball chain ring on her finger. How had she managed to keep it all this time? As soon as the doors opened, she was gone and he was not permitted to follow.

God, please. Please, don't let her die now that I've finally got her back.

Declan returned after what felt like hours, but in reality was less than ten minutes. He collapsed into a waiting room chair, scrubbing his hands over his face before he looked up.

"You're Walters?" Declan asked, sounding dead-tired. Walt knew the feeling well. It was especially bad after a long mission with little sleep and almost constant adrenaline.

He nodded, too sick to speak even though he had a week's worth of questions.

"Tell us what you know." Conor sat across from his brother, leaning forward to rest his elbows on his knees.

Iris nudged Walt toward the chairs. He numbly sat beside Conor, bracing himself for the worst.

"Nadia is one tough cookie," Declan began. "They're prepping for surgery and taking the baby. When they get some antibiotics into Nadia and get her hydrated, she has a fighting chance."

"And what about the baby?" Iris's hand was on her flat abdomen, as if she remembering when little Jonny had occupied it.

Walt nearly spat on the floor. *Who cares?*

"I dunno." Declan sighed. "Nothing is beyond God. We just gotta pray."

What were they talking about? Wouldn't the best case scenario be for the thing to die?

"When do you think we'll be able to see Nadia?" Walt asked instead.

"Probably not tonight, man." Declan offered an apologetic grimace. "Your name was the first word out of her mouth in Yemen. I think this might belong to you." Declan dug in his pocket and pulled out the small makeshift ring, dropping it into Walt's outstretched hand. "They had to remove it for the surgery."

He blinked against a rush of mixed emotions as he closed his grip around the ring. Relief, sorrow, worry, and anger warred inside his chest.

"I should have been there." He gritted his teeth and slammed his fist into his thigh.

Iris rubbed circles on his back, which only irritated him further. He didn't need comfort. He needed vengeance.

"Tell me your guys killed every last one of them."

Declan studied him intently for a second before giving a singular nod.

"No one was left breathing inside that compound. And we ran across some alarming intel in the process." Declan stood and waved a hand at a few of his team members approaching from the hospital entrance. "Those guys were working for Abdula Hamdan, and I don't think he's finished with Nadia yet."

*****

Nadia awoke with a gasp, feeling a trickle of water travel down her arm.

"Easy there." A grandmotherly woman with short graying hair and kind blue eyes lifted a sponge off Nadia's arm and stood back. "You're safe, honey. Out of surgery and stable."

Nadia's hands flew to her stomach as reality caught up with her. Tubes and wires ran from her body to various monitors and bags of fluid.

"My baby!" she cried.

"Shh-shh. The baby is in good hands."

"Whose hands? Man or God?"

"Depends who you ask." The woman snorted, but sobered in the next instant. "That is, the baby is in the best *mortal* hands for her condition."

"Her?" Nadia choked on the word, throat too dry.

The woman immediately grabbed a cup with a straw from beside the bed and held it to Nadia's lips. Cold water hit the back of her throat, giving her an instant headache and making her cough and sputter. She'd forgotten what ice water felt like and wasn't sure she liked it anymore.

"Where am I?"

"You're outside of Washington D.C., at Inova Fairfax Hospital." The woman tentatively offered her the water again, and Nadia took more care with her second sip. "Best neonatal intensive care you could hope for . . . if you can keep this water down, I'll get you some broth."

"Is my baby going to live?" Nadia asked after swallowing the liquid.

"I'll let the doctor talk to you about that." The woman pushed a button on the bed and took Nadia's hand.

A moment later, another woman with red hair and bright green glasses stuck her head through the door.

"Molly, can you call Dr. Emmerson." When Molly vanished, the older woman said, "My name is Amy. I'm a nurse—your nurse. I'm gonna see you through this, Nadia, whatever may come."

Tears filled her eyes as she gripped Amy's hand and nodded.

Less than two minutes later, a female doctor entered—blonde hair pulled back in a tight bun. Nadia attempted to sit up, sending a grateful smile to Amy for quickly noticing what she needed and raising the top half of the bed. Pain broke through an odd numbness in her abdomen, reminding her that she'd been separated from her baby *girl*.

"Ms. Hamdan," Dr. Emmerson stood at the end of the bed. "The cesarean went quite well, and I'm confident you will make a full recovery, though it will not be a swift one. We've got you on an intravenous nutrition therapy and—"

"I want to know about the baby," Nadia snapped.

"Of course." Dr. Emmerson cleared her throat. "I'll be frank. She's…not as premature as we initially thought. Her lungs are completely formed. However—"

Nadia's breathing shallowed as she clung to every word.

"Due to the malnourishment you experienced, her birthweight is low—just under five pounds—still better than we anticipated. She's going to need intensive care while she gains some weight, and we can't make any sort of guarantee that she will survive."

"I understand." Nadia sank further into her pillow as tears spilled from her eyes. "You'll do everything you can?"

"Of course."

"And I can go see her now?"

"Not quite yet."

"Please. Please, let me go to her. Just for a moment."

"It's not possible." Dr. Emmerson grimaced apologetically. "Your fever has decreased, but it isn't gone. We can't let you into the NICU until we're certain you don't pose a risk. If you bear with us, we'll get you to your baby as soon as possible. You have my word."

"I see." Nadia fought the sob building in her chest.

Dr. Emmerson clasped her hands in front of her. "Do you have any family members who could check on her for you? Perhaps that would bring you some peace of mind for the time being."

"The baby is my only family." Nadia lifted thin fingers to wipe her eyes. "I don't know if any of my friends even know I'm here."

Amy snorted, drawing the attention of both the doctor and Nadia.

"Sorry." She pursed her lips. "I know for a fact there's a man named Walters who's been giving the staff . . . a hard time since you arrived. And he's got an entire posse huddled around him."

Nadia sucked in a breath and rubbed the place on her finger where Walt's ring used to rest. When had she lost it? Ten months of keeping it safe and now it was gone.

"Walt is . . . was my fiancé. How long have I been here?" As much as she craved a glimpse into Walt's warm brown eyes, to hold his calloused hand, and hear his southern accent again, she wasn't sure she could stand to have him in the room. How could she face him like this?

"Not quite a full day." Amy's brow furrowed. "What's the matter sweetie?"

Nadia swallowed the lump in her throat. "I-I don't know what to do . . . about Walt. We were supposed to be married by now. But with all of this? What if . . ."

"Oh, honey. Something tells me he'd burn the whole world down to get to you, no matter what has happened." Amy patted Nadia's arm like a mother comforting her child. "If a man ever loved me that much, I probably wouldn't have three cats waiting at home."

*****

"Sir, please don't make me call security. I've already told you—" the useless nurse blinked at someone behind Walt at the same time as a hand touched his elbow.

Turning around, he met Iris's stern blue gaze. "Walk with me."

"No. What if they come to get me? I'm not going anywhere."

"Then sit with me," she commanded, lips turning down in annoyance.

Walt followed his friend, skin crawling as he slid back into the seat he'd spent too many hours in.

"I'm losing my mind, Sully."

He rarely used her Marine nickname anymore. It hardly suited her these days, but his brain didn't have the capacity to override factory settings. Was he the only one who felt the urgency in the air? No one seemed to be bothered by the fact

117

that they were sitting idly by when they ought to be doing *something*. At least Conor was sending up flares about Abdula Hamdan's ability to terrorize and kill his children from federal lockup.

Iris took Walt's hand and drew in a long breath. Her eyes slid closed and he growled internally, knowing what she was about to do and not in the mental state for it. He ground his teeth and squeezed his eyes closed anyway. Nadia would be ashamed of him if she knew how little he'd talked to God in the last year. He was too angry. Angry that Tarif was dead. Angry that Nadia had been missing—and the new knowledge of all that had happened only made matters worse. Where was God during the last year? How could he have let all of this happen?

"Lord, thank you for bringing Nadia back to us. Please help us to trust that you are going to take the bad and make it good somehow. Heal Nadia's body, heart, and mind from the things she has endured." Iris's voice wavered. "Br-bring us peace and understanding, God. In Jesus' name, Amen."

Despite his anger and impatience, Walt felt the edge wear off as Iris prayed. He hated it. This wasn't the time to feel comforted. Too much was left unsettled around them. What came next? When would he be able to see Nadia? At least Iris hadn't prayed for the "baby" this time.

She narrowed her eyes at him like she could read every thought running through his head. She saw too much. Knew him too well.

"Nadia will be okay, Walt." Iris finally released his hand, which automatically clenched into a fist. "They both will."

"Stop it." He couldn't take it anymore. "Don't talk to me about that *thing*—"

He swallowed the burning sensation in his throat.

"Baby," Iris stated flatly. "It's an innocent human child."

He scoffed, not shying away from Iris's hard stare.

"It's a monster's baby."

"By that logic, Walters, you're no more than the son of a drunken deadbeat. And Nadia is the same as her child, the offspring of an irredeemable terrorist. Do you even hear yourself right now?"

"It's different." Walt's gut twisted.

"That baby had no more choice in a father than you or Nadia did. Take a freaking breath. That is *Nadia's* baby, like it or not." Iris's expression softened. "You need to prepare yourself to support whatever she decides to do here. Don't add to her worries. I'll beat you senseless if you hurt her any more than she's already been . . ."

"I could never hurt Nadia." Walt crossed his arms. "You know that."

"I know it wouldn't be your intention, but that doesn't mean you won't destroy her with the hate I see in your eyes." Iris squeezed his shoulder. "You had the same look after every mission that resulted in a casualty on our side. You've got to let go of the idea that a baby is the enemy here. If I know Nadia Hamdan, she's not going to abandon her child."

"How could she want to keep it? How would she be able to look at it every day?" The gutted feeling that tore through him brought more terror to Walt than he'd felt in all his years of war. Iris was right. "How will I?"

"Walt—" Iris began, but someone else cut her off.

"Mr. Walters?" A middle aged woman stood in front of them.

"Yes." He leapt to his feet.

"Ms. Hamdan is awake, but ..." The woman's eyes darted to Iris and back to him.

Walt's heart faltered in his chest.

"What's happened?" Iris voiced the words that Walt couldn't form.

"She's fine. Stable," the nurse assured them. "Physically, anyway."

"Can I see her?" His eyes burned with a sudden rush of relieved tears. He'd do whatever he had to—face down the devil himself to hold Nadia in his arms again.

"You may, but I need to warn you." The lady squared her shoulders. "She's scared. Nadia needs every reassurance you can give her."

"Of course." He took a step toward the door that would lead to his fiancee, but the nurse stopped him with a hand to his arm.

"She's scared to see you just as much as I know she's desperate for it."

A pit opened up in his stomach.

"Scared of me?" He was going to be sick.

"She's worried that things will be different between you. You love her, don't you?"

"More than anything. Nothing could change that."

The woman's wrinkled forehead smoothed out a bit. "That's what I hoped you'd say. She's going to need to be convinced of it. If I take you in there, I need to know that you won't upset her. She's got a hard recovery ahead of her on so many levels. Can I trust you, Mr. Walters?"

"Yes ma'am."

"Whatever she needs from you—"

"Whatever she needs." He nodded, desperate to get beyond this point. "I'll do whatever it takes."

"Good man." The woman turned and led the way. "I'm Amy. We're in this together. All of us."

Chapter 4

Nadia licked her dry lips and smoothed the extra blanket Amy had draped across the hospital bed. The beeping of the monitors grated on her frazzled nerves. Everything was jarringly pristine, like being in the New Orleans mansion she'd grown up in—just after the cleaning staff had been there.

She'd spent countless months in third-world countries after losing that lifestyle, trying to right the wrongs her father had orchestrated over the years. She'd surprised herself, learning to live on next to nothing and appreciate eternal things more than earthly comforts. But nothing could have prepared her for the squalor she'd been subjected to during her captivity. And now, the shock of being in an American hospital overwhelmed her senses.

"God give me strength." She'd prayed those words so many times. How had she thought being rescued would mean immediate relief? She squeezed her eyes shut and hummed Noah's hymn to herself, not hearing when the door opened and closed.

"Dee?" The familiar voice made her suck in a breath and silenced her song. Fear kept her from looking at the man she'd been desperate to see since the day she'd left him.

Tears streamed from her eyes. It wasn't a dream. She knew that, but still her tormented mind warned her not to trust anything. Warm fingers grazed hers.

"Walt?" she whispered. "I'm so sorry."

"Hey." His hand cupped her cheek, making her flinch at the touch. "Baby, look at me."

Finally, she forced her eyes open. He was there, right in front of her, apprehension on his beautifully familiar face.

"I'm sorry," she repeated.

"Don't say that." He sat on the edge of her bed. "I love you and you're here—alive and here. The only one who has anything to be sorry about is me. I should have found you sooner."

"You're not angry?"

Walt's nostrils flared slightly. "I'm plenty angry, Dee. But not at you—never at you."

"I don't know what to say." A tickling in her throat made her cough and grip her sore abdomen as a burning pain surfaced. Walt's eyes darted over her like she might die if he didn't help her.

"What do you need?" He frantically stood and backed toward the door. "Should I get Amy? Or a doctor?"

"Walt." His worry made the tightness in her chest subside. "Wait. I'm okay."

As quickly as he'd left her side, he returned. Hesitantly, he took her hand. "I can't believe you're really here—"

His words were lost in the emotions that overtook him. He still loved her. It was written in the tears dripping from his long eyelashes.

"*Albi*, I missed you so much." She tested the waters, reaching her hand up to wipe tears from his cheek.

A breath escaped his lips, and she could see the questions in his deep brown eyes as he leaned into her touch.

"We're going to be okay." She nodded, attempting to convince them both. "But I need you to do something for me."

"Anything."

*****

Anything but that, Walt wanted to scream. But he'd promised Amy and himself that he'd be the man Nadia needed him to be, so Walt forced one foot in front of the other as Amy led him to the last place on earth he wanted to be. The teal paint on the walls was likely meant to comfort desperate people, but all Walt could see was red.

"Wait." He halted in the middle of the NICU hallway. "I-I can't do this."

Amy turned to face him, a deep breath lifting her shoulders. She gestured toward a waiting area.

"Let's sit."

All the strength seeped out of him as he slid into the chair next to Amy.

"You need backup," she declared after a beat of silence. "I'll go see if one of your friends will come—"

"No." Walt cut her off. "Nadia asked me to do this. I just need a second."

Amy's wrinkled hand gripped his forearm. "Young man, it's okay to ask for help. Stay put, and I'll be back in a flash."

He didn't have the will to argue with her. But he called after her in a hail Mary attempt to avoid making everything worse. "Amy?"

She turned raised eyebrows toward him.

"Not the blonde. She . . . won't be helpful right now." He wouldn't survive a battle on two fronts. It was one thing to force himself to visit Nadia's baby. No way would he keep his cool if Iris was fawning over it and trying to convince him to love the thing. "Tell her I need Conor for this."

Amy nodded once and disappeared around a corner. Walt tried to pray. He took deep breaths. He watched people come and go from various rooms—some of them smiling and others crying. He counted the tiles on the ceiling and listened to the medical jargon of doctors and nurses passing by without taking notice of him. When Amy returned, Walt was shocked to see Declan behind her instead of Conor.

"I'll be at the nurse's station when you're ready." Amy patted Declan on the shoulder before walking away.

Declan settled into the seat next to Walt.

"Sorry about this." Walt sighed in defeat. "I didn't mean to drag you into it. I—"

"Hey, man." Declan turned in his chair, facing Walt head on. "God didn't bring me here by mistake. Conor may have solid advice for most situations, but this one calls for someone with a dog in the fight."

"Pardon?"

Declan pulled his phone out and flashed the lock screen in Walt's direction. It was a family photo of Declan with a pretty brunette and four kids. The eldest looked nothing like the rest of the family—with sharp features and hair as black as Nadia's. The three other kids wore mischievous smiles and had red hair like the Flynn brothers.

"That's Phoenix." Declan pointed to the raven-haired teen that leaned into his side like he was her hero. "She is the best thing that ever happened to me."

"But she's not your kid." Walt saw the logic of sending Declan. He'd adopted another man's child. It wasn't the same.

"She is one thousand percent my kid, even if we don't share DNA."

"Listen," Walt began. "I see where you're headed—"

"Nah." Declan shook his head. "You couldn't possibly."

Walt closed his mouth, not wanting to argue with the man who'd saved Nadia's life.

"Phee is the brightest, sweetest, most innocent human I've ever met. She stole my heart the instant I laid eyes on her. My wife, Claire, raised her alone before I came into their lives." He held up a hand when Walt opened his mouth to interrupt. "For eight years, Claire didn't know any more about Phee's father than that he was the man who raped her. She was barely out of high school when it happened. Every odd was stacked against her. The only good thing that came out of the darkest days of Claire's life was Phee."

Walt blinked at the man sitting next to him. He hadn't expected that, and he didn't know how to respond.

"Her life has immeasurable value, Walt. She had value at the moment of conception, no matter how evil the circumstances. I thank God that Claire saw that, despite everything the world says to justify a different perspective. We can't imagine life without Phee in it."

Walt deflated, sinking deeper into the chair. "I don't know how to do this."

"Of course you don't." Declan crossed his arms. "Only God can redeem something like this. The question is, do you trust him to do it, or are you going to let the enemy keep winning?"

A surge of adrenaline coursed through him at the challenge. It was a calculated move that backed him into a corner. With a huff, he stood and squared his shoulders, begrudgingly rising to Declan's challenge.

"Nadia wants pictures of the . . . baby." He forced the words out.

"That's good." Declan stood and waved at Amy. "We have a mission objective. Everything is gonna be okay, buddy. You'll see."

It might be a cold day in hell before he ever loved the living, breathing reminder of Nadia's captivity, but that was a fact he'd keep to himself.

Just get it over with.

After washing their hands and listening to Amy's every instruction for keeping a safe environment around the baby, they entered a room with more machines and monitors than where Nadia lay in recovery. Walt held his breath as he stepped closer to the incubator. The whimpering creature inside kicked its tiny legs. It was beyond fragile looking—impossible to view as a threat, even if he wanted to.

"You can reach a hand in, if you'd like," Amy prodded. "But she can't be taken out for a while."

Walt only shook his head, retrieving his phone to snap a few pictures of the pitiful thing. Thankfully, neither Declan nor Amy pressed him to do more or stay in the room for long. All the way back to Nadia's room, he tried to ignore the irritating thought that maybe everyone was right. His instincts told him the baby was just one more of Abdula Hamdan's victims—and *she* needed protection. He simply couldn't imagine being the one to give it to her.

So what if she looked a lot like Tarif? What did it matter if she reminded Walt of his little sister, who'd also been born prematurely?

This. Is. Different.

*****

"May I have this dance, ma'am?" Walt's brown eyes glinted in the New Orleans sunset.

Jackson Square was brimming with the excitement of a wedding reception. Of all the things—good and terrible—that Nadia had experienced in this city, watching her ex-boyfriend and ex-nemesis-turned-sister exchange their vows and pledge their lives to one another had to be the best. She glanced back to where Barrett and Iris smiled and danced, all their worries forgotten.

It was their fault, bringing Walters into her life. And now she couldn't shake the Marine who had weaseled his way into her heart. This was the moment they'd been building up to. There was no safe distance between them, no time to carefully draft and edit her replies to his flirting over email.

"I did make you a promise." She placed her hand in his, butterflies taking flight in her stomach.

"I've been dreaming about this moment for over a year, you know?" He stared down at her, so strange and yet alarmingly familiar. "You're the most beautiful woman I've ever seen, Nadia."

"Don't you dare say that around the bride." She tried not to smile. Recklessly, she added, "I couldn't take my eyes off of you the entire ceremony, Walt."

"Oh, I noticed." His teeth sank into his lower lip as a satisfied smile lit up his face. "Were you thinking about how much you wish it was us getting hitched? We could be leaving for our honeymoon right now."

"Ugh." She feigned gagging at the suggestion. "You're such a brute."

His hearty laugh sent a thrill through her.

"I booked my flight for the same time you're leaving on Monday." He grew a bit more serious. "Can we . . . spend the next two days together and see how things go?"

Nadia held her breath, searching his eyes as she formed her reply.

"I-I think that would be okay."

Walt slowed their dance and pulled her closer. "Do you know how much I want to kiss you?"

"Probably as much as I want to kiss you." And she almost gave into the temptation, but turned her face at the last moment and offered her cheek instead. "However, you'll have to take me on a proper date before that happens."

Walt rolled with the punch, grinning like a fool. "Challenge accepted."

"Nadia?" A woman's voice called her out of the pleasant dream and back to her hospital bed.

"Iris." Nadia took her friend's hands, tears instantly filling her eyes. "I was dreaming about your wedding."

Iris's face crumbled. It was alarming to see raw emotion overtaking her friend. Iris gripped her hand tighter, pressing Nadia's knuckles into her forehead as she bent over and wept.

"Shh, shh, shh." What had happened to the woman who rarely showed an emotion other than righteous anger? "Iris, pull yourself together. Since when are you the emotional one?"

Iris chuckled through her tears. "Since becoming a mother. The pregnancy hormones were just the beginning."

"Ah." Nadia fought against her own emotions. "That tracks."

Iris took a deep breath, as if trying to regain control. Clearly, it was out of reach.

"I'd say I can't imagine what it was like—"

"But you can." Nadia finished for her. Iris had spent twenty-three days in an ISIS cave in Syria. Mercifully, she hadn't been harmed in all the ways Nadia had.

"Not really. Only parts of it." Iris finally calmed. "Oh, Nadia. I'm so sorry for what they did to you. And that it took us so long to find you. And Tarif—"

"W-was his body recovered?"

Iris nodded. "We buried him near my parents in New Orleans. If you want to have him moved …"

"No." Nadia shook her head. "Thank you for doing that. New Orleans was our home longer than anyplace else. It's appropriate."

"How are you feeling?" Iris relinquished Nadia's hands and wiped her own eyes.

"Better than I have in a long time." She forced a smile. "The nightmare is over, anyway. And it's amazing what a bit of hydration can do. And whatever this nutritional IV stuff is."

"You look really awful, Dee. Worse than I did after ISIS."

"Of all the things I missed, Iris Jones, your brutal honesty wasn't one of them."

The women shared a short laugh that ended with Nadia gripping her abdomen and Iris wincing in empathy.

"I had a cesarean with Jonny." She swallowed hard, eying Nadia's stomach. "The recovery isn't too horrible."

"Pictures," Nadia demanded. "Show me that sweet boy right this instant. Have you told him about me?"

"Of course I have, and we look at pictures of you all the time. He's going to know his Auntie Dee when he sees you."

"I love that." Nadia swiped through images of Jonny, pausing on one where Iris's foster brother held the boy. The contrast of an NFL linebacker with a tiny baby was almost comical. "Oh. My. Gosh. Silas Landry holding a baby instead of a football has got to be the most precious thing. *Ever.*"

"They're a hoot." Iris rolled her eyes. "Silas spoils Jonny worse than Maggie and Ash—"

"Maggie and Ash? H-have they, um." Nadia nearly dropped the phone at the mention of Walt's mom and sister. "Have they been to New Orleans a lot while I've been . . . gone?"

"Yeah. At the beginning, mostly. We were all a bit worried."

"Walt went off the deep end, didn't he?"

"For a few weeks. But he pulled himself together." Iris seemed surprised by her own memory. "Looking back, I'm not sure I gave him nearly the credit he deserved. He really could have been way worse. But that's neither here nor there. He's got his ducks in a row now, and—you'll see."

Nadia digested the somewhat cryptic information as she swiped through more photos of Jonny.

"This kid is *seriously* adorable, Iris."

As they gushed over ten months worth of baby photos, Walt quietly entered the room and sat next to Iris. When she'd finished bragging that Jonny's first word—spoken two weeks ago—was "mama," Iris put her phone away and turned her attention to Walt.

"Is it finally my turn?" The lightness of his tone seemed forced, and his expression unreadable. "I've got pictures too."

Nadia ripped the phone from his hand when he held it out to her. The first glimpse of her baby overwhelmed her.

"She's so tiny," Nadia whimpered. "D-did she seem okay?"

Walt blinked at her, clearly not knowing what to say.

"Of course she didn't. How could she?" Nadia studied the picture again. "She's malnourished and barely clinging to life, right?"

"Actually," Walt leaned forward in the chair. "The doctor came in before we left, and she said the baby's vitals are promising. And . . . I think she's got your fighting spirit."

"Good." Iris looked between Walt and Nadia. "That's really good, right?"

"Yeah." Nadia sucked in a breath and let it out slowly, hands shaking as she held the phone out to Iris.

The woman seemed to melt a bit as she studied the pictures. "She looks like Tarif, doesn't she?"

Nadia took the phone back with new curiosity.

"I actually thought the same thing." Walt sat up straighter. "She, uh, didn't open her eyes when I was there. Don't know what color they are. Lighter brown like Tarif, or almost black like yours, or . . . I dunno."

His discomfort was palpable. In her desperation, Nadia hadn't considered how difficult her request would be for Walt. She wanted to ask how he felt about the entire situation, but fear of the answer kept her from speaking a word.

Amy came in a moment later, heading straight for a computer beside Nadia's bed. Everyone fell silent and studied the nurse until she glanced over her shoulder at them.

"Don't mind me. I'm just making my rounds." She asked Nadia, "Are you ready for some pain medication, hon? It's time that you can have some, and I do suggest it. Even if you don't feel any severe pain yet, you don't want to let it sneak up on you. Best to stay ahead of it, if you know what I mean."

Nadia glanced at Iris automatically. Her friend nodded, saying, "Do it. You don't want to mess around these first few days. Save the tough act for later."

"Okay. Yes, please."

Amy tapped away at the keys some more before approaching the IV line with a syringe. "This medicine will make you drowsy again, but you need to rest anyway. Did you want someone to stay with you or have them clear out?"

Nadia licked her lips and turned to Walt. "Um, do you want to stay?"

He released a gust of air and leaned forward, taking her hand. "If I never take my eyes off you again, it'll be too soon."

Amy snickered and Iris raised a knowing eyebrow. Nadia's cheeks warmed as she squeezed Walt's hand.

"Good to know, *Albi*."

Chapter 5

Several hours later, Walt stared at Nadia as she slept off the effects of more pain medication. At some point, he dozed off as well, and when he woke, Iris was nowhere to be found. Now it was dark outside, and he was wide awake. No matter how much he tried, Walt couldn't stop his thoughts from drifting to the baby in the NICU. He didn't want to care. The intrusive thoughts about Declan's family photo wouldn't relent. It was unfathomable that he might grow to love that little girl in the same way Declan cared for his wife's daughter, yet here he sat wondering.

God, is it possible? I hate the thought of it, but somehow you're going to force it on me, aren't you? I can't have Nadia any other way, right?

She moaned in her sleep, eyebrows pulling together. Was she having a nightmare? A moment later, her lips lifted into a small smile.

"Just you wait," she mumbled, then let out a tiny snort.

Walt couldn't help himself. He smiled back at her. He'd bet the brand new transmission in his Silverado that she was dreaming about their third date. She'd said those same words to him when he'd shoved a paintball gun into her dainty hands. He'd insisted that it was "on brand" for how they'd met and that she'd love it, but she'd protested the entire way—right up until the horn blew and the paintball war ensued.

That's when he learned that Nadia Hamdan was rabidly competitive and a dang good shot. If he hadn't known better, he would have sworn she'd been through all the same tactical training as him. At any rate, he'd fallen more in love every time he'd taken a hit of pink paint, and he'd been ready to drop to one knee by the end of that date.

"I'm going to marry you, you know that, right?" He'd swept her off her feet and ducked behind a cinderblock wall.

"Yes. You remind me every chance you get." Nadia had shocked him with a devastatingly passionate kiss before she'd asked, "What makes you so sure I'll say yes?"

It was the first time he hadn't known what to say to a woman. She'd laughed as he'd scrambled for a response, then she'd leapt from his arms and aimed three shots to his chest before vanishing back into the fray.

Nadia cried out from her hospital bed, ripping Walt from the comfort of his memories. He scrambled to her side and pressed the button that would bring a nurse to the room.

"Dee, what is it?" He gently gripped her shoulder, terrified of hurting her or leaving one more mark on her skin. The bruising on her left cheek made him nauseous every time he looked at it.

"*Laa.*" She gasped and scratched at his arm. "*Laa.*"

She was saying "no" in Arabic.

"Nadia, wake up." He released her and took a step back.

A nurse he didn't recognize entered the room at the same moment Nadia opened her eyes and blinked up at Walt. The tension in her body vanished in an instant.

"I'm sorry." She gripped her stomach. "It hurts."

"Don't apologize," the nurse took the words right out of Walt's mouth. "I should have checked on you twenty minutes ago. That's on me. Let's get you something for the pain."

Nadia averted her gaze to the end of the bed. She kept her answers short with the nurse and didn't look at Walt again until the woman had left the room.

"Did I—" Her words seemed to lodge in her throat.

"I think you were having a nightmare."

"Yeah." She reached for her water, wincing at the movement. Walt rushed to help her and settled on the edge of her bed, holding the cup as she took a long drink. When she relaxed again, she said, "You can't imagine how good it is to have clean water so readily available."

What did he say to that?

"Where did those flowers come from?" Nadia pointed to the small table behind him.

"Iris and Conor both brought some. The rest, I'm not sure."

When he turned back at Nadia, she looked terrified.

"What's the matter?"

"Nothing." She shook her head. A moment later, she winced again. "I need the nurse to come back."

"Are you going to be sick?" He pressed the call button at least five times.

"No. No, something is . . . um." She huffed a frustrated breath and crossed her arms. "Can you give me a minute when she comes in here?"

"Of course." His pulse raced. "But I'm going to lose my mind if you don't tell me what's wrong."

"Nothing is wrong." She insisted as her cheeks darkened with a blush. "I think . . . my body is doing what it's supposed to."

"Okay?"

The nurse came back in and sent a questioning look at them. "Did I forget something?"

"Um." Nadia squirmed in the bed. "I think something is going on with my, uh, lactation?"

Walt jumped up and backed away from the bed.

"I'm going to get a cup of coffee." He cleared his throat. "Need anything?"

Nadia only shook her head, not meeting his eyes.

"It wouldn't hurt you to learn about this, Dad." The nurse called toward him.

"No!" Nadia barked. "He doesn't need to be here."

"Fine, fine." The nurse waved and started to dig into a cabinet.

Walt rushed out of the room and wandered the halls in a daze. He didn't know where to find coffee in the middle of the night and hardly paid attention to his trajectory until he found himself in the NICU.

"Sir?" A nurse looked up from where she sat behind a desk. "Visiting hours ended at eleven."

"Right. I'm not here to—" He glanced toward the end of the hall where Nadia's baby was. "Do you know how the Hamdan baby is doing?"

The nurse studied her computer screen and stroked a few keys.

"Why don't we have a look?" She grinned like she was doing him a massive favor. "Follow me."

He didn't argue. What difference did it make at this point?

Like a rusty old boat in the bayou, he'd been taking on water for months without an escape plan, and if having Nadia back wasn't the lifesaver he'd hoped for, he may as well go down with the ship.

But what is it called when a wave engulfs the entire vessel all at once?

That's the question that hit him when he locked eyes with the wide awake baby in the incubator of room N2107.

*****

I scared him away for sure. Nadia gulped, pulling the blanket up to her chin as she stared at the door Walt still hadn't returned through. Did it take an hour to find coffee? Did he think she was still dealing with the "milk" situation, or had that been the straw to break the camel's back? This was too weird.

God, what is your plan? Why does it feel like I'm still in captivity? Please release me from this torment.

Nadia yelped in surprise when Walt burst into the room. His face was red as he panted, staring at her for a moment before he pressed his fists into his temples and started pacing.

"What is it? What's wrong?" Fear gripped her around the throat.

"The baby. Sh-she was awake."

"Is she okay?"

"Yes." He paused at the foot of the bed, deflating. "She looked me dead in the eyes, Nadia."

"Oh. Um . . ." The urge to climb from the bed and run to her baby was maddening.

"She has your eyes. Darker than Tarif's." He resumed pacing. "I-I'm so confused."

"It was a fifty-fifty chance that she would get my eyes, right? Why is that confusing?"

"That's not what I meant."

Nadia took a deep breath. She'd avoided this conversation all day. Would he ask about her time in Yemen? Would he reject her and the baby that wasn't his? She wouldn't blame him. It was beyond obvious that he'd been struggling. For most of the evening, he'd had that glazed-over look in his eyes like when he used to get orders for a deployment in the Marines. She knew then that this wasn't going to go well. But why had he gone back to the NICU? She hadn't asked him to do that.

"I don't know what to say, Walt."

"Neither do I." He collapsed into the chair beside her bed.

Nadia reached out her hand, relieved when he immediately took it.

"You don't have to walk this road with me. It isn't fair to you and I know that. I'm so s—"

"Stop apologizing to me." He squeezed his eyes shut. "I made you a promise. I'm all in."

"I remember." Nadia took a fortifying breath. "You said, 'No matter what.'"

"I did." His Adam's apple bobbed, and pain contorted his face. "And I meant it."

"*Albi*, neither of us knew this would be the outcome. We can't go back. I don't know how to go forward. I'm broken in ways only God can heal, and I trust him to do it. But I refuse to make you suffer along with me."

A dozen Walt-worthy quips saturated her brain. A year ago, he might have joked about love being pain, both of them being broken, or the struggle being worth it. But it wasn't just the two of them anymore, and it never would be again.

"Is this where you tell me that I should let go and move on? That's not going to happen, Nadia. I'm not going anywhere."

"You will if I ask the nurse to call security." She was only half kidding.

"Try it." A devious grin pulled at his lips.

He was still the same Walt, with slightly deeper worry lines. What torment had he endured in her absence?

"Walt, we should talk—"

"No." He shook his head. "We both need sleep. Talking about . . . everything. That can wait."

"The nurse said my test results are clear of anything contagious." Nadia changed the subject. "I think they'll let me see the baby in the morning."

"Have you thought about her name?" His eyebrows pulled together.

He looked more conflicted than Iris trying to pick a restaurant after church on Sundays. The woman never could decide—it always fell to someone else.

"Honestly? No. I don't suppose I had faith strong enough to imagine I'd get the chance. And even now I'm struggling to go there in my heart and mind."

"Because she might not make it?" Walt blinked at her as he intertwined their fingers. It was strange how his touch could be so familiar and foreign all at once.

"Yeah."

"Sh-she's a person." His words sounded rehearsed. "Everyone should have a name."

"You're right." Nadia yawned, feeling the weight of her exhaustion returning. "I'll pray on it."

Walt sighed and leaned closer.

"I couldn't pray most days," he whispered when her eyelids grew too heavy to hold open. "You'd be so ashamed if you knew how I've acted. I don't deserve you, Nadia. I never have. If you send me away, let it be for that."

Chapter 6

Urgent talking outside of Nadia's room drew Walt from his restless sleep. Early morning light streamed in through the window. Nadia didn't stir, not even when the door opened and Iris hissed for Walt to come outside of the room.

"What's going on?" he demanded in a hushed tone.

"Disturbance at ADX Florence while our guy from the Denver office was *inside* the prison." She pulled on his arm until they were several feet away from Nadia's room. "There was a lockdown and everything."

"Tell me Nadia's father didn't escape." Walt gritted his teeth. "No, wait. Tell me he did. I'll take him out myself."

"No one has ever escaped ADX, Gomer. Calm down." Iris pointed to where Conor approached. "Here's our update now."

"False alarm . . . as far as we're concerned." Conor slid to a halt in front of them. "It was just a clash between two rival gangs. Not associated with Hamdan or anyone I think we need to worry about."

"Is he in solitary or not?" The hair on Walt's neck raised.

"He is. And that's what worries me most." Conor scratched the stubble on his chin. "Hamdan has been in solitary confinement, uninterrupted, for two straight years."

"That doesn't make sense." Iris glanced between them. "If he's not the one sending out orders, who is?"

"That's what I aim to find out. Agent Woodhouse is still there and says he won't leave without some clarity." Conor started to back away. "Don't count Hamdan out just yet.

Solitary doesn't mean what it once did. If I've learned anything from dealing with corrupt agencies, it's that the enemy is often the one with the strongest alibi. And the people you should be able to trust are usually the ones holding the knife."

"This can't be happening." Walt scrubbed his hands over his face and leaned against the wall, sliding to sit on the floor once Conor was gone. After a moment, Iris sat next to him and sighed.

"I always knew this stuff with Nadia's father might come back to bite us, Walt. You did too. We'd be fools to think we'd escape the wrath of powerful men like Hamdan." She pulled out her phone and started tapping on the screen. "We need to warn Sanchez."

Walt swallowed hard. He'd lost touch with most of the Marines after his discharge, even the one who had helped them take down Nadia's father.

"Tell Sandy I say hello." Walt pushed himself to standing and didn't wait to hear the conversation before he slipped back inside the hospital room that felt more like a safehouse from the world beyond. Nadia smiled weakly at him. "Babe. You're awake."

"Only just, Captain Obvious." She sounded groggy. "What time is it?"

Checking his watch, he answered, "Seven-forty." With a gulp and sheer determination he added, "Should we get you ready to meet your baby?"

Suddenly, the NICU was the least of his worries. No way was he going to burden Nadia with the situation unfolding in

Colorado. He forced a smile to match the hopeful one on her lips.

One foot in front of the other.

*****

Guilt niggled at Nadia's insides. She didn't *need* Walt to be with her when she made her way to the NICU, but he seemed determined to stay glued to her side. He'd brushed off her suggestion to discuss the elephant in the room, despite the fact that something was relentlessly gnawing at him.

"What are you thinking about, *Albi*?" She gripped his arms as he helped her stand from the bed, two hours after the NICU opened up for visitors. Waiting was torture, but she was at the mercy of the medical staff.

"Later," he insisted as he stood behind her. "Focus on this walk—proving your strength to these yahoos—and meeting your baby. Everything else can wait."

She let it go and started her walk in the hallway to appease the doctor.

Walt didn't touch her, but she could feel the warmth of his hovering hands, ready to catch her should she fall. The man clearly didn't know his own worth. How could he think he didn't deserve her?

Sure, she'd joked with his mom and sister over the years, telling him how lucky he was, but she'd always known the truth. She was blessed beyond measure that God had orchestrated their meeting and everything that followed. And if they somehow survived the next few weeks and months, and he continued to love her as much as he always had, she'd be the luckiest woman on the planet.

How did she put that into words? And were they words she should speak at all? Whatever she said to him, she couldn't manipulate the situation or guilt him into a life that would rob him of peace. Equally, she didn't want to rob either of them of the life that had so clearly been God's will before her time in Yemen. Was it still his plan for them?

Nadia swayed after she turned to walk back toward her room and the wheelchair that would carry her to the NICU.

"Dee?" Walt's arms were around her in an instant.

"I'm dizzy." She closed her eyes and let him hold her up. "Don't tell them. Please."

"We should get you back in bed. Maybe it's too soon."

"No," she pleaded, turning to face him. "Just pretend you're hugging me."

"Why would I pretend?" He gently pulled her into his chest, arms wrapping fully around her and swallowing her whole.

At first, she feared being in his embrace would summon negative emotions associated with all of the months men had harmed her, but those feelings never surfaced. Every second she relaxed deeper into the warmth of him, more tension left her body, and the feeling of safety she'd craved for so long blossomed around her.

"I missed this," he whispered, kissing the top of her head. "Dang it all, Nadia, I can't live without you. Please don't ever leave me again."

If she let her emotions get the best of her, she really would wind up back in the hospital bed. Gripping his shirt, she fought with all her might to keep her tears at bay.

"I promise." She leaned back enough to look up at him. "If you promise to be honest with me."

He gulped and nodded.

"Can you accept . . . both of us?"

A breath escaped his lips as apprehension lit his eyes.

"Ready?" Amy's cheerful voice broke the silence that had fallen around them.

Turning around, Nadia spotted the blessed wheelchair that would transport her to the NICU. She gladly let Walt and Amy help her into the contraption and met Walt's eyes when he knelt down right in front of her.

"Will you let me try? One day at a time? I can't give you the answer you want to hear . . . yet."

She nodded. It was a fair request, though her heart fractured in her chest. He'd been right to suggest waiting longer to talk about it. Her first time seeing her baby in person would be tainted with the hard reality that the man she loved might not be able to love her child. It wasn't a shocking revelation, but it hurt all the same.

"Can I still come with you?" He didn't budge from in front of her. "I'll do whatever you want."

"Call Iris?" She wiped hot tears before they could run down her cheeks.

Walt's eyes slid shut as he stood and pulled his phone from his pocket. He walked away as he put the phone to his ear, talking low.

"Don't fret, hon." Amy patted her shoulder. "He'll come around. He's a good one."

"He is." Nadia watched as Walt's hand fisted at his side, and he seemed to be arguing with Iris.

"Love conquers all." Amy's attempt at reassurance made Nadia's stomach churn.

She didn't have the strength to argue about context and misquoting scripture. There was danger in applying God's love for his children to the ability of humans. No one understood better than Nadia how a person's love could turn into a deadly poison in their soul. Hadn't her father once loved her?

No. Love is of God. Abdula Hamdan does not know God. He cannot know love.

She offered a weak smile over her shoulder and reminded herself of the full truth of God's words, praying them over herself, Walt, and the baby. Whatever each new day brought, God's love would remain the same, and if they would seek him first, he could redeem the broken pieces.

Love is patient, love is kind. Love does not envy, is not boastful, is not arrogant, is not rude, is not self-seeking, is not irritable, and does not keep record of wrongs. Love finds no joy in unrighteousness but rejoices in the truth. It bears all things, believes all things, hopes all things, endures all things.

"Love never ends," she whispered to herself.

Chapter 7

Walt followed at a safe distance, knowing the way to the NICU by heart now. Nadia and Iris would be none the wiser about his presence, but he wasn't letting them out of his sight. The ache in his chest doubled in size as he dipped his hand into his pocket and pinched Nadia's ball chain engagement ring. He'd nearly forgotten it was there.

"God, what am I supposed to do?"

Everything was all wrong. It had taken entirely too long to get his arms around Nadia, and as soon as he did, he'd ruined it by breaking her heart. She may have worn a brave face, but the light in her eyes had dwindled to nothing in the moments after his admission. Why hadn't he just lied to her—to himself?

His phone buzzed in his pocket, making him pause and duck into a restroom to be sure he wasn't caught stalking the ladies.

"What is it, Conor?"

"Woodhouse was granted access to Hamdan. He claimed to have no knowledge of Nadia being kidnapped or even that she was a missionary. The man didn't even know his son was dead, Walters. I think we've got a bigger problem on our hands."

"He's got to be lying." Walt gripped the side of the sink.

"Woodhouse is convinced the shock and emotions were genuine." Conor must've walked outside. The sound of a car engine came and went before he said, "And Hamdan has been out of the loop for so long, he doesn't have a clue who would target his kids. At least not a list short enough to give me any hope of figuring it out in a timely manner."

"What does that mean, Conor? What am I supposed to do?"

"Nothing. Let me worry about it for now. You just focus on your . . . family."

Walt took a deep breath and stared at the ceiling tiles. "For a seasoned FBI agent, Flynn, you are the worst at reading the room."

"Not the first time I've heard that." Conor hung up without another word.

Walt pocketed the phone, eyeing himself in the mirror. He'd never backed down from a challenge. The newest situation had the potential to hurt more than rattlesnake venom—which was worse than bullets and shrapnel—but there was only one way to find out.

*****

"You know he's lurking in the hallway, don't you?" Iris spoke low beside Nadia.

Both women had been staring at the baby for a full ten minutes. Nadia hated the thought of leaving, but she could feel the last shreds of strength seeping out of her body.

"I don't know what to do, Iris. I won't let him be a martyr."

"Oh, please." Iris crossed her arms over her chest and glared at Nadia. "You don't have the monopoly on martyrdom. Besides, the only way to rid yourself of that adorable parasite of a man is to kill him."

"Be serious." Nadia lowered herself into the wheelchair, giving up hope that she might be able to power through the pain, nausea, and dizziness. "Iris, what if this isn't something we can overcome? We owe it to each other to do what's best for all of us, even if it hurts."

Iris sighed and puckered her lips. "It's not gonna come to that, Nadia. Trust me. He's stubborn—we all know how infuriating he can be—but that's his best quality when push comes to shove. Right now, he's trying to wrap his head around everything. He needs time to let go of the picture-perfect life he imagined."

"He shouldn't have to give up on that."

"Maybe in a perfect world. Just like Tarif shouldn't be dead and you shouldn't have spent ten months being tortured. That's not the point."

Nadia rolled her eyes. "Then what is your point?"

"Walt is the most loving person I've ever met, Nadia. He can't help it. He's a fierce protector, a perfect brother, and he's going to be an amazing father if you give him the chance. You just have to let him get there on his own terms."

Nadia glanced back at her baby girl and blinked away tears.

"I was so scared to see him. I'm even more scared to tell him all that happened. But now, it's burning a hole through my soul, Iris. I need him to know everything."

"Oh, absolutely. And the sooner, the better. Rip the bandaid off, sister."

"Really? He keeps deflecting when I bring it up."

"Don't let him do that." Iris snapped her fingers and shook her head toward the hallway where Walt was surely hovering.

"He's more scared than you are, but the quickest way through this is to face it all head on."

"I-I have to agree. Do you think he'll eventually love the baby?"

Iris sputtered and waved her hand flippantly. "I'm placing a wager—"

"Don't you dare gamble in front of my child." Nadia swatted at her friend. "You're the worst aunt ever."

"Hogwash. I'm the fun aunt, and I'll be her best friend. That being said, I'd bet Barrett's trust fund that Walt points a shotgun at the first kid who tries to date . . . you really gotta give this kid a name, Nadia. Honestly."

"Joa." Nadia's cheeks warmed as she spoke the name aloud for the first time.

Iris stared wide-eyed at the baby and nodded. "Hmm. Joa."

"You hate it." Nadia chuckled. "I did too, sort of."

"Yep. I'm going to need an explanation."

"In Yemen, I shared my small prison with a woman—"

"Josephine Bain." Iris retrieved a rolling stool from the far wall and sat next to Nadia. "She's the reason we found you."

"What?" Nadia gripped the arms of the wheelchair. "Is she alive?"

Iris's shoulders sank as she shook her head. "She gave us your location with her last words, Nadia."

The news was a confirmation of what she'd already believed, but the reality of it cut deep into Nadia's chest.

"And Noah?" She rasped out.

Iris blinked in confusion, not offering a word in response.

"What about Noah?" How had she not asked about him sooner? "The German soldier that was with us."

"Th-this is the first I've heard about him." Iris gripped Nadia's forearm when she started to gasp for air. "It's okay. We'll look into it."

"It's not okay. None of this is okay." She hugged herself and looked at Joa. "Jo and Noah got me through each horrifying day. And Jesus, of course. The combination of their names came to me this morning, and I asked Amy to look up the meaning."

"And?" Iris prodded.

"It means *Jehovah increases*." Nadia closed her eyes and thought back to the morning Jo had put her faith in Jesus. "Even in the darkest places, God's mercy is there. He's forever robbing Death of a victory."

"Joa. It's perfect." Iris held Nadia's hand and let her cry until Amy came back into the room.

"It's time for you to rest, Mama." Amy released the brakes on the wheelchair. "You have the perfect little motivation, don't you?"

Nadia glanced at her sleeping daughter one last time before Amy wheeled her away.

"I sure do."

Chapter 8

In his hurry to beat Iris and Nadia back to her room, Walt strode right past the woman who had brought him into the world and threatened, on occasion, to take him out of it.

"Mom?" He skidded to a halt a few feet away from Nadia's door.

"DuWayne." She rushed to hug him, crying into his shoulder. "How is Nadia? Where is she? How long does she—"

"Slow down." Walt held his mother out at arm's length. "How did you even know we were here?"

Her look of indignation and annoyance wiped the fondness and worry away in an instant.

"I *should* have heard it from you. I have half a mind to bend you over my knee." She slapped his hands away. "It's all over the national news, DuWayne. How could you keep this from us?"

"Us?" He darted a glance up and down the hall. "Is Ash with you?"

"Of course she is." Mom smacked his chest hard. "You know, I raised you better than this. I can't believe you didn't at least let us know that Nadia is alive."

"I'm sorry." He squeezed his eyes shut. "It happened so fast and everything is . . . complicated."

"You're talking about my new baby niece, right?" Ashley's words hit his eardrums a millisecond before her fist slammed into his low back.

"Mmm." Walt grunted and turned to face his little sister. "You've got to be kidding me."

"Ha." She crossed her arms over her chest, green eyes flashing. "That's exactly what I said when my boss called me into his office to ask why I was at work and not on my way to DC to be with my sister-in-law."

"She's not—" Walt growled in frustration. This situation couldn't possibly get worse.

"Maggie? Ashley!" Nadia's cry from a few feet away drove the nail into his coffin. No way was he coming out on top with the three of them ganged up against him.

He watched in silence as the reunion unfolded—all tears and rapid-fire questions. The smile on Amy's face made Walt roll his eyes. The nurse would be in their girl-gang in no time. It took all of three seconds for the women to forget him entirely and disappear into the hospital room without him.

Iris cleared her throat next to Walt.

"They're going to make everything worse." He stared at the door that stood between him and all the women he held a healthy fear of.

"Or . . ." Iris shoved him toward the waiting chaos. "They're the catalyst you both need to get your heads on straight."

"I can't deal with this right now." He turned and crossed his arms. "Can't I go find Conor and deal with the threat of more retaliation from Abdula or whoever?"

Iris outright laughed in his face. "No."

"How did this get out to the media? Doesn't anyone care about OPSEC anymore? They may as well hang a banner over her door that says, 'Come and get her while she's super vulnerable.'"

"Those are really great questions, actually." Iris chewed on her bottom lip and narrowed her eyes in contemplation. After a few seconds, she shrugged and pushed him another step back toward Nadia's door. "And you don't need to worry about that either. Let me do my job. If we feel like Nadia isn't safe here, we'll set up a protective detail."

"I can protect Nadia," he argued.

"Oh, please. You can't even hold your own against a couple of five foot three redheads." She gestured toward where his mom and sister were waiting to rip him a new one.

"You're the worst."

"You know you love me." She snickered. "Now, get in there and face the firing squad. You've earned it."

"Sully," he called after her as she walked away.

"Hmm?"

"Pray for me."

"You got it, pal." She laughed until she was out of earshot.

*****

"When can we meet her?" Maggie held Nadia's hand tight. "Will they let us into the NICU even if we aren't *officially* family?"

Walt entered at the worst possible moment, earning a glare from his mother. He cleared his throat and darted a deer-in-the-headlights look at Nadia before slinking toward the couch under the window.

"Let me worry about that," Amy answered. "Special circumstances apply here."

"Thanks, Amy." Nadia sent a grateful smile toward her nurse. Turning to Ashley, she asked, "Are you still dating, um, Marcus?"

Ashley snorted. "Heck no. He's old news. I'm . . . talking to a guy I've known for years, but the dating part is new, long-distance, and not important right now. When are the two of you going to finally get married?"

She raised her eyebrows at Walt.

"We've got some things to figure out." Nadia refused to look his way.

"Oh, for crying out loud." Maggie sputtered. "What is it now?"

Silence fell in the wake of her question. When she didn't get an answer, she released Nadia's hand and stood, pacing to the end of the bed.

"I don't get it." Maggie shook her head. "You've both used every excuse you could muster for years."

"Mom—"

"Not a word out of you." She pointed a finger at Walt. "First, it was endless emails and getting to know what you both already knew from the day you met—you're made for each other. Then, it was missionary and Marine business. Now? What? Surviving a death cult and full year of separation is the reason to *not* do what you'd finally decided on?"

"It's more complicated than that." Nadia fought the drowsiness pulling her body toward complete surrender.

"Oh, honey." Maggie rushed back to her. "I know that. I get that you've been through horrific trauma. I'm not trying to brush that off. It's just—"

"Mom, can you and Ashley *please* give us a minute?" Walt stood and made his way to the side of the bed opposite Maggie.

The woman took a deep breath and nodded, gesturing for Ashley to follow her out of the room.

"If you screw this up . . ." Ashley threatened through gritted teeth before she followed behind Maggie.

Walt sat on the edge of the bed and held Nadia's hand.

"They're right." His brown eyes bored into Nadia's. "I'm sorry about earlier. I wish I could be the best kind of man without any effort. I'm just trying to wrap my head around everything, but it doesn't change how I feel or what I want."

"How can you say that?" She sank deeper into her pillow. "I haven't even told you about everything. I lost a baby before this pregnancy, you know?"

Walt's muscles tensed, but he made an obvious effort to not react to the bombshell.

"I'm sorry you went through that. It doesn't change anything for me."

"What if you can't get over Joa's . . . origin?"

"Joa?" He tilted his head to the side, eyebrows pulling together as if allowing the name to marinate. "It suits her."

"Walt." Nadia willed her eyelids to stay open, but his name was no more than a whisper on her lips. "I need to tell you everything."

"Okay. How about after you take a nap?"

She yawned and agreed with a singular nod.

"I have something of yours." He dug in his pocket, pulling out the pitiful length of ball chain that had grounded her in the hope of their life together.

Nadia gasped, the effects of the drugs subsiding for a moment.

"I thought I'd lost it."

"I can't believe you managed to keep it in the first place." He slid the ring on her finger. It didn't fit as snugly as the day he'd made it. "Don't give up on me, Nadia. Marry me. Today or next week or next year, I don't care. I can do *anything* but survive losing you again."

"Okay."

The word slipped out of her mouth before she could stop it. Was she doing the right thing? For herself, definitely. But what about for her child? What sort of life was she establishing for Walt and Joa? Was it selfishness, fear, or faith controlling her now?

"I'm so tired." She stopped fighting the need to close her eyes. "You know what I realized?"

"What did you realize, beautiful?" Walt kissed her forehead.

"Even if you never love Joa, you'll still be better than my father. He did this to us, you know?"

"No, Nadia." Walt's words grew distant as consciousness slipped further away. "I don't think it was Abdula."

"It was. I can prove it."

Chapter 9

"She can prove it?" Conor settled into a chair across the cafeteria table from Walt and Iris. "She said that?"

"Yeah." He scrubbed his hands over his face. "I'll find out what she meant as soon as she's awake."

"Is it best or worst case scenario if Hamdan is really behind it all?" Iris questioned before biting into a grilled chicken sandwich.

"I don't even know." Conor shrugged. "At least we won't be looking for a ghost. But how he managed to get the orders out is beyond concerning."

"What about his lawyer?" Walt drummed his fingers on the table, growing irritated.

"That's the first thing Woodhouse checked on." Conor nodded. "Everyone from Hamdan's old life who didn't end up in prison ran for the hills. He's got a public defender with a spotless record and no association to any other known terrorists. He's a Colorado native with three little kids and a minivan. We can dig deeper, but I don't think he's our guy."

"And Hamdan's old cell mates?" Iris interjected.

"Dead ends." Conor grimaced. "Literally. He had three and they were all dead prior to his stint in solitary."

"Ugh." Walt cracked his knuckles out of habit. "It doesn't add up. I have half a mind to interrogate the guards myself. Somebody knows how this happened."

"We'll get to the bottom of it." Iris elbowed him. "Incoming."

Walt caught sight of his sister, stomping toward him. She stopped beside Conor, stealing a fry from Iris's plate.

"It's time to visit my niece, *brother*. They won't let us go without you."

"Will you ever stop being a pain in my butt?" He narrowed his eyes up at her.

"Nope." She popped the P and stole a second fry. "You coming or not?"

"Fine." He slid the chair back and rose to his feet. "I'm right behind you."

Ashley crossed her arms and didn't budge.

"Or we can stand here wasting time." Walt mirrored her defiant pose.

She huffed a breath and did an about face toward the door.

To Conor and Iris, Walt hissed, "Get the names of every guard who has had contact with Hamdan, or I'll take matters into my own hands."

Iris rolled her eyes and Conor sighed, but neither of them argued.

Walt took deep breaths all the way to the cafeteria door, pausing before he stepped beyond it.

One foot in front of the other.

He ignored the excited chatter of Mom and Ashley, all the way to the NICU. Ashley complained about not being allowed to give the baby a stuffed giraffe as they washed their hands and prepared to enter the room. The now familiar sounds of the monitors and incubator calmed his nerves when the women hushed their jabbering long enough to ooh and aah over Joa.

Joa Hamdan. Someone had added her name to the whiteboard hanging on the wall.

"Can I touch her?" Ashley whispered the request to the NICU nurse.

"No." Walt answered before the nurse could, pulse spiking.

"Physical touch is really beneficial, actually." The woman pursed her lips.

Walt gulped when Joa let out an angry little cry. Did *she* already know how to defy him too?

"She needs to know she's not alone, Son." Mom pushed him toward the incubator. What was happening? "If you don't want your sister to beat you to it, you better solidify your place in the pecking order."

Before he could gather his wits, Joa's eyes were locked on him, and he felt her tiny hand wrap around his pinky finger. With a gasp, he looked at the point of contact. A lump formed in his throat when he looked into her eyes again.

Dang it all.

He was a goner. Even if he tried to hold on to the negative emotions, they wouldn't survive for long. This was what everyone wanted, right? For him to tolerate Joa's existence and have that grow into something more? Could it really be like Declan Flynn said? Could Joa be a blessing and not just the consequence of evil? Running his thumb over her impossibly small fingers, he thought that maybe she already was.

A commotion in the hallway broke through the racing thoughts in his brain, drawing his eyes away from the baby. A woman screamed and someone hit the wall just beyond the door.

"Stay here." Walt barked at the women. "And barricade the door."

The scene in the hallway sent adrenaline coursing through his body. A man in a janitor's uniform lay on the floor with two security guards pinning him in place. Two nurses hovered over a third who had blood trickling down her forehead.

The man on the floor spit blood from his mouth and smiled at Walt, sending ice into his veins. In that moment, he knew without a doubt he would kill to protect Joa just as readily as he would to protect—

Nadia.

He took off at a sprint and ignored the staff who yelled at him along the way. Bursting into Nadia's room, his heart stopped. She wasn't in her bed, and Amy lay unconscious on the floor at his feet.

*****

Nadia's shallow, rapid breathing wasn't helping her to hold on to consciousness. The walk from her bed to the toilet had been enough to make her dizzy, but the horror that ensued from there was how she'd ended up locked in the bathroom with her hands shaking and her heart racing. She slid to the floor and prayed that Amy wasn't dead, and that Walt or someone else would find them before the man in her room figured out how to unlock the door protecting her.

Over and over he slammed into the door, no match for the heavy wood and steel of the deadbolt. After a dozen attempts to reach her, the banging stopped and the room grew completely quiet. She'd seen this movie before. The moment she unlocked the door, he'd burst through it and slit her throat.

God protect me. Save Amy. Please, Lord, don't let anyone else get hurt.

Panic seized her at the thought of her defenseless baby in the NICU. Would the man try to get to Joa?

"No. No, no, no," she whispered. "God, please shield her from harm."

She tried to stand, if only to keep the man from turning his attention elsewhere, but in her attempt to open the door, her vision went black and her head hit the floor with a thud.

Frantic banging on the door drew her back to consciousness.

"Nadia!" Walt's terror filled her with urgency.

She tried to push herself up from the floor, but it was no use. Pain kept her down as the room spun around her. A moment later, the sound of a key and bolt sliding made her reach a hand toward the door. Before she could attempt to speak, Walt lifted her off the bathroom floor and carried her to the hospital bed. Nurses and doctors swarmed the room along with a security officer, Conor, and Iris.

"Walt, the baby!"

"She's okay." He was at her side. "They didn't get to her."

Tears flooded from her eyes. "Is Amy okay?"

"She has a concussion, but they said she'll be fine."

"Can we get the room cleared out, please?" Dr. Emmerson called over the chaos. "We need to assess Ms. Hamdan for injuries."

Everyone but Walt moved toward the door.

"I'm not going anywhere, Doc." He stepped back, but planted his feet and crossed his arms.

"Fine." She gave no warning before lifting Nadia's gown to check the cesarean incision.

Walt spun around and Nadia covered her burning cheeks. How she had a shred of modesty left, she didn't understand.

When the medical team was satisfied and started to leave one by one, Nadia cleared her throat.

"How many men did my father send for me?" She met Walt's weary eyes.

"We don't know. At least two. Nadia, why are you so sure it's Abdula?"

"I just know." She gritted her teeth, eyes landing on the table of flowers beside him.

"I need you to be specific if we're going to figure out how he's doing this and how to stop him."

"Those flowers showed up the first day I was here, right? Desert verbena. The pink ones." She swallowed the lump in her throat, pointing where her eyes were locked. "That was our . . . thing. He started giving them to me after we left Yemen. It was a piece of home—something to remind me of my mother and the flowers she kept in our house there."

Walt looked at the potted plant. "That could be a coincidence."

"When the men in Yemen told me that my father sent them to kill Tarif and capture me, they presented me with desert verbena just like this. They told me it was from my father and that my life would last only as long as I could keep the plant alive."

Walt sucked in a breath and sat next to her, brushing the hair away from her face.

"What if they were lying?"

"Why are you trying to defend him?" Anger bubbled in her gut.

"I'm not." He shook his head. "I'm not trying to defend him. But, Nadia, it's next to impossible that he's behind this. At the very least, it's impossible that he sent men today."

"Why?"

"Because he's been under twenty-four hour surveillance and the only person he's spoken to is an FBI agent that Conor trusts."

"It had to be planned in advance. They're finishing the job he ordered a year ago."

"That's the other thing. Unless a guard from the prison helped him—which we are absolutely looking into—he hasn't had contact with another soul for two years."

"I need to speak to him, Walt." She gripped his hand with all her strength. "I need to look my father in his eyes and find out how he did this."

Chapter 10

Walt paced the hospital room floor, waiting for Iris to get the video call connected. It took more than one major power move to get clearance for Nadia to talk to Abdula, and part of Walt wished it hadn't worked at all.

Did they need clarity as soon as possible? Yes. Did he want it to come at the expense of Nadia's mental health? Heck no. She'd told him years ago that the shame of being her father's daughter was something she carried every day. She'd never been able to fully hand that over to God, which caused her even more guilt. It was a constant struggle. What would speaking to the man do to her, especially as fragile as she was now?

"We're on." Iris adjusted the computer screen, so Nadia was the only one in the camera's frame. Walt, Conor, and Iris stood back, able to see Abdula Hamdan without being seen themselves. "Go ahead, Nadia. He can hear you."

She stared at the computer, not speaking.

"Hello, Nadia." The man's deep, accented voice made the hair raise on the back of Walt's neck.

"I know you did this, father."

"I didn't." The desperation in his words was almost believable. "I did not kill my son. I did not …"

"They gave me the verbena plant." Nadia's voice grew cold. "No one else knew about that flower. Only you."

"What?" He leaned closer to the computer's camera. "What did you say?"

"The desert verbena. They knew what it meant to me and they used it against me, just like you wanted."

"Nadia, I didn't do this."

"Not even Tarif knew about the flowers, *Ab*—father." She punched the bed and winced in pain. "You're the only one who knew."

"No." He blinked, shaking his head in earnest. "No, I'm not the only one."

Nadia seemed to hesitate, darting a glance over her shoulder at Walt.

"Then who did know?"

"Qasim," Abdula growled the name like a curse. "Qasim is the one who would bring the flowers back from Yemen."

"I saw him." She gasped and looked at Conor. "I saw this man in Oman, but I didn't think he saw me."

"When?" Conor knelt beside the bed.

"A week before the attack? Maybe two weeks." Tears fell to her cheeks as she looked back at her father. "Do you swear to your god that it's true? You didn't know he would do this?"

"*Wallahi*." Abdula practically yelled his oath. "Qasim killed my son, and I will not rest until he is destroyed."

"Get this away from me." Nadia pushed the computer toward Conor, who took it with him and started barking orders to Agent Woodhouse on the other end of the call. Iris followed her boss from the room.

"Well, there you have it." Nadia whimpered, head falling to the side like she didn't have the strength to hold it up. "Abdula Hamdan did not kill his son, Walt. Did you hear the good news?"

Walt gulped, not knowing what to say. Wasn't it a good thing that her father hadn't plotted to harm her and Tarif?

"Nadia, I don't understand. Isn't it better this way?"

"Of course."

"What aren't you saying, babe?"

"He only cares that Tarif is dead. He wants vengeance for my brother, but not for me. What kind of father is that? I belonged to him as much as Tarif did, but he thinks nothing of me."

Walt sat on the bed, reclining next to her and pressing his lips firmly to her forehead.

"You belong to me, Nadia. Me and Jesus and Joa. We love you. No one else matters. Do you hear me?"

"I hear you." She shifted to lean her cheek into his shoulder, crying for a minute before she spoke again. "Are you ready to hear me, *Albi*?"

Walt pulled in a deep breath and nodded.

He sat, sick to his stomach for the next ten minutes while she described her life in captivity. Instead of anger resurfacing as he held her, something inside of him broke. Nadia drifted off to sleep as he wondered how her trauma would affect their marriage and life together.

For the first time in a long time, he felt the urge to pray in earnest.

God, please take this pain away. All of it. We can't survive without your help. I've been a fool, drowning in my anger and running away when I should have clung to you and grown stronger in my faith. Show me how to be the man Nadia deserves, the one who won't let her heart be broken or burdened. Remind us both that it doesn't matter how much our earthly fathers failed us, because you are with us.

Acts 20:24 surfaced in his mind.

But I consider my life of no value to myself; my purpose is to finish my course and the ministry I received from the Lord Jesus, to testify to the gospel of God's grace.

The things they had each endured were more than enough to destroy the average person. But God. Like Paul in the Bible, they were not average people. They both belonged to God. For years it had fallen to Nadia to remind Walt of that fact, and he'd begrudgingly accepted it most days. It wasn't enough, being lukewarm with his faith and efforts. That wouldn't cut it if he were going to be worthy of Nadia . . . and Joa. If he didn't step up now, he might not get another opportunity, and that revelation scared the last shreds of cowardice out of him.

Carefully, he extracted himself from Nadia's bed and exited the room. Finding Conor and Iris with their heads together in the hallway, he approached them with determination.

"I need to go check on Joa." He interrupted their conversation. "Will you stay with Nadia until I'm back?"

"Of course." Iris didn't hesitate, moving in front of the door like a guard dog. "Take all the time you need."

All the way to the NICU, Walt prayed and planned the words he would say. It was ridiculous, developing a speech for a newborn. When he finally stood in front of the incubator, staring into Joa's open eyes, all of his carefully crafted words evaporated from his mind. He hesitated for a moment before slipping his hand into the machine.

When tiny fingers wrapped around his thumb, all he could say was, "We're in this together, kid. You won't ever know what it's like to have a father who doesn't value and protect you. I promise."

*****

"What's going on?" Nadia groggily looked at Maggie and Ashley, who both had conspiratorial grins on their faces. The hospital room had transformed from clinical to whimsical, with flowers on every surface and presents stacked in the corner. The desert verbena wasn't anywhere to be found. "Exactly how long have I been asleep?"

"A few hours." Ashley shrugged. "I ordered you a steak dinner. Hope you don't mind. You're too pale."

"That sounds enticing, if I can stomach it." She gestured to the flowers and gifts. "What is all of this?"

"It's for your wedding-slash-baby shower," Maggie piped in. "DuWayne said we have today to get it all done, because tomorrow he's taking charge of the situation."

"The situation?"

Ashley grinned, looking proud as she said, "He's finally come to his senses, Dee. He said he's not letting you go another day without his last name—both of you."

"What?"

"Listen, we tried to tell him it isn't his decision alone, but there's no reasoning with him when he gets like this. He insisted that you turned over all the wedding planning authority to him a year ago, and he's holding you to the promise you forced him to make." Ashley shrugged. "May as well just roll with it."

170

"He wants to get married?" Nadia pointed to the bed she lay in. "In this hospital? Tomorrow?"

"He wanted to get married today." Maggie chuckled. "But the hospital chaplain won't do it until tomorrow."

Nadia closed her eyes, trying to slow her racing thoughts. Was she okay with this? Should she be angry that he was making all of her choices? She couldn't argue with his reasoning, when she'd been the one who'd suggested it on the night of their engagement. But had he completely lost his mind while she slept? And what about Joa? They hadn't discussed her place in their life since he'd all but admitted he might never be able to accept her.

"I need to talk to him." Nadia crossed her arms over her chest. "Now."

Ashley hummed. "That's impossible. He's gone to the county clerk's office to get the marriage license."

"Oh. My. Gosh." Nadia shook her head in indignation. "He's serious about this."

"Honey," Maggie sighed. "You know my son. It may take him an infuriating amount of time to figure something out, but when he does . . ."

Nadia fought a smile at the surprising jolt of excitement that hit her in the chest.

"He's such a brute." She couldn't contain her chuckle. "I really do love him, you know? Even if he's crazy and reckless."

Ashley clapped her hands together and jumped up from where she sat. "Are you ready to see your wedding dress options? Iris has been busy."

"I suppose that's the logical next step." Nadia took a deep breath. "First, I really need to go see Joa."

"I was so hoping you'd say that." Maggie pressed the call button on the side of the bed. "Prepare yourself for the protective detail. The FBI has this place on lockdown. It's impressive."

Nadia swallowed the sudden lump in her throat. No matter what merriment they orchestrated, the fact remained that someone out there still wanted her dead. She worried about the danger they were in right up until she entered Joa's room and noticed that her last name had been scratched out and replaced with *Walters*. Peace surrounded her at the sight of his messy scrawl. He'd done it himself—claimed Joa as his own without permission or prompting.

Okay, Lord. I guess we are doing this.

Chapter 11

"Unreal." Iris stared at the marriage license Walt proudly held in front of her face. "I can't believe they really gave you one."

"I may have played on the lady's sympathies to expedite the process, but it really isn't difficult to get a marriage license in Virginia."

"Mmhmm." Iris nodded slowly, doubting it was as easy as her buddy suggested. "And what does Dee say about all of this?"

Walt squared his shoulders. "I haven't talked to her about it, but Ashley texted that she seems to be on-board."

"You're insane."

"You're my best man." He smiled at her. "You owe me."

"You've been waiting four years to get me back, haven't you?" She snorted. "Aren't we beyond all that? You've got Silas and Barrett on route. Conor is willing and able. Heck, even Declan is waiting on the sidelines, and—"

"Oh, no." He leaned in to emphasize his point. "*You* are doing this, Sully, with a smile on that pretty face of yours. I saved your life more than once and you made me a bridesmaid in the end. This is happening."

She dragged in a deep breath. "Yeah, I deserve that. But what about Dee? I'm her best friend."

"Don't kid yourself. Ashley may look harmless, but she'll stuff you into a supply closet if she thinks you're vying for her position."

"Oof. Good point." She held her hands up in surrender. "Where do you want your bachelor party to happen? Oncology wing or The Screaming Peach cafe?"

"Funny." He rolled his eyes and turned toward Nadia's room. "Time to face the music."

"She's not in there," Iris called after him.

"Oh." He turned back around. "She's with Joa?"

"Yes." Iris narrowed her eyes. "Joa . . . Walters?"

"It's like you said. Joa didn't have a choice in who her father was. But I have the chance to make it right. And that's what I'm going to do."

"Roger." She slapped him on the arm, turning to walk with him toward the NICU. "I knew you would."

"How?"

"I know you better than you know yourself, Gomer. You're just a little slow on the uptake."

*****

Nadia held her breath when Walt slipped into Joa's room. Suddenly, being near him made her nervous—like when her eighth grade crush walked into third period algebra and sat next to her. She didn't know if she should be the one to say hello or wait for him to make the first move.

Walt laid a piece of paper on the countertop before joining her next to the incubator. Joa had fallen fast asleep a few minutes ago, and Walt seemed content to stare at her. What was he thinking?

"Before you say anything—" He intertwined his fingers with Nadia's, making her knees go a little weak.

Leaning into his side, she waited for him to say his piece.

"I prayed about all of it. A lot." He sucked in a breath and blew it out, like he was nervous. "I know what I'm supposed to do now."

"You really think a shotgun wedding at a hospital is the answer?" Nadia turned to stare up at him.

He blinked down at her, but didn't falter. "I do."

"And don't I get any say in it?"

He slowly shook his head. "Nope. You said anywhere and anytime, so long as I was the one standing next to the preacher, waiting for you."

"Walt." She couldn't help but to smile at his determination. "It's too fast. There's so much to figure out."

"I disagree. We already waited way too long, and then you missed our dance in Jackson Square, which—by the way—was going to be a surprise wedding."

"What?" She slapped his arm. "I so wouldn't have gone for that."

"Oh, I know you would have."

"Fine," she stated flatly, ignoring the grin she'd missed so much. He looked more like the Walt she remembered from a year ago. "I totally would have."

"Dee." He sobered. "After everything. Years of beating around the bush, plans falling to the wayside, and the attempts on your life, we can't keep putting it off."

"What about Joa?" She glanced at the sleeping baby.

"She and I hashed it out hours ago." He gently turned her face back toward him, cupping her cheek in his hand. "She's all in, just like me. We're just waiting on you."

"You're crazy." She pressed her cheek into his palm.

"You love me." He moved to kiss her like he used to, but stopped short. Blinking, he inched back. "Sorry."

Dread pooled in her stomach, but not from the near intimacy. The fear and hesitation in his eyes sent a shooting pain through her chest. They had talked about the details of her captivity, but not how the things she'd endured would affect their physical relationship.

"You can kiss me, *Albi*," she whispered, wrapping her arms around him. "If you want to."

"Of course I want to." He studied her eyes intently. "Do *you* want me to?"

She let the question settle over them for a moment before she said, "I really, really do."

The tender way he held her and tempered the kiss she knew him capable of made her love him more. Joa chose that moment to cry over a wet diaper, which somehow caused a painful ache to build in Nadia's breasts. She stepped back and hugged herself, unsure what to do until the NICU nurse appeared and began the task of changing Joa's diaper.

"Can you show me how to do that?" Nadia stepped closer.

"Of course." The nurse instructed and praised Nadia through the process. When the new diaper was secure, she lifted Joa and placed her right into Nadia's arms. It was her first time holding her daughter, but somehow it felt as though they'd never been separated.

Noah's hymn automatically began to tumble out of Nadia's mouth in a soothing, quiet tone. Walt didn't question why she was singing in German, but he tilted his head in curiosity.

"Would you like to try nursing her?" the nurse asked when Nadia stopped singing. "The doctor said a little while ago that it would be okay. Best to start as soon as possible. The more she eats, the sooner you'll both get to go home."

"I have no idea what to do." Nadia slowly sat in the wheelchair with Walt supporting her and Joa all the way down.

"I'll step outside." Walt took a step toward the door, but hesitated.

"Okay." Nadia suddenly got the sense that she was taking a test she hadn't studied for. Should she ask him to stay? No. That was too much pressure for both of them. "Walt, don't go far. Please."

"I'll be right outside, babe. Yell if you need me."

The nurse sent a questioning look at Nadia when Walt was gone. "That was weird. I've seen dads uncomfortable with nursing, but they usually stick around anyway."

Nadia groaned. "It's so complicated."

"Hmm." The woman grinned and crossed her arms.

"Do I just . . . take out the . . . um—"

"Breast." The nurse nodded. "Yep. And pop it right in there. Joa will know what to do. If you don't get a good latch, I'll help."

Nadia took a deep breath and carefully moved the gown aside, trying to remember the tips she'd been given when the other nurses had helped her pump and coached her on how the real deal would differ. Just like they'd all said, Joa knew what to do, and even though it hurt for a moment, it seemed to be working.

"You're both naturals." The nurse smiled approvingly. "Now, tell me what's so complicated about that hottie waiting outside the door."

"He's my fiancé . . . but not Joa's biological father."

"Right. I do know that part of the story, and I'm so sorry for what you've been through. You both seem to be taking it all in stride. I heard he's determined to marry you tomorrow, and I walked in on him changing her last name himself. I mean . . . so not okay, but also, how adorable? I couldn't even scold him for it. Of course, the birth certificate form is what really counts."

"I have no idea how to make this transition. Maybe once we're married, it will be easier?"

"Ha." The woman chuckled. "Marriage never makes things *easier*. That's a fantasy we tell ourselves."

"In this case, I actually mean that it might not be as strange for him to see me nurse the baby." Nadia's cheeks flamed. "Oh, this is so embarrassing."

Understanding filled the woman's face. "He's never seen you . . . exposed, has he?"

Nadia shook her head, staring down at Joa.

"Then, yes, I do think marriage will make it easier. Feeding a baby isn't something anyone should ever feel ashamed or uncomfortable about, but I suppose your situation is really unique."

"Do you think it's crazy? To marry him when everything is so complicated?"

"Do you love him like he clearly loves you?" The woman crossed her arms and studied Nadia's face intently.

"More. I love him more."

She hummed and narrowed her eyes. "Then it would be crazy to hesitate, wouldn't it? Sure, the whole ordeal is complicated and bizarre, but the love between you isn't."

Chapter 12

Conor, Iris, and Declan were hovering together outside of Nadia's room when Walt pushed her wheelchair around the last corner on the way back from the NICU.

"What's going on?" Nadia asked before Walt got the chance.

"One of Hamdan's leads miraculously panned out." Conor's hands landed on his hips. "We've got a group under surveillance."

"Where?" Walt gripped the handles on the wheelchair.

"Upstate New York." Iris supplied. "And here's the crazy part. The chatter we're picking up is about a German soldier they captured eight months ago and still have in Yemen."

"Noah." Nadia sat forward. "He's alive?"

"Sounds like it." Conor spoke again. "And we may know how to get to him."

Declan stepped forward then. "They're planning to use him to draw out more UN forces for an ambush. But thanks to your father, we've narrowed down where they could be in Yemen, and we're going to strike first."

"We?" Walt stood straighter.

"My team and some . . . other guys I know." Declan nodded. "I told you we eradicated the entire cell, but I was wrong. I won't let you down a second time."

Nadia looked back at Walt with a questioning gaze.

"Before you try to go on this mission, Walters," Iris began, "the answer is still no."

"I'm not leaving Nadia and Joa." Walt was only slightly conflicted. A small part of him would still love to personally wipe out the evil in Yemen.

"You have to save Noah," Nadia pleaded. "Declan, you just have to."

He nodded once before turning to walk away, determination in every step.

"I don't even know what he looks like." Nadia sounded weary. "I only know his voice. He was in the room next to me and Jo, but they only ever took us out one at a time."

Iris knelt in front of Nadia, holding out her phone with a picture of a German soldier on the screen. He had kind green eyes and light brown hair.

"We have the advantage now," Iris pointed out.

"We've always had that, Iris," Nadia whispered.

Walt sent up a silent prayer for Nadia's fellow captive. He prayed like he should have all along, that God would lead the charge and remind everyone that the victory had always belonged to him.

*****

"We don't have to do this gift thing today or get married tomorrow, Dee." Walt had been unusually quiet since they returned to her room ten minutes prior. "It doesn't seem right, with everything else going on."

She took a deep breath and studied him for a moment.

"You know what doesn't seem right to me?" She waited until he met her eyes. "That I didn't marry you on your birthday last year."

He gave a weak laugh and shook his head. "There wasn't time. The courthouse was already closed."

"You say that like you have thought about it before."

"I kicked myself for a full month that I didn't ask you that morning and take you to the courthouse and then announce it to our friends over dinner."

"Of course you did." She moved over in the bed and patted the empty space beside her.

Walt settled in and wrapped his arm around her shoulders, relaxing when she snuggled against his chest.

"Are you saying you still want to go ahead with my insane plans, or do you agree that the timing is all wrong?"

"Oh, I'm saying that you aren't getting out of it now. I don't care about the wedding-slash-baby shower, but I'm not going a minute longer than I have to without taking your last name. I'm just sorry you are missing out on all the best parts of a wedding day and . . . night."

His arm tightened around her.

"The best part is that you'll finally be my wife, Nadia. I don't care when the rest of it happens."

"You're really the greatest, you know that?" She yawned, closing her eyes and listening to his heart beat against her ear. "The total package."

"I'm glad you think so, babe." He sounded as drowsy as she felt. "I'm gonna need you to repeat that to my sister. Really put her in her place."

"Nah. She keeps you humble."

They must've both fallen fast asleep, because it was dark when Walt jostled her and Nadia moaned from the pain in her stomach.

"About time," Ashley griped. "You missed your party. Now, Mom has gone to the hotel to take a nap in the hopes that you'll at least open your gifts after dinner."

"You had the party without us?" Walt stretched, but kept Nadia tucked against his chest.

"We cancelled it, dummy." Ashley rolled her eyes. "Everyone left anyway."

Walt tensed. "What do you mean everyone left?"

"Declan Flynn is long gone. Iris and Conor were called in to some big FBI thing." She shrugged. "But don't worry. There's still a bunch of guys here protecting Dee and Joa. Just no one that was invited to the party."

"What about Barrett and Silas?" Nadia asked. "Shouldn't they be here by now?"

"They said they were twenty minutes out." Ashley averted her eyes and started to pick at the hem of her blouse. She was dressed for the party, despite cancelling it. "That was half an hour ago."

"I'm sorry, Ash." Nadia tried to push herself up, but Walt wasn't having it.

"For what?" Her soon-to-be sister-in-law looked alarmed.

"I know you worked hard to plan the party. You look so nice. Maybe it's not too late to celebrate."

Ashley stood then and glanced down at her flowy green shirt and dark wash jeans. Why did she seem so nervous?

"Th-this is just something I threw in my bag. It's nothing special." She backed toward the door. "You're probably starving. Let me ask when that steak dinner is coming."

When she'd gone, Walt turned narrowed eyes on Nadia.

"Did she seem extra shifty to you?"

"A little." Nadia agreed. "Do you think she's really upset about the party?"

"No." He stared at the closed door. "I think she's hiding something."

Before they could theorize about what Ashley was hiding, the door swung open and in walked Iris's husband, Barrett. Behind him was the NFL's golden boy, Silas Landry, with a huge smile on his face, a toddler asleep on his shoulder, and three large gift bags dangling from his hand.

"There she is." Silas beamed at Nadia. He dropped the bags on the floor and wasted no time handing little Jonny off to the boy's father. "Dee, you're a sight for sore eyes. We haven't been the same without you."

"I missed you too, Si." She grinned when he bent over to plant a kiss on her cheek. "But I wasn't expecting you to make the trip here. What about football and . . . everything?"

"You're more important to me, Dee. And no way am I missing your wedding. But I'm only missing practice—no games." He squeezed Walt's shoulder before taking a step back to look at the two of them. The room seemed cramped with Silas's massive form towering nearly to the ceiling tiles. "God is good." He slowly shook his head back and forth, hazel eyes glistening. "Didn't I tell you God would bring her back to us, Walt?"

"Yeah, buddy." Walt smiled. "You sure did."

"Hey, Dee." Barrett stood at the end of the bed, cradling his son who stirred in his arms. "Wanna meet Jonny?"

"Please." She moved out of Walt's embrace and reached her hands out toward the toddler.

Walt stood and nudged Silas away from the bed, speaking so low she couldn't hear what he said, but she didn't care once Jonny opened his eyes to stare back at her. He blinked and touched her face, then looked back at Barrett.

"This is Auntie Dee, Jonny. You've seen her in pictures."

Just then, Ashley walked in and held the door open for a woman carrying two trays of food. The hushed conversation between Walt and Silas ceased, and Ashley's eyes went wide when she looked at them.

"You guys made it." She laughed nervously. "Cool, cool. Super cool."

Nadia darted a glance at Barrett, who had his lips pursed like he was holding in a laugh. She looked back at Ashley, who was staring at Silas and Walt.

"Enjoy." The lady with the food deposited the trays on the rolling bed table and exited as swiftly as she'd entered.

"You didn't tell him." Silas's massive hands landed on his hips as he spoke directly to Ashley.

An awkward silence blanketed the room.

"Can I talk to you?" Ashley blurted out. "Alone?"

"To me?" Walt asked.

"Um." Ashley gulped, shaking her head.

"To Si?" Walt seemed to grow six inches taller. "Why would you need to talk to my friend?"

"Because," Silas flashed a smile as he backed toward the door. "I'm her boyfriend, bro."

"Dang it, Silas Landry." Ashley grabbed his hand and yanked him through the door, letting it swing closed behind them.

"What the—" Walt took a step toward the door.

"Eat your dinner, *Albi.*" Nadia barely contained her snort. Turning to Jonny, she asked, "Want some of my mashed potatoes?"

The boy nodded enthusiastically and crawled to sit right next to her on the bed.

"You'll be his bestie for the restie, Dee." Barrett sat at the foot of the bed. "The boy loves to eat."

"You get that from your *mama*, don't you Jonny?"

"Mama!" He threw his hands up as if saying the word was a victory.

"Are you all seriously going to ignore what just happened?" Walt stared at them in disbelief.

"Is it really so bad, Walt?" Barrett wasn't helping with his ridiculous grin. "He's already like a brother to you."

"It's . . . it's—"

"Adorable," Nadia supplied. "They're cute together. They both love Jesus and you."

"No." Walt looked back at the door. "Just no."

"Guess Ash likes the ones with melanin just like her brother." Nadia snickered with Barrett.

"You're not funny, Nadia." Walt grabbed his tray of food before sitting on the chair Ashley had vacated. "Nothing about this is funny."

"It's a little funny." Barrett argued.

"My future just flashed before my eyes. I love Silas but— right now—I wanna kill him." Walt gulped and turned wide eyes on Nadia. "What's going to happen when it's Joa all grown up and telling us she has a boyfriend?"

"There are a lot of years between now and then, *Albi.* It's going to be okay."

"I wouldn't be so sure. Iris has her own plans for Joa and Jonny." Barrett shrugged as if it were decided. "They're basically betrothed already. I've got the paperwork with me, if you're ready to sign."

"Jones." Walt shook his head. "I will toss you out that window."

"Sure, but then you'd have to deal with my wife." Barrett pinched off a piece of Nadia's dinner roll and popped it into his mouth with a confident smirk.

Chapter 13

"Ready?" Walt whispered in Nadia's ear as they waited for Amy and another nurse to maneuver the transport incubator into the hospital chapel. It was a small room with modern benches in place of traditional pews, and the same shade of teal that covered the walls of the NICU streamed from the light fixtures.

"Yes." She smoothed out her simple white dress. The fact that Iris and Ashley had managed to cover her bruises and make her look almost like her old self was miraculous. "I'm so ready."

"What is with these people and the color teal?" The Marine dress uniform fit Walt perfectly, despite the fact that he'd borrowed it from a friend of a friend stationed nearby.

"It's calming?" Nadia shrugged. "Do me a favor."

"Anything, baby."

"Don't let me fall down."

"Are you feeling dizzy?" Walt gripped her arm, and she saw worry flash in his eyes.

"No, *Albi*. I'm a little nervous though."

"Me too." He blew out a breath as they took a step into the chapel. Everyone was chatting and paying them no attention. "Why do you think that is? It's just our family and friends. And a few random strangers."

"And us making a covenant before God Almighty." She squeezed his arm and leaned into his shoulder. "It's kind of a big deal."

"Right." His eyes darted to every corner of the room but not to her.

She reached up to frame his face with her hands and pressed a kiss to his lips, leaving a smudge of red on them.

"Skipping ahead a bit?" Silas murmured as he walked by them with Ashely on his arm.

Walt growled under his breath, but didn't look away from Nadia's gaze. She'd talked him off of an emotional cliff late last night. His mind had spiraled from protectiveness over his sister, to how he never wanted Joa to look at a boy at all, and then to a dark place of what might have happened if the rescue had been delayed by only a few days.

"Do me another favor?"

"Hmm?" Walt rested his forehead on hers.

"Don't overthink today."

"That's a really big ask, but I'll do my darnedest."

Seventeen minutes later, the ceremony ended with applause. As people started to file out, on their way to a conference room that the hospital administrators had allowed them to use for a reception, Nadia stopped Iris and Walt from leaving the altar.

"Iris, can you keep everyone entertained for half an hour? I need some time with my *husband* and Joa."

"You got it." Iris winked and started to usher the stragglers out.

Amy stood by the incubator waiting for them. "She did great, didn't she? Not a peep."

"Do you think we could wake her up?" Nadia squirmed uncomfortably. "And make a pit stop on the way to the reception?"

"I thought you needed some time with us." Walt's eyebrows pulled together. "I assumed we were gonna stay here to pray or something."

"That's a really great idea." Nadia swallowed the lump in her throat. "But, honestly, my milk let down like half way through the ceremony, and I feel like I'm going to . . . explode."

Walt's jaw went slack as his eyes darted to her chest and back to her face.

"Follow me." Amy snickered and pushed the incubator toward the door. When she had them settled in a room not far from the chapel, she shut the door, leaving the new family alone for the first time.

"You don't have to stay, Walt, but it's going to be awkward whenever it eventually happens, right?"

"Mmhmm." He nodded.

"And I kind of need help with this dress. The zipper."

"Right." He kept on nodding. "The dress. Zipper. Dress."

"Maybe by the time we are able to be intimate, there won't be any awkwardness." She grimaced. What was she saying? "Sorry. I shouldn't be asking this of you."

"You asked me to unzip a dress." He shrugged. "That's not awkward. We're married."

"You're so full of it."

"But you knew that when you married me." He gave her a pointed look. After a beat of silence, they both burst out laughing, which startled Joa awake.

"I love you, Walt." She turned and moved her hair so he could unzip her dress. "We're gonna be okay."

"You know"—he kissed the back of her neck before stepping away and settling into a chair—"I think you're right."

"I usually am."

*****

By the time they made it to their reception, Walt's stomach hurt from laughing. The last thing he expected was to feel completely normal so soon. The year of separation and horrors hadn't changed him or Nadia at their cores. At least not when it came to each other. If anything, he felt closer to her now, and she still laughed at his jokes.

"*Albi*?" Nadia purred before kissing him on the jaw.

"Yes, my love?"

"I probably should have asked this sooner, but where are we going to live, and do you have a job?"

He gripped his chest, feigning hurt feelings.

"You have been a bit self-centered here lately, haven't you?"

She smacked his arm. "I feel bad enough without you pointing it out."

"I've got a private security job, but I'm not planning to do it forever. We can figure out what's best for us now that you're back. And I've had my eye on a piece of property near Lake Pontchartrain." He caught her hand and ran his thumb over Nadia's ring. "I didn't want to buy anything until you saw it."

"You don't want to consider looking in Florida? What about Maggie and Ash?"

191

"Oh, I have a feeling they'll be in Louisiana before too long." He sighed, resigned to the inevitable.

"Really?"

"Sure. Mom was already talking about it. Now Ashley is hung up on Silas, and he's not leaving New Orleans. I don't see the point in moving away from our friends when you know Joa and Jonny are bound to be joined at the hip soon."

"You think they'll be like brother and sister?" She looked up at him with a gleam in her eyes.

"Nope. Iris has her heart set on arranging a marriage. Barrett wasn't joking about those contracts."

"Stop it." Nadia laughed and gripped her stomach. "Ouch."

"We should get you back to your room."

"Not just yet." She glanced up and down the table, a smile pulling at her lips. "I want to enjoy this for a little while longer."

"You know we're having a big party when we get back to NOLA, right?"

"Obviously." She rolled her eyes and let them land on him. After a moment, her face fell. "When do you think we'll hear from Declan?"

"Hopefully in the next two to three days."

"And when do you think we'll be safe?" She swiped a tear from her cheek.

"When have we ever really been safe, Dee?" He hated to see their banter end, but they could only ignore reality for so long. "We aren't those people."

She gulped and looked at the incubator. "Couldn't we be? Isn't there a way?"

"The world isn't a safe place." He squeezed her hand. "But we have each other and God. That's enough. The rest of it we will deal with one day at a time, just like we always have. *Our* daughter will be strong, Dee. And you know what?"

"Hmm?"

"She will be loved by both her parents."

Nadia met his eyes then.

"I don't deserve you," she whispered.

"That's my line, babe." He smiled into the kiss he planted firmly on her crimson lips.

Epilogue

Six Months Later

ADX Florence, Colorado

Father,

I hope this letter finds you well. My soul has been unsettled and weary for some time. You know that Tarif and I converted to Christianity and that our years since then were filled with serving people in the name of Jesus Christ. I don't expect you to understand or accept this, but I need you to know what it means. We both knew what our conversion could cost us, and we were both ready to pay any price to bring just one more soul to salvation in Jesus—something Tarif was much better at than I am.

My brother died before my eyes, and I know he stood before Jesus in the next instant, beside our mother who believed in the same God we chose. They are in Heaven now, waiting for me and for my husband and our daughter. That is where we will spend eternity—of this I have no doubt. Jesus offers the same to every man. It is my deepest desire that you would turn to the truth of Jesus as well.

For a long time, I blamed you for all the things that went wrong in my life, and for the things you did in the name of Islam. Even when I knew it was Qasim who killed Tarif and held me captive, I still blamed you for bringing that evil into our lives long ago. I hated you. But that was a problem in my own heart and mind. I was wrong.

Through the blessing of my baby, I can see how God brings good out of the evil other men do to us. How can I hate, when God has given me so much love? How can I dwell on things such small things in the vastness of eternity and next to the infinite glory of my creator?

It is through Christ's power that I can choose forgiveness for all transgressions against me. I hope you can forgive me for holding a grudge and failing to pray for you as a daughter should pray for her father. Know that I am praying for you now, every day, until eternity.

I love you,
Nadia

Author's Note

A little over a decade ago, I was blessed to hear the testimony of Bill and Darla Moxon who had served as missionaries in Haiti. During the course of their ministry, they experienced two home invasions by men who travelled from a distance to target them in the small town where they had worked tirelessly to become a part of the community. They were terrorized and feared for their lives and the lives of their three young daughters. The story was hard to listen to, and it was evident that the more graphic details were omitted for the Sunday morning crowd of Colorado Christians.

The part that struck me was how Bill and Darla returned to Haiti years after their traumatic experiences—because they loved the Haitian people and longed for their salvation. Had I been in their shoes, I can't say I would have had the intestinal fortitude or the care to return to a country that had taken my peace and nearly cost me my life. Their message was one about forgiveness and God's redemptive grace. It has stuck with me all of this time.

The thing about stories—real or fictional—is that they have the power to edify our hearts and minds. My Aunt Cathy once said to my mom, "Fiction is like boot camp for real life." Her point was that when we read a story, we are given the opportunity to put ourselves into the character's shoes and ask the hard question, "What would I do?" We can take time to assess our hearts and know how we'd like to react given a similar situation. Would we love our enemy when they are determined to harm us? Would we allow God to redeem a situation that has the power to destroy us? Would we fight to stay on the path of righteousness, even when the world around us says it's okay to take the easier road because we've already endured enough?

When the opportunity arose to write this story, I immediately knew it was meant for Nadia and Walt. They are two of my favorite side characters from another of my books, *The Glory of Light*. The pro-life element writes itself whenever a woman is captured, trafficked, and rescued. My earliest draft was more focused on the question of whether or not Joa should be born alive, but it didn't work well with the length of the novella, so I decided to address the issue from the easier position of whether or not Joa could be loved and raised by her biological mother and the man who said he was all in—*no matter what*.

Most adult women have already asked themselves how they would respond to a pregnancy forced in a situation like Nadia's because it's a huge part of the debate surrounding abortion. A lot of people—even in the pro-life camp—call this a gray area. Many concede that abortion is acceptable in cases of rape and incest. The pro-choicers tout this argument as if it makes up the majority of the issue, even though it only applies to a small percentage of annual elective abortions. And some Christians agree that abortion is acceptable after rape. I strongly disagree and pray that my stance on the sanctity of all human life was well received by the reader.

Of course we can't really know how we'd react until a hypothetical situation becomes reality, but forethought is a step in the direction of preparation. Having these thoughts in the back of our mind prepares us to be more receptive to hear the voice of the Holy Spirit. And being primed to recognize hard truth is vital when we are bombarded with pretty lies.

Take a moment to dwell on Matthew 7:13-14 and remain vigilant to keep your feet firmly set on the narrow road that leads to *life*.

Acknowledgements

I'd like to express my heartfelt thanks to Brave Authors for not only inviting me into their community of writers who aren't shy when it comes to hard topics, but for trusting me to tell a story worthy of this collaboration. It was a joy to work with my friends, Kelsey Gietl (cover designer) and Sarah Everest (editor). Thank you ladies for making these stories shine!

When I saw that I'd be working alongside Aubrey Taylor and Jennifer Q. Hunt, I knew it was going to bless me beyond measure. My first memory of Aubrey is seeing her with tears in her eyes and a guitar in her hands as she sang praise to Jesus at a writing retreat. It was thinking about this memory and Aubrey's love for German people that inspired me to add Noah and his comforting hymn to this book. Jennifer Q. Hunt has read all of my stories before anyone else. She's been my developmental editor since my first book, and this project was like a natural evolution of our working relationship. I don't have words to express how honored I feel to be published alongside these beautiful women. Thank you both for your friendship and support. I love you!

Born For Adversity

Aubrey Reiss Taylor

Chapter 1

Lorraine, France
(Formerly Lothringen of the German Reich)
April 1920

My sister grasps my hair as I heave forward into the basin. There is nothing left in my stomach. Monika coughs and waves a hand over her face. "Ugh, could you at least eat something?"

"I've tried."

She tends to the bucket while I splash water on my face and rinse my mouth. I slump to the floor and run a hand over my hair. Monika reappears. "Lani, you have to tell Mama."

"There is no way."

"What are you going to do, hide it forever?" She pinches my side. "You know you can't do that."

"No, I know."

"Once you start to show she's going to send you away."

"Would she really do that?"

"Why do you think Käthe went to Switzerland?"

"Because she got married."

"Not at first."

"Why did no one ever tell me?"

"Because you weren't around." She washes her hands. "Once you came back, it was old news."

"So, what? We just don't talk about it? I have a niece or nephew out there no one's ever told me about?"

“The baby died,” Monika says matter-of-factly, “which for Käthe’s sake is good.”

“Why is it good?”

Monika huffs as if to imply that I should *know* why. “The last thing we need is that kind of drama in our family.” She lifts me to my feet. “It’s bad enough you’re following in your sister’s footsteps by getting pregnant. Does Gunter know?”

I fold my lips into a thin line.

“You haven’t told him?”

I shake my head.

“You have to tell him. Maybe he will come back.”

“He won’t.”

“Why not?”

I follow her into the kitchen where she begins to chop ginger and boil water.

“Mama’s also going to notice that the ginger keeps disappearing, Lani.”

“Can you buy more at the market?”

“Yes but it’s not my job to hide this for you.”

I sigh heavily.

“Why do you think Gunter won’t come back?”

“He has his life. I have mine.”

“Running guns and fighting is no way to live. Not permanently.”

“Have you *met* any of the young men who came back from the war?”

“Certainly. They come to the *Gasthaus* all the time. Some of them never leave. They sit there all night, drinking and singing. One of them particularly loves to bang on that out-of-tune piano. He’s sweet as can be—just—more comfortable around the boys." She places the knife on the counter. "Not in any particular way, mind you. He's not introverted or anything."

"Well, I'm glad to hear that."

"Mmm." She sighs wistfully.

"Moni?"

"Ja?"

"That wasn't just any sigh."

"Yes it was."

"I'm sorry, it wasn't."

My sister bustles about the kitchen as if it's going to keep me from pressing her about the young man at the piano. "So, what's his name?"

"What's whose name?"

"The sweet young man who plays the piano and likes men but not in any particular way."

"Wilrich."

"Sounds dignified."

"That's not the word I would use." She slumps into the chair beside me. "But he's handsome. If only he wasn't so—"

"Wedded to his weapon?"

Moni nods.

"So you see why I don't think Gunter will ever settle down."

"A girl can hope."

"You think Wilrich might stick around, then?"

"I doubt it. The others didn't."

"Well, you never know. Is he from around here?"

She shrugs. "We don't…talk much."

"What do you do?"

She taps her fingers against her cup.

"Monika!"

"Please." She gestures to my middle. "It's too late for me anyway. You were the sister who wasn't supposed to mess up."

"I guess Mother and Father are three for three now."

She presses her finger tips against the cup as if in an effort to make it shatter. "That is how it was for girls during the war, *oder*? We were out on the streets with nothing to do. Sex was a pastime. Käthe got lucky because she met Simon early on."

I put my hand on hers.

"Was Gunter your first?"

"Yes."

She smiles sadly. "I always knew he would be."

"I'd hoped I would be his." I look down at the table. "You know how it is with soldiers, though."

"Do I ever." She places the cup on the table and rises. "Anyway, chastity is overrated."

"You better not let Mama and Papa hear you say that."

"Or any of the church ladies."

I play with the lace on my bodice. "I don't think it's overrated."

She reaches into the cupboard and pulls out a bottle of Schnapps. "You're still chaste. One time with one guy—"

"Twice."

"With one guy." She shrugs. "Gunter was the sweetest young man in the world. I'm sure he was worth it."

"Except he's gone now."

She tosses back a mouthful of booze. "Who knows what life would be like if this war hadn't damaged all the men in Germany. You and Gunter would be married, expecting this child together. I probably would have married one of Simon's friends…"

"You don't want that."

She nods. "No. But I might've been foolish enough to go ahead and do it."

"You might have met Wilrich at a dance over in the next town."

"Maybe."

"Käthe would still be here."

"On the other hand, maybe we'd all be in Amerika."

"I don't want to go to Amerika."

She huffs, takes another swig and tucks the bottle back behind the flour tin. "You'd be safe and happy. Your baby might have a future."

I rub my stomach, dreading the day my belly starts to show.

Monika gazes out the window. "At least we have each other, Lani."

"Ja."

With Käthe gone, Monika no longer sees me as the annoying little sister they were forced to allow to tag along. When I returned from France, Moni and I spent many late nights bonding over hot cups of coffee, bemoaning my unfortunate engagement to François Durant, and pondering how I could get out of it.

There was also the occasional mention of my childhood sweetheart, Gunter Schrader. I'd always believed I would marry him, and though I'd abandoned him in the middle of the war, I began writing him letters, only to crumble them up and throw them in the *Kachelofen*.

Until one day, I finally sent one.

And then, there he was.

I rub my stomach again. If I had known what would come of that letter and his response, would I have sent it?

"Come on, Lani. A walk might help."

"Ja."

Chapter 2

I wrap my arms around Gunter, not willing to let him go. I've lost him too many times. "Why must I let you go again?"

He rests his chin on top of my head. "I'm not asking you to understand. I'm just asking you to trust me."

"Trust you to come back."

"Trust me that this is for the best."

"I don't see how this can possibly be for the best."

The reverie vanishes. The conversation I wish I could have had with Gunter, except we never had the chance.

These German men and their cursed sense of duty.

I close my eyes and reenter the fantasy, indulging myself in imagining another way the conversation could have gone.

"Please stay."

"I can't. Besides, you still have François." Though he gives lip service to his *duty*, his body language betrays his true feelings.

"I don't want François. I want you."

"He can give you a good life."

"You can give me love."

"I know." He covers my mouth with his own. Hungry kisses send tingles throughout my body. *Ach, he was such a good kisser.* "I want you too, Lani."

"Then don't go."

The spell is broken. Nausea forces me from my fantasy and out of bed to the bucket, where I release whatever is left in my stomach from last night. Shaking and disheveled, I fall back onto the floor and run my hands over my hair.

You're a stupid girl, Lani.

*****

Seated at the kitchen table, I fidget nervously with a pencil and stare at a blank sheet of paper, hoping that I can get a letter off to François before he arrives to collect me. The poor man fell in love with me while I was in France during the war. Though he is desirable and has a secure job, my father insisted we wait another year before getting married.

I was grateful for father's intervention. He sensed that I was not in favor of the union—and he certainly was not in favor of me marrying a Frenchman.

François went on his way, and I remained in my parent's home, hoping and praying for a way out. I think we all secretly hoped that Gunter would be that *way out,* that something would finally come of our childhood dreams of a life together. But Gunter had changed. He was restless, and no longer desired to settle down. I curse myself for believing that if I let him make love to me, he'd stay.

Nausea burgeons in my abdomen. I dart into the root cellar and thrust my head into an empty bucket.

Behind me, the back door opens. A market basket drops on the floor and Mother rushes in, dropping to her knees beside me. "*Mein Gott,* child, what's wrong?"

She simply had to arrive home from the market at this moment.

I release the contents of my stomach and sink back into her arms. She pulls a handkerchief out of her bust and wipes my mouth. "You haven't been yourself lately."

"Broken heart."

"Broken hearts rarely end in vomiting."

Monika appears in the doorway, her hands crossed in front of her chest.

"Stay away, Monika dear," Mother snaps. "I don't want you catching it as well."

"Oh, that won't happen. Of that I'm sure."

"You can't be too sure." Mother's voice trembles. "The last thing I need is to be caring for two sick daughters. It's you two who should be taking care of me. God, I wish I could marry you two off." She throws a glance at Monika. "The men at the Gasthaus are nothing but loafers and miscreants. And you, Lani Margaret—"

"It's not what you think, Mama." My voice trembles. If I don't tell her the truth now, it is just going to be harder. I rise, straighten my hair, and wipe a few tears from my eyes.

"If I had a *Pfennig* for every time Gunter Schrader has come and gone and left you in the lurch—"

"You would have two Pfennigs." My words are sharp. "I'm not sick, Mama." I press a hand against my stomach. She purses her lips. Her eyes bore into me. Realization dawns. "Oh, mein Gott. What did he do to you?"

"He did nothing to me, Mother. I—I wanted him to."

Monika bites her lip while Mother rings her handkerchief in horror. "Monika, did you know about this?"

My sister looks down at the floor.

"How long have you two been hiding this from me?"

"Just a few weeks, Mother. Lani didn't know how to tell you. Neither did I." Monika grinds the toe of her shoe into the dirt floor.

Mother glances back and forth from Monika, to me, to Monika, and back to me, as if my sister is somehow to blame for the fact that I am pregnant. Monika thrusts her hands into her pockets and continues to toe the floor. "Mother, we don't live in the world we used to. Lots of girls lost their virginity during the war. There wasn't much else to do, all these soldiers marching through, young men coming home from the front—"

Mother holds up a hand. "The war is over."

"And yet here we are. Our world is still upside down, and no one seems interested in righting it."

Mother looks at me with disgust. "What are you going to tell your father? What about François? He's due here in two weeks."

I shake my head. I've had many ideas, none of them good.

Mother huffs and rises to her feet. "Well, if you were looking for a way to get out of the arrangement, I would say you've found one." Her voice is not hopeful. She grabs the bucket, exits the room, and heaves the contents into the backyard. I imagine her marching to the water spout, rinsing the bucket, and dumping it again.

"The church will be open for confession later," she announces as she returns to the storage room. "I suggest you go."

She exits, saying nothing more to me, but Monika remains in the doorway, arms still crossed.

I sneer at my sister. "You, of all people, should not be judging me."

"I'm not."

It is then that I realize she is fighting back tears. "I am mad at you, Lani, but I don't judge you." She turns and walks away brusquely, as if it's all she can do to escape my presence before the floodgates burst. The door to her room slams shut, and I hear whimpering from behind it.

I lean back against the wall of the root cellar, extend my legs, and cross one ankle over the other. I willingly gave in to Gunter, hoping the questions that have lingered between us for seven years would be answered. I gave him the one thing I had to give, but in the end, it did nothing to make him stay.

The possibilities run through my mind again as I brush my fingertips across the hardened dirt floor. I can only hide this for so long. Now that Mother knows, Father will know too. He will insist that I tell François as soon as possible.

I could disappear. Go to Switzerland and live with my sister.

There is another option. I run my hand across my stomach. It is forbidden, and I don't even know how I would go about obtaining such a thing, but it would give me complete freedom and set my life back on track. It would be like none of this had ever happened. I could marry François and do what everyone has been urging me to do for two years: learn to love him.

Chapter 3

I pull a scarf tightly over my head and make my way to the center of town. The church presides stoically over one end of the square. Monika walks with me that far before continuing on to the Gasthaus where she is due to work through the evening.

She grasps my hand. "Be brave, all right?"

I nod. She kisses my cheek. I turn and head through the great wooden door, where the priest waits inside, crouched in his little confessional like a spider waiting for flies

He coughs as I approach. There is still time to turn around—

"Come in."

Pfarrer Ignatz is not as warm as the priest who served this little congregation when I was a girl. Surely Pfarrer Andreas would have encouraged those who come to confession with his gentle voice and tacked the words *my child* to the end of his invitation.

I step into the booth and close the door behind me. Making the sign of the cross, I beg his blessing and admit that it has been months since my last confession.

Since about the time Gunter arrived.

"Go on."

"I am eighteen, Pfarrer. Unmarried, unbetrothed—" I pause, realizing my mistake. "Engaged to be married. My fiancé has been gone for a year. He will be returning soon to collect me, except I do not want to marry him."

Behind the screen, I sense the priest nod.

"These are my sins." I bite my lip. To speak the words as if they were a sin would be to betray my heart. I am angry that Gunter left. My heart lies in pieces. But if I had it to do all over again, I would still do it. A thousand times, I would do it.

Perhaps this is one of those moments where actions have to precede feelings. I draw a breath and push the words out. "An old friend arrived in town a few months ago. He was actually much more than a friend. I used to believe I would marry him someday. I committed—fornication—with him twice. I enjoyed it. In my heart, I still feel as though I would do it again, though I know this is wrong."

"Is this all?"

"I'm pregnant."

"I see."

"I've been considering finding a way to—" I clutch my stomach. Mein Gott, this is hard. "I've been thinking about ending the pregnancy."

There is silence on the other side of the screen. I take a final breath. "I hid it from my parents until this morning. For these and all my sins, I am truly sorry."

The priest is silent for a moment. "You say you would do it again if given the chance."

I search my heart one more time, hoping to find a different answer. There isn't one. "Yes, Pfarrer, I would."

"The first thing you must do is rid your heart of these desires. There can be no absolution if you intend to return to your sin like a sow returns to her wallowing in the mud."

"I know, Pfarrer. My friend has left. He will not be back. I have no opportunity to have intercourse with him again."

"Sin is a matter of the heart, not the body."

Again, a *my child* might make these words a little easier to take. "I know. Forgive me, Pfarrer."

"I cannot grant you forgiveness on this matter. Until you are ready to turn from your sin, you must do the following: you must fast and pray every day. Read and meditate on the Gospels. You must be honest with your fiancé. After that, you must carry this child through birth, and find a respectable home for it. I would advise you to go to a place of refuge, far away from the village, that you may avoid the stigma you will certainly face."

"Many girls have—"

Through the screen, he holds up a hand to silence me. "I have seen too many young women try to use the upheaval here at home to excuse their behavior. You are a child of God. You must behave like one."

"Yes, Pfarrer."

"You must come to confession each time the doors are open."

I nod.

"And you must never see the young man who impregnated you again."

I tremble at his words. Tears wet my eyes, and my heart enters my throat. "I won't. Of that I'm sure."

I am still shaking as I exit the confessional and find my place in a pew nearby. I fold my hands and kneel, staring up at the stained glass windows. I can't pray. Not when I know how severely I've offended God, and that I'm not even sorry.

Instead of praying, I imagine myself lying back against Gunter's chest, clutched in his arms, his steady voice reassuring me instead of leaving me high and dry. "I'm doing this for you, Lani. For our homeland. For our peace. For our freedom. For our safety."

"You will return."

He pulls me closer. "Yes. As surely as I survived the war, I will survive and come home to you." He presses his lips to my cheek and whispers, "And I will never leave you again."

A heavy dose of shame accompanies the thoughts I've allowed into this holy place. I lean forward and focus on the list of penances Pfarrer Ignatz has just given me. Perhaps if I pour enough effort into those things, I will stop longing for Gunter's embrace, and I will know what to do about this child he's given me.

*****

Father arrives home. I recognize his footsteps. He hangs his scarf and jacket and hat. His boots come off. He greets Mama. There is silence. Silence that breaks the routine I've known for the better part of eighteen years.

His footsteps begin to ascend the stairs. I check my mirror and tuck a few pieces of hair behind my ear, splash water on my face, and gather a Bible into my lap, turning it to the Gospels in respect for the penance Pfarrer Ignatz laid out for me.

Father knocks on the door.

"Come in, Papa."

He opens the door and stands in the doorway. He is not a tall man, but he stands with the stature and pride of a German, in spite of all that has befallen our people in the last two years.

His dark hair is freshly cut, his face clean shaven except for a trim black mustache that spans his upper lip.

I look away.

"Lani," he says tenderly, a hoarseness cutting into his voice.

I stare down at my hands, twisting my fingers in the hopes that the physical pain will relieve the sting of shame.

"Lani," he says again.

"Yes, Papa."

He moves forward and places his hands on my shoulders. "Did Mama tell you?"

"She told me you have something you need to tell me, and that it is urgent. She is very concerned." My shoulders sag. He gives them a squeeze. "*Liebchen*, has there ever been anything you couldn't tell me?"

This man has never given me a reason to fear him. Why would I start now? "No, Papa."

He drops to his knees, his hands still raised to my shoulders. "Then why don't you spare us this awkwardness?"

I stare into his dark, compassionate eyes and whisper, "Papa." I want to throw my arms around him, have him pick me up and swing me the way he did when I was little, but there will be none of that. Once he realizes his innocent, virgin daughter has not only been deflowered but is carrying a bastard child, a chasm may form between us that I will never be able to cross.

With a sigh, I push the chair back and rise to my feet, turning my back toward him.

"Your mother said it was important that I come up and see you right away."

My throat tightens with threatening tears. I refuse to meet his eyes. Gripping the windowsill, I take a deep breath and force my confession for the third time today. "Papa, I'm pregnant."

Silence falls heavy in the room. His breathing stops. The reflection in the window pane reveals a man who is staring at the wall, thinking. Seconds tick by. He approaches me. I spin and run into his arms. "I'm sorry, Papa." Tears burst from my eyes, and I bury my face against his neck.

My father grips me tighter and sways me back and forth gently. Several moments pass. Finally, words come. "You will always be my little girl, Lani. Nothing will ever change that."

I wish I could believe him. I wish I could discern whether it is sorrow or shame in his voice. He releases me and descends the stairs in silence. Until this moment, I've always felt secure in his love. My time in France did nothing to diminish his opinion of me, his concern for my wellbeing, or his willingness to take me back in. He did so with open arms. He recognized the difficulty of my circumstances and gave me a way out of a relationship I was not happy with.

Yet what have I done in return for his love and grace towards me?

Chapter 4

Hesitantly, I settle into my place at the breakfast table. Mother sets a plate of buttered bread in front of me, along with a hot cup of coffee. "What will you do today?"

"Market as usual, I guess." I take a bite of bread.

Papa peeks around the paper. "Good morning, Lani."

"Good morning, Papa."

"Monika is in the backyard gathering eggs. She got a late start." Mama dusts her apron. "I have a few things to attend to. If you two will excuse me…" her voice fades as she darts off. I am alone with Papa, something I had hoped to avoid.

He reaches a hand across the table and grasps mine. "I meant what I said, Lani."

I squeeze his fingers in response.

"We'll figure this out. I promise."

I stare down at the plate before me.

"The first thing you must do is tell François."

"I know, Papa."

"The sooner, the better."

"I know." When I was younger, the words *I know* meant *I know, but I don't care what you say, I'm going to do what I want.* Today, a more accurate translation would be *I know, I just don't know what to do about it.*

Silence hangs between us. His stare works slowly to elicit words from my mouth. "What do I tell him, Papa?"

"Begin with the truth."

"People don't like to hear the truth."

"That is true, Lani dear, but in this case, I'm afraid that does not matter."

*****

Frustrated, I sit down to write, tapping my pen to my lips as I agonize over what to say. Do I tell François that I suffered a momentary lapse of reason? That I was tricked? Violated? Victimized? Or do I tell him the truth, that I *chose* to express my love to Gunter physically?

From the moment Gunter reappeared, my every thought was how good he looked, how wonderful he smelled, and how badly I wanted to be close to him. My only concern was how I could convince him to stay forever.

At long last, I scribble something I hope will make sense to François, fully intending to drop it off on my way to the market.

Except I don't. Once more, I put off the inevitable, hoping for a way out. For a miracle. For a miscarriage. To wake up beside Gunter and realize this was all a bad dream.

I know it isn't, but that does not stop me from hoping I will see him rounding the corner as I make my way into town.

With the note to François stashed safely beneath my mattress back home, I give in to the same pathetic fantasy I've been holding onto for weeks, lingering in the still-too-familiar sense of Gunter's presence until I bump a passerby on the shoulder. "Excuse me."

The old woman gives me a dirty look, as if I have a sign hanging around my neck that says *Unwed and Pregnant.*

I was hoping to avoid going to confession, but the incident is enough to force me to turn and head for the church. The market will have to wait.

I enter the booth, sit, and go through the motions of making the sign of the cross, begging for blessing, and confessing my latest batch of sins. "When I was here last, you asked me to read the Gospels, pray, and fast every day."

"And have you done those things?"

"Yes. Well—I can't fast. I am carrying a child."

"Indeed."

"I have been drinking water and eating bread. Mostly. I spoke to my father about my—predicament."

"And?"

"He is kind."

The priest's silhouette bobs a little behind the screen.

"I have not told my fiancé."

The priest's silence forces me to continue. "I tried. I wrote him. I stuffed it under my mattress." Something that sounds too much like a sigh of desperation escapes my lips. "I keep thinking about the baby's father. Fantasizing that he will reappear and everything will be solved, though I know it will never happen. I do not think"—I wipe a stray tear from my eyes—"I do not think I can be faithful to my fiancé. Even if he agrees to marry me, I will always secretly wish that it was Gunter lying beside me."

Again the priest waits for me to finish.

"These are my sins. I want to do the right thing, but I can't force my heart to feel any differently toward Gunter."

"The first thing you must do is stop thinking about him. You must only think about what is real. Spend the time in prayer instead of fantasy. Read the Gospels. Get involved in some kind of service work. Your feelings will lessen, but you must do these things."

Where is this man's compassion? He can't possibly understand because he is a *man* and sworn to celibacy. My hands curl into fists, as if gripping my feelings, refusing to let go. To satisfy him, however, I force out the words: "I will do it, Herr Pfarrer."

"Will you, young lady?"

Of course, he sees right through me. He would not be a man of God if he didn't. Deep down inside, I know he's right. There is nothing to be gained by holding onto these feelings. "Yes, Pfarrer, I will."

He leads me in a prayer of absolution. I step out of the confessional and kneel again on the bench. How do I let go of someone for whom I've carried a torch all these years? Hope that I've held out when there was so little hope around me? I whisper. My lips move, though no sound comes out. "God, I don't know what to do. I don't know where to start. I only know that I can't do this alone."

Somewhere, a lone singer works on his tune for Sunday.

With motherly hands
Leadeth He His own
Steadily to and fro.
Give our God the glory!

My eyes flit around the stained glass sanctuary. The voice echoes from deep within.

Of false gods, make derision…
Give our God the glory.

The words are aimed like an arrow at my heart. All at once, they are comforting, convicting, and condemning. I am unsure how to receive them.

Still shaken, I rise to my feet. There is probably little to be had at the market anyway, and what is left by this hour is certainly not worth shopping for. As I begin the walk home, I am reminded of the exchange with the older woman half an hour earlier. The condemnation stings.

With motherly hands.

I've never known my mother to be condemning, although her correction can be quite pointed when it needs to be. Painful, even. Yet she has never once steered me wrong.

I don't know where this journey will take me—the only thing I know is that I must begin.

Chapter 5

There are now multiple letters to François under my mattress. A few have made their way into the masonry oven. There are a few words still floating around in my head. None of that matters now.

François enters the kitchen behind Father. His wild, dark hair has been trimmed, and he now dons wire-rimmed glasses, a button-down shirt, and a bowtie. No longer the war-weary soldier I met in France, he fits the image of an office-bound civil servant to a T.

He smiles nervously as I rise from the table to greet him. I'm sure he can sense the tension in the room, but he pulls me in and kisses my cheeks one at a time. "I've missed you, Lani."

I nod demurely. "I can't believe it has been a year."

"How are you, my dear?"

"I am fine." I retreat to the safety of my chair and take a seat. Mother places coffee and cake before us. François produces a bottle of wine. "A gift for the mother of my intended."

"Lovely, François, thank you." She receives the bottle, clutching it as if it provides some barrier to the awkward conversation that is about to take place.

I don't have to proceed directly into that.

"I am sorry I didn't write more often, François."

"It was my understanding that we were not to write."

I nod. Thank God for that caveat.

He grasps my hand. "It is all right. We will have the rest of our lives to talk."

"Yes, I suppose we will."

He removes his hand. Mother glances at Father. He reaches for the bottle she recently set on the counter. "Come, Schatz. You and I will enjoy a glass of wine in the sitting room while these two catch up."

Mother follows his lead, leaving François and me alone.

"Is something on your mind?" Clearly, he is playing the fool. He must be able to tell that this is not the happy reunion he has been expecting.

"I'm not feeling well, that's all."

Once again, his hand moves on top of mine. "Are you sick?"

"No, just… tired."

"I see. Perhaps you're just nervous. It has been a year, after all."

He is right. I am nervous. I turn my hand and squeeze his. The least I can do is show some appreciation for this poor man who has obviously been pining over me for the last twelve months. "Look, François, I am very happy to see you, but there is something I must tell you before we take this any further."

Be brave. I breathe a silent prayer, squeeze his hand again, and force myself to look into his eyes. He seems expectant, perhaps a little fearful, of what I'm about to say.

"There is no easy way to say this, François, but I believe I owe you the truth. While you were gone, a childhood friend returned for the first time in years. For a while, before the war, we were very much in love."

He nods slowly, urging me forward.

"I do want you to know that he is gone now. I don't expect he will return."

Relief spreads across his face, and it pains me to continue. I release his hand, and place both my hands in my lap. "There is something else, François… While he was here, we slept together. *Twice*. I'm"—I breathe deep again—"I'm pregnant with his child."

It's his turn to suck in a breath. His body stiffens. He stares at me in disbelief. It is impossible to tell whether it is anger or pain in his eyes, though perhaps it is both. When he speaks, his voice is clipped, almost as if he's being choked. "You slept with him."

"Yes."

His body relaxes. He tilts his head back and forth and rolls his shoulders. "Well. It is a new era, *non*? Women are free to do such things. We had our trysts at the front, I suppose you ladies feel this entitles you to a little freedom yourselves."

He is forcing the words out, as if trying to rationalize something that makes him want to vomit.

"That is not how I feel, François. It was a mistake, that's all."

"Do you love him?"

"I don't see what that has to do with it."

"It has everything to do with it." He stands up and turns toward the window, running a hand over his now-cropped hair. "A man has his pride." His hands drop to the edge of the sink, and he leans heavily on it as he stares into the yard. I rise and approach his side. He waves me off.

"I know this is not what you wanted to hear."

"You're right about that." He curses. "I've always known you carried a torch for that *Gunter*. Don't think I didn't notice the smile that would spread across your lips when you'd say his name. The way your eyes would light up. I assumed it was some childhood reminiscence. Figured he'd probably gotten killed off in the war. To know you'd sleep with him the second he came back—how am I to know you wouldn't do it again if he suddenly reappeared someday?"

"He won't." I reach for his hand.

He recoils. "How can I be sure of that?"

"I don't know."

"I'm sorry, Lani. I'm going to have to think about this."

"I understand."

He turns and heads for the door. I follow hesitantly. He pulls on his shoes and cap and turns to me. "Will you be going away then?"

"I am considering it."

He nods. "Very well."

Without another word, he throws open the door and steps out onto the street. I stand in the door and watch him walk away. Father's hand comes to rest on my shoulder. I turn and throw myself into his arms. In spite of the wretched choices I've made, he comforts me. Gunter is gone. Now François may never come back. My father could have beaten me, berated me, disowned me, pulled me into a back alley to have it *taken care of,* but he stands here holding me, allowing me to wet his shoulder with my tears. He runs a hand over my hair. Mother stands in the doorway between the hall and sitting room.

Somehow, I know this is going to be all right.

Chapter 6

"Are you still up?"

"Ja. Can't sleep."

Monika slips into my room and lies down next to me. "François is staying at the inn."

"I assumed so."

"It doesn't look like things went well. He was at the bar all evening."

"Really? I've never known him to drink heavily."

"I didn't say he was drinking heavily. Nursed a few glasses of wine. A shot or two of Schnapps. Wrote a few things in his notebook."

"Did he recognize you?"

"No. I introduced myself."

"What did he say to that?"

"Heaved a sigh. That's when he finished his first glass of wine. Asked for a shot of Schnapps. Then he started to open up."

"Achso. And?"

"Said he has some thoughts. He wants to stop by tomorrow and talk a little more about the…*situation*."

I shrug. The light flickers.

"You know, you're a pretty lucky girl, Lani. He's willing to try to work through things. Most men wouldn't." She places a hand on mine. "Maybe you could just listen to what he has to say."

"Did he tell you what his thoughts are?"

“Only that he had some friends that might be able to help.”

“The last thing I want is for anyone else to find out about this.”

Monika rises and stretches. “You’re a fool if you do not at least listen to what he has to say. Now I’m going to bed. You should try to get some sleep, too.” She puts out the light and moves toward the hallway. “Goodnight, Lani.”

*****

François arrives at midday, looking as though he hasn’t had more than a few winks of sleep. Some dried blood rests on his chin from where he cut himself shaving. In spite of the fact that he is part of the occupation, I get the impression that he is trying hard to look more *German*.

“Hallo.”

He nods and steps inside. “Are you up for a little walk?”

“I suppose.” I retreat to the kitchen and announce to Mother that I’ll be skipping lunch today. She scolds me that I am pregnant and should not be fasting, no matter what the priest says. I promise to take some thin soup and bread when I get home. At that, she lets me go.

Wrapping a shawl around my shoulders, I follow François out onto the street.

“How do you feel today?” There is little emotion in his voice.

“I feel all right. The nausea has subsided a bit.”

“I’m sure you’re glad of that.”

“Yes.”

We walk a bit until we are quite alone and take a seat on a worn stone bench. He rubs his thighs and looks around. "Quaint little town you have here."

"It's home."

"Yes, I can see why you would want to come back to it after all these years."

Behind us stands a statue of Saint Anne holding the Virgin Mary. *Anne, patron saint of unwed mothers.* A few candles lay burned out at her feet. I gaze at the figure. François gazes into the distance. "Monika told you my ideas?"

"Only that you had some, and that you had friends who would be willing to help."

"Yes, well"—his gaze shifts about again, nervously—"this may not be what you want to hear, Lani, but I think it is for the best. If you are inclined to try to follow through on our marriage plans, it will have to be a precondition."

"All right."

"I know of someone in my district. He is a doctor by trade, but very…*forward thinking*. Looking to improve the lives of young women who've gotten themselves in trouble."

I begin to shake. I know where this is going. I've had similar thoughts myself. I open my mouth to speak, but he raises a hand. "He would be willing to do the work. He is even willing to negotiate a fee."

The patron saint seems to be hovering over our shoulders, a party to every word. I do not believe I can have this conversation in her presence.

"What do you think, my dear?"

I fold my hands and rest my mouth against them, squeezing my eyes shut and trying to ignore the holy presence behind me.

"I don't see what other options you have."

"I could send the child to an orphanage."

"Yes, I suppose, but that would mean months of absence. You know people will talk."

"People will always find something to talk about."

"But do you want to be the subject of their conversation?"

"Of course not."

"It is better for everyone if you just get rid of it." He grasps my hands. "It will be like it never happened."

"And you would want to be with me after that?" It's not that I am hoping for any answer in particular. I only want to understand what the conditions are. At this point, he is correct. I have no other prospects, and I am not about to allow myself to become an old maid simply because Gunter Schrader could not make a commitment.

"Yes, Lani, I would like to be with you. Very much."

"You wouldn't hold it against me for the rest of my life?"

"Absolutely not. We all make mistakes."

I wonder if this will end up being like the time he told me I should not be ashamed of being half German, nor of the fact that I grew up as a German, only to have him turn around and begin cursing my people and referring to them as *the Boche.*

I pull my hands from his grip. "Now I'm the one that has to think, François."

He nods. "Indeed. Only don't think too long. What must be done, must be done quickly."

I grip my stomach. The decision is not as easy as he would like it to be.

"What, darling?"

"Don't you feel that it is wrong, François?"

"Of course it's not ideal." He strokes his mustache thoughtfully. "Lani my dear, millions of men spent years slaughtering each other. It was not ideal, but you have to admit it was necessary."

"I don't see that it was."

"See what you want, Lani, but mankind does not have a very good track record when it comes to solving their problems peacefully." He rises. "Anyway, would you like me to walk you back home?"

"Actually, François, I believe I should stay here." I glance up at the kindly face that was chiseled into stone generations before my birth. "If only she were here now. Surely she would have some wisdom."

"I think we're both well aware of the type of advice she would give."

"Perhaps it is good advice, then."

He heaves a sigh. "Have it your way, but I know your parents would like to see you married, even if it is to a Frenchman. I can care for you. I'm only asking you to make this small sacrifice." Without another word, he walks back into town.

I face the young saint again and shake my head. "What would you do in my place?"

Ashamed, I admit to myself that she would never have gotten to this place to begin with.

Chapter 7

The moments I spent sitting before a block of chiseled stone were more cathartic than any conversation I've had with the priest, who himself is like a stone: cold and not comforting.

As I step inside the house, the smell of coffee and Father's pipe tobacco immediately hit me. I did not realize how long I had been gone.

"Father, you're home."

He is seated comfortably in a padded chair, reading glasses on, a book in his hands, coffee at his side. Without lifting his eyes, he reminds me that he always comes home on Wednesday afternoons.

"Right." Have I truly been so distracted that I don't even know what *day* it is?

"Your mother went out for *Kaffee und Kuchen*."

In other words, coffee, cake, and gossip. I perch on the stool at his feet. "You don't think—"

He finally looks up. "I don't think what, Lani dearest?"

"You don't think she'd ever say anything about my…predicament."

"Oh, Lani." He sets the book down and leans toward me. "No, I don't think your mother would say anything. Not to those hens."

It elicits a small giggle, but my heart is so burdened that the levity does not last long.

Father's deep-set brown eyes take me in. I place a hand on his. "Papa?"

"Ja, Liebchen?"

"I'm so ashamed." My voice is small. It cracks.

He moves his hand on top of mine and squeezes. That is when the floodgates burst, releasing everything I've been storing up inside from the moment of Gunter's arrival, to our nights together, to his refusal to tell me he loved me, to his disappearance, to my pregnancy, to François's arrival, to his insistence that I kill this child—

Father pulls me into his arms and rocks me slow. I put my arms around him and hold onto him for all I'm worth, realizing afresh how badly I need this wonderful man I am lucky enough to call *Father*. He strokes my hair. I feel him tremble a little and move back. Tears wet his eyes.

"Papa? You're—"

He grasps my hand. "It's all right, Liebchen." His eyes glimmer through his tears. His mouth turns up in a sad smile. "If a man is unable to cry over his little girl's suffering, then he is in danger of losing his very soul."

"That's beautiful, Papa."

He pulls me back into his arms. "I've known all this time you were barely holding it together. I—I haven't known what to say myself."

"It's all right."

A few moments of silence pass between us. He pulls out his handkerchief and offers it. "It's clean, don't worry."

I take it in my hands and dab my eyes while he stares thoughtfully at me. I can tell he wants to speak. "Yes, Papa?"

"I have an aunt in Bavaria, near the border with Austria."

"Aunt Waltraud?"

"*Richtig.*" He moves away only far enough to pull on his pipe and exhale. "I am thinking it might be a safe place for you to go for a while."

I nod. He senses my hesitance and leans in again. "You are welcome to stay here, Lani. I am only thinking of your comfort."

"I couldn't do that to you and Mama."

"We are going to have to answer questions about your whereabouts anyway."

Yes. People saw me around town with Gunter, and then he was gone. Word will get around one way or another. Father does not seem resentful or even resigned. He is simply matter-of-fact about the whole thing. He *will* have to answer questions.

"I hardly know Aunt Trudi."

"She is a wonderful woman. You will get along well."

"How does she feel about—" I gesture, hoping I won't have to speak the words.

"I don't think that matters, Lani. You can go there and refresh yourself, enjoy summer in the mountains."

"What will I do about the baby?"

"Trudi will be able to give you direction. She is, or was, a midwife."

I breathe a sigh of relief. Father raises an eyebrow.

"I'm sorry, Father. It's just that François insisted I do something about the baby *immediately.*"

"He did, did he?"

"Yes."

"And what did he want you to do?"

Again I gesture, this time unable to find the words to describe the sin he wants me to heap on top of all my others.

Father leans back and nods, clutching his pipe and examining me.

"I couldn't, Papa. I just couldn't. I know it's the easiest way—"

"The easiest way is usually the wrong way."

"I know that too." Although my choices have not always evidenced this knowledge.

Father continues to suck his pipe thoughtfully. "This ought to tell you something about François."

"It's certainly not something I expected to hear from him."

"How does he propose to have this done?"

"He says he has some friends."

"The Bolsheviks are keen to allow these things to go on."

The thought hits me out of left field. "Are you saying he's a Communist?"

"I'm not saying anything, Lani. I'm just observing, but it ought to tell you whether he's the kind of person you want to spend the rest of your life with."

"He's got a stable job. He will be able to support a family. He's willing to stay with me even after I slept with another man—"

"All well and good. I'm just asking that you consider what he's asking you to do."

"I will, Papa, thank you." I lean forward and reach my arms around him. For a moment, I feel like a little girl again. "I love you."

He kisses my cheek. "I love you too, Liebchen."

Chapter 8

"I've made my decision, Pfarrer."

He nods, waiting for me to continue.

"My fiancé insisted that I end the pregnancy. I went home and wept in my father's arms." Even now I wipe a stray tear. "I had considered it myself—that option—but only for a moment. Once it came out of my fiancé's mouth, I knew I could never do it."

I can practically hear the priest rubbing his chin, as if he has not yet shaved this morning.

"My father cried with me. It was so wonderful to hear a man cry. I have never had reason to doubt his love. He has been so kind through all of this. I can't help but feel even more guilt after everything I've done—running off to France, getting engaged without his approval, and now this—"

"But you are working through your penance."

"Yes."

"Some time ago you indicated that if the father of your child were to come back into your life, you would not hesitate to commit fornication with him again."

"Yes, I know."

"Do you still feel that way?"

My shoulders sag. I bite my lip. "I know it's wrong, Pfarrer. Of course I want to say no, but I'm scared that I might be lying to myself, and you, and God."

"The fact that you are being introspective about it is proof that you are on the right path, though perhaps you have not yet arrived."

I nod—as if he can see me.

"You mentioned that you have made a decision."

"Yes."

He waits for me to continue.

"I am going to go to Bavaria to stay with my father's aunt. I have not seen her in years, but he seems confident that she knows how to handle young women like me."

"And you will give birth there?"

"Yes. She is a midwife."

His silhouette bobs behind the screen. "And when do you leave?"

"As soon as possible."

"And you will continue your penance and attend confession?"

"Of course. Father says the church there is simply beautiful."

"Indeed. Bavaria is a special place."

I leave the booth a few minutes later, feeling like all the weight in my chest has finally begun to lift. If Pfarrer Ignatz was a physician, I would say he had no bedside manner. He is certainly not the warm, kindly priest that blessed this village for the last fifty years. However, I believe we are beginning to have a little rapport.

After I've made my prayers in the back pew, I step out onto the street and am nearly scared to death by François's sudden appearance.

"I thought I'd find you here."

"Yes, I was attending confession."

"Mmm. Something you've been doing often, I presume?"

I clutch my prayer book.

"There's no shame, Lani. I can't imagine a better place to turn when you are in the midst of such difficult circumstances."

"Yes, well…"

He stops and places his hands on my upper arms. "Have you given any thought to our conversation?"

I look down at the cobblestones to his right.

"Oh, Lani. If you've been to confession all this time, certainly you must know there is forgiveness waiting on the other side of whatever has to be done."

I wiggle out of his grip. "That's no way to talk, François."

"Why not?"

"Because I'm not going to go presume upon God by killing this child in cold blood and then asking for forgiveness."

"I hardly think it's in cold blood."

"What would you call it?"

He reaches for me once more. I dodge him. "You can only talk like this because you would not be the one living with an immense sense of guilt and loss."

"Loss?"

"Yes! Loss."

"I would say you have nothing to lose, but everything to gain."

"That's where you're wrong." I press my hand to my stomach, suddenly aware of fiery indignation and a desire to protect this little life. "I'm sorry, François. I can't do what you're asking of me."

He reaches for me again. "Please. I know where you can have it done safely and privately. In another town, far north of here where nobody knows you."

I stop fighting long enough to look into his eyes. I'm flattered that he feels so strongly about us that he's fighting to get me to see his point of view. On the other hand, it's incredibly selfish. "You want me to kill this child so that we can have a happy life together."

"I would not have put it that way, *ma Cherie*, but yes. It will enable us to go forward with our plans."

"Your plans." Once more I pull my arms from his grip and turn. "I have to go."

He stares at me as I begin to walk away. "You always did carry a torch for Gunter Schrader."

I stop in my tracks and turn back to him. "What does he have to do with anything?"

"Everything." He extends his arm and indicates my abdomen. "It's his child you carry. Perhaps you are just determined to keep a piece of him with you, since you know he'll never stay."

François knew exactly where and how to strike in order to maximize the effect of his words. I grip my stomach. I want to weep, but anger surges in place of my tears. "*Ach, du Lieber.* You have always been a selfish *Schwein.* You pretend to have my best interest at heart but then you go and say something like that. That is why I don't want to marry you." I pull the ring from my finger, grateful that all the throwing up has prevented me from swelling or gaining weight.

He reaches out his hand reflexively, and I press the ring into his palm.

"I'm sorry you feel this way, Lani." He closes his hand around the bauble and stares at me incredulously. "I think you are making a big mistake."

I look him up and down. Not only do I not love him, I no longer find him the least bit attractive. I sigh deeply and square my shoulders. "On the contrary, François. I think that this is the first good decision I've made in a long time."

Without another word, I turn and make my way home, but I do not turn onto my street until I've sat on a bench to pray and gather my thoughts.

I clutch the little prayer book to my chest and rub my thumb against its soft, aging leather. For a moment, I indulge myself in imagining I'm pulling Gunter close—making the memory of him what it *should have* been, rather than what it was.

My heart squeezes like it did that first morning when I trudged over to his hotel room, unaware that I was about to lose my virginity. Gunter pulled me into his arms. I looked at the bed, where the covers were still strewn and the sheets wrinkled.

From behind, Gunter's brother hollered, "I'll go hunt down something to eat. Back in an hour?"

Gunter nodded. Jochen winked, and shut the door. We were alone.

"That was quick," I breathed.

"He was on his way out already. I think your arrival just sped up the process."

"Is he bringing back something for you?"

"Don't know." Gunter pressed his lips against mine and added a muffled, "Don't care."

My mind and body began to war inside me. I wanted him—every part of him.

But now, I can see the future. I can see him abandon me for another chance to fight. See the baby that is going to grow up without a father. See me, somewhere in a tiny village in Bavaria with a great aunt, giving birth alone, giving the baby up, going back to a town where people *know* why young women go away.

I've gone away twice now. *I* know my reasons for going to France in 1917, but do they? Or did they assume *then* that I messed up, just like they are going to now?

In my mind, I push Gunter away rather than allowing him to lay me back on the bed. He looks at me, hunger still in his eyes.

"I'm sorry, Gunter. I can't do this."

He works his jaw. I take a few steps backward, reach for my handbag and motion to the door. "Let's take a walk. Hopefully we'll meet up with Jochen on his way back."

Gunter purses his lips. He's thinking about it. I extend my hand. "Come on."

He nods. We make our way to the street. Somewhere, between the cemetery and the park, he suddenly spins me around and pulls a ring out of his pocket, infinitely more beautiful than the one François offered me.

I shake myself out of the fantasy and look around at the people passing by. My heart sinks. There is no use in turning this into something that will never happen.

Am I finally beginning to regret climbing into bed with Gunter?

Chapter 9

June 1920

The train jerks into motion. Papa places a hand on my forearm as if to steady me.

"Thank you for coming with me, Papa."

"I couldn't have you travel alone. Besides, I haven't seen her since you girls were little. I believe I owe her a visit." He settles more comfortably into the seat beside me, though his hand remains on my arm.

"How much does she know about what's going on?"

Father considers his words. "Your Aunt Trudi is accustomed to these things."

"This is a little different."

"Is it?"

I flex my hand, wiggle my fingers and gaze with remorse at my ring finger.

"She's worked with unwed mothers before, Lani.

I touch my hands to my stomach. *Unwed mothers.* He makes it sound so harmless. In reality, it is a stigma that could follow both me and my child for the rest of our lives. I'm finally beginning to feel little butterflies. Mother says they are baby kicks or baby hiccups. This season of life that was intended to be so beautiful is laden with shame and regret. "Did Käthe go to her?"

Father stiffens. "How did you know about that?"

"Monika told me."

"Naturally. Käthe and Simon married shortly after they found out."

"Achso." I want to ask more questions, and I know he would answer them to the best of his ability, but he is my father. And I am scared.

We are alone in our compartment. Father uses this as an opportunity to ask me the serious questions I've been avoiding back home. "Have you given any thought to what you plan to do afterward?"

"How could I even *consider* bringing this child home and subjecting him to a life of shame and stigma?"

Instead of answering my question, Papa crosses one leg over the other. "Him?"

Embarrassed, I turn away from Papa. "I guess it feels natural to say *him*." A moment passes. I grip my stomach. "I don't want to give him up, Papa."

Father sighs. "It's going to be hard either way, Lani."

"I know."

"I am sure Aunt Trudi is more equipped to give advice than I am."

I still can't get past the fear of what she'll think of me. Even if she has dealt with unwed mothers before, I am family. Her own nephew's daughter. Father is a kind, upstanding member of the Church. Mother too. Käthe got away with it because she got married and moved to Switzerland. The baby died. No one will ever know.

Monika has let my parents down in plenty of other ways. I was the last ray of hope for two devoutly religious people whose eldest daughters have both fallen short of their expectations.

And now I've failed too.

*****

Father nudges my arm. "Liebchen?"

"Ja?"

"We will be arriving soon."

In a haze, I realize I must have fallen asleep under my weighty thoughts.

"I haven't been here in years." He pulls me in to his side, and I savor his familiar, comforting scent as we stare out the window.

"I've never been anywhere."

"Haven't you?"

"*Doch.* Home and Grandpere's little village in France."

"Achso."

I cannot even be angry at him for patronizing me. After all, I'm the one who ran off to France. In spite of his kindness to me and my many apologies, I do not feel I've said enough. "I am so sorry I left you and Mother during the war."

"All is forgiven, Lani. I've told you this."

I shake my head. "It can't be."

He turns so that we are facing each other, grasps my shoulders, and looks pointedly into my eyes. "Lani, I have forgiven you. So has your mother. Perhaps it is time to forgive yourself."

I shake my head.

"Why hold onto it?"

"I'm not holding on on purpose." I grip my stomach and look down at the bump forming beneath my dress. "I'm just afraid this shame will always be with me."

244

"Haven't you talked about this at length with the priest?"

"Yes."

"And he gave you absolution."

"Yes."

"So, what still bothers you?"

I shake my head. "I just feel wrong inside. Like damaged goods."

Father inhales deeply.

"Father?"

Whatever is behind his eyes pains him. "Lani, life is rarely as pure, simple, and beautiful as we want it to be. There is an ideal that we all strive for—or at least, an ideal we are expected to strive for. It is wonderful when we manage to obtain it, but when we fall short, we cannot live as if we are beyond repair."

The train begins to slow. He glances out the window. "Looks like we've arrived."

I nod and stare down at my fingers again, twisting them to relieve the empty, unpleasant feeling inside. He places a hand on mine. A subtle but reassuring smile lifts the corner of his mouth. "It will be all right."

*****

Aunt Waltraud is a strong, squat woman with a long braid that was probably once brown. The plait has been curled into a bun, and gray flyaways frame her face. Other than that, she looks like my father. *A good, solid, southern German composition.*

"Lani, my goodness, how you've grown. The last time I saw you, you were—" she presses a hand toward the ground.

After a kiss on the cheek, she adds, "I guess I know which one of you girls inherited all of your mother's looks."

"Come now, Aunt Trudi. Our side of the family has its own brand of charm."

"Have you looked in a mirror lately, Ferdinand?"

He rubs a hand over one cheek and then the other. "An acquired taste, I'm sure."

She winks. "Let's go. I had one of the young men from town drive me up here. He'll need to get back by sundown."

"We have plenty of time," Father observes. "It is the height of summer."

"That is *not* a good thing," Trudi hisses.

We wind our way through the crowd, which eventually thins until we're standing before a modest wagon and a *very* good looking driver.

"Leopold, this is Herr Schumacher."

My father extends a hand, and Leopold gives it a firm grasp.

"His daughter, Fräulein Schumacher."

"Lani—you may call me Lani."

"Pleased to meet you." He bows slightly, then rises and rubs his hands together. "Let's get you folks home."

Aunt Trudi hurries us into the wagon. Leopold gives her a hand, then hops up and snaps the reins. I can't help but notice how strong and attractive he is, although he's not much taller than I am. I grew so fond of Gunter's height and blond hair, his North German accent, and the way *Plattdeutsch* would sometimes slip into his speech even though he tried his best to avoid it. This young man wears a pair of worn Lederhosen. Beneath them, his legs are toned and strong.

What am I thinking? Here I am escaping my hometown because of the mistakes I've made. I'm no longer engaged, and the man I had *hoped* to marry refuses to stop fighting even though the Armistice was signed a year and a half ago.

Gunter once told me that another name for rifle is *the soldier's mistress*. Apparently, it was no exaggeration. Leopold probably only uses a rifle for hunting.

I want to smack myself, but Trudi raises her voice. "Do you remember Bavaria at all, Lani dear?"

"I was too young to remember much."

She nods. "Well then, your father had better watch out. Ferdinand, she may grow to like it here. Never go home."

Father chuckles. "I might too, if her mother would permit it."

Leopold shakes the reins and grins, revealing a dimple on his left cheek. *Stupid girl.* There is no man in the world who is going to want me now. And if one does, I will be forced to resign myself to keeping a secret from him for the rest of my life.

I turn toward Father. His strong, solid presence brings me a kind of comfort. I want to snuggle against him as I did on the train but the current seating arrangement would not allow for such a thing. Instead, I reach for his hand.

"Your father was a special young man," Trudi remarks. "I was always so proud to show him off around town when he would come to visit."

He leans toward me. "She says that as if I am no longer special."

"I say that as if you are no longer young."

Once again, I inadvertently notice Leopold's silent, amused smile and the dimple on his cheek.

Chapter 10

When I awake the next morning, Father has already taken off on a morning hike. Trudi pours me a cup of tea and slides a hand-rolled pretzel in front of me. "Your father told me you were a tea drinker. Do you take butter on your *Brezel*?"

"Yes, please."

She hands me a crock of butter and sits beside me, clutching her own cup. We haven't talked much about my reason for being here, but now that we are alone, she gets right down to business. "Your mother told me you are between four and five months along."

"Yes."

She nods and sips her coffee. "Tell me about him."

"About who?"

"The father."

I pull off a piece of Brezel and chew on it to give myself time. I have finally begun to find a modicum of success at pushing Gunter out of my mind. Now she wants me to talk about him?

She raises an eyebrow. "He is not your fiancé."

"No. That was François. Former fiancé, actually."

Trudi nods.

"It's hard to talk about Gunter..." My voice fades.

"This was not simply a moonlit rendezvous, then."

"Ach, no."

"This wouldn't be the young man that used to visit every summer?"

"Yes. My childhood friend."

She nods thoughtfully. "If you were so close, what makes you think he won't yet come back to you?"

"He has changed. The war changed everybody. Some men are bloodthirsty and hungry to keep fighting. Even if they are not, they don't fit into society the way they used to. Monika says they sit at the inn, singing old songs and drinking Schnapps until late into the evening. She never sees them with proper women, only prostitutes."

"From what your mother says, I assume Monika is one of the latter."

I glance at her with disbelief. "I know my sister has had some—flings—but I'd hardly call her a prostitute."

Trudi waves the thought away. "We're not here to talk about Monika, my dear."

I peel another piece off the warm Brezel and shove it in my mouth.

"Mein Gott, do you always do that when you're nervous?"

"Do what?"

"Stuff your face like a pregnant sow?"

I slow my chewing and take a sip of tea to help masticate the remaining doughy morsel. "I'm sorry, Aunt Trudi. You're right. I'm incredibly nervous."

"Well, you don't need me to tell you that it's completely natural for a woman in your position."

I look down at my plate. *In my position.*

"What I mean is that any woman having her first child is going to be nervous. Your mother was certainly nervous when Käthe came along. Even more so because she had lost a child prior to Käthe's birth. Then Monika came along and then she lost another one. She was terrified she would lose you." Trudi sips her coffee. "From her letters, I can guarantee she is still nervous about the way she handles things. Being a mother will give you nerves of steel, that's what I always say."

"How so?"

"There are so many times when you wonder if you are doing the right thing. There are no guidebooks, you know." She shrugs. "I suppose people try to write them, but really, something is always going to come up that you are not prepared for and which no one could have predicted."

"Like your daughter getting pregnant."

"I don't think that is as uncommon as you think. Especially not since the war. No one knows what to do when their idea of the way things are supposed to be gets shot to bits."

"It's not an idea, Aunt Trudi. It's the way God tells us we are supposed to live."

She nods. "That may be true, but I think the Good Lord is well aware that things do not always go that way, and He has made provision. That doesn't mean we're supposed to go around doing whatever we want. It just means that—" the front door swings open and the sound of Father knocking his boots off and stepping inside interrupts her train of thought. She inhales and searches for the end of her sentence. "It just means that when we mess up or choose to go our own way for a while, he is there waiting for us to come back. Sometimes he lets us go. Other times, he draws us back quickly. I guess a lot of it depends on our own hearts. Are you stubborn or are you malleable?"

Father appears. "What a beautiful morning. Lani, you should have been with me. Perhaps tomorrow?"

"Perhaps."

Trudi rises and pours him a cup of coffee. I wonder how many years her husband has been gone. She serves my father as automatically as she would've the man of the house.

"It's smaller than I remember it, Aunt Trudi," Father comments. "It seems as if the woods have encroached on the property a bit."

She raises a hand. "I cannot take care of all that land myself. Would that some nice young family would come along and cut down the growth and raise their children here. They'd never want for something to keep them occupied."

Oh how I wish I could provide that for my baby. I shake my head at the thought. It's no use. By New Years, he'll be gone to the orphanage and I'll be home.

Chapter 11

"I have some mail for you, Frau Schumacher." Leopold appears with a few pieces of mail. He stops in his tracks when he sees me, bows, and gives the typical regional greeting. "*Servus*."

"Guten Morgen." Ach. He really is short.

Leopold pulls a letter from his hand and offers it. "Fräulein Schumacher—I mean, Lani—I believe this is for you."

"Thank you." Instantly, I recognize Monika's handwriting.

Aunt Trudi directs Leopold to the backyard where he is to do some work around the grounds. There isn't much left of the place, and what is there is being maintained by the efforts of an old woman and a teenage boy.

At least I think he's a teenager.

I turn my attention to Monika's letter.

Dear Sister,

The house is quiet since you've been gone. I have no one to talk to. Mother and Father have been harder on me since you left—I'm not blaming you, I just feel they are more determined to see me "shape up" and settle down with a young man. Preferably nearby, not in Switzerland.

It is Mother who is the worst. Father has been quiet and contemplative, smoking his pipe and going to confession more often.

I think he blames himself for the way things have turned out with his children. Käthe disappearing to Switzerland with a Jew, me working at the inn and staying late with the young men in the parlor, drinking and singing and then, "God knows what." And you. He's worried about you.

We can all count ourselves lucky that Father is not an angry, controlling man, but I fault him for being *too* soft, permitting things he should have spoken up against.

It is a tough balance, isn't it?

Ach, Lani. I miss you. I have considered joining you in Bavaria myself, at least for a few weeks, but that might put Father over the edge. I'll make the trip closer to your delivery. For now, I am going to start coming home earlier, to give our parents less occasion to worry.

Much love,
Moni

Aunt Trudi bustles in. "Leopold is such a nice young man. I can't imagine what I would do without him."

The poor woman lost both her sons in the war. An unfathomable tragedy. Her husband was a member of the *Jägerkorps*, and both boys followed him into the battalion. Those men were known for their bravery and ability to survive extreme conditions. One of Trudi's sons was killed in action in France, almost immediately. The father and the other son were eventually sent to the Carpathians, where the latter fell off a cliff. The father's health was greatly weakened by the bitter cold, and he spent many months in a medical hospital before, as Trudi says, "He died of a broken heart."

She had been a midwife before marriage, and when her husband and sons left in 1914, she found solace in caring for other people once again.

"Leopold reminds me of my Thomas," she comments. "Helpful and friendly."

"And what of Hans?"

"Hans had a darker personality." She begins to scrub the basin. "Thomas was the light of my life."

If I remember correctly, it was Thomas who fell off the cliff. "He sounds like an incredible young man."

She stops scrubbing and rests her hands on the edge of the sink. Breathing deeply, she stands straight and wipes her hands on her apron. "Yes, my dear girl. He was."

Bravely, she walks to the living room and retrieves a photograph. "You may have been too young when you visited, I don't suppose you remember him. This was my Thomas."

He is a young soldier, dressed in a handsome Bavarian uniform with a *Shako* helmet. "This was the day he left for the war." Her voice evidences both sadness and pride.

"He was handsome."

"Indeed. Ach, the ladies loved him, but he was always too caught up in his hunting and dancing."

"He danced?"

"Oh yes, he loved traditional Bavarian dancing. Was the best shoe slapper in the *Kreis*. I can only imagine how much better he would be now. As I said, he was too caught up in it to notice the way his partners loved him."

"Really!"

She smiles and pulls out a wooden box. "He always wore his awards with such pride." Opening the box, she reveals a chain that hangs heavy with coin-like medallions.

"How old was he?"

"Young to have this many awards, I'll tell you that."

"How wonderful."

"Leopold dances too—though no one dances like my Thomas did."

That explains his nice legs. I immediately push the thought away. Leopold must know why I'm here. If it's not obvious already, within a few months' time, there will be no denying why I've come.

Trudi tucks the chain back in its wooden box. "I have you in Hans's room. I still keep Thomas's room somewhat"—she is almost ashamed to admit it—"as it was when he was alive. Perhaps you would like to see some of his other things?"

"Bitte."

She leads me upstairs to a door which has remained closed the entire time I've been here. She hesitates a moment before opening it, as if she's whispering a silent prayer, then pushes into the room. It is small and simple, but clean. Not a speck of dust on the bedside table, the mirror, or the wash basin. A vase with fresh flowers accents the small dresser. In the corner is a wardrobe, to which she advances immediately.

Trudi turns the key and swings the doors open, revealing his linen shirts and Lederhosen. At the bottom, a worn pair of shoes stands beside an immaculate pair of adult men's dance shoes. "They've never been worn," she whispers sadly. "We were saving these for his return from the war."

I move closer as she picks them up and examines them. "Mein Gott, can you imagine, Lani? If he were here now—"

Leopold's voice interrupts from below. Trudi places the shoes back in the wardrobe and shuts it quickly before bustling out into the hallway. "We are upstairs, *Junge*. You may come."

His feet sound up the stairs, and he announces, "I've finished with the trimming. Is there anything else I can do for you this afternoon?"

"I don't think so, young man. Not at the moment."

"All right. Send word if you need anything."

"Of course."

He pokes his head in the room and bids me goodbye. Trudi walks him down to the door. "Give my best to your mother and father."

"I will."

She closes the door behind him and returns to Thomas's room. "You may feel free to look around any time, my dear. I do not normally allow my guests in here, but—well, you are family. I think you and Thomas would have enjoyed each other's company."

"That's kind, Aunt Trudi."

"I have a few things to attend to. Stay as long as you like." She exits again quickly, as if another second in this room would cause the floodgates to burst. I settle down onto the bed and run my fingers over the quilt while my eyes wander around the room. There are a few things on the shelf, books about beetles and birds and trees, a few books about war, and some maps. A small collection of toy soldiers. I wonder what kind of boy he was, what kind of man he would be if he were alive now, and in what ways Leopold reminds Trudy of her late son.

*****

Trudi places a piece of cheese neatly on her slice of bread. "Maybe next time Leopold comes to help around the yard, I will send you out to help him."

"I can help you any time you need, Aunt Trudi."

"Achso. That's not what I meant. It would be nice if you had someone your age to talk to."

I shrug. Clearly, Leopold and I are in different stages of life. "I can't imagine we'd find much in common."

"Wouldn't you?"

"The very reason I'm here is because I grew too close to a boy."

"I don't think there's any fear of *that* happening. Besides"—she gestures to the kitchen window, which faces the backyard—"on the outside chance that anything does happen, I'd be the first to know. I have a sixth sense about these things."

I laugh a little too sardonically.

"I'm quite serious, young lady. We had more than enough girls running around without fathers in their homes during the war."

"So, you specialize in serving unwed mothers."

She shrugs and reaches for another slice of cheese. "I wouldn't call it a specialty. I have served plenty of married women as well, and they pay better. But, I happen to have some experience serving unwed mothers *pro bono*. Girls seem to love men in uniform, and soldiers are known for enjoying—

extramarital pleasures—when given the opportunity. I guess you would say I just happened to get back to my profession at the right time.”

There is not a hint of discomfort on her face. She’s simply stating the facts.

“I only saw one picture of Gunter in uniform.”

“Na ja, you didn’t have to. You already loved him.”

I nod.

“Anyway, in case you are wondering, I am not trying to play matchmaker with you and Leopold. I simply thought you would like someone your age to talk to, since I know you are not comfortable going into town and getting to know some of the other young women. I have resisted inviting you to church, but your father did say your parish priest requested that you attend confession.”

“I know.”

“Perhaps we should go up into town tomorrow and see to that.”

“Perhaps.”

“If I am to go with you, of course, it will involve Leopold.”

“It’s fine, Aunt Trudi. I am not avoiding him.”

“One has to respect you for being cautious. A lot of young women would fall right back into the trap that got them here in the first place.”

Chapter 12

The cessation of clip-clopping hooves tells me Leopold has arrived. I peer out the window in time to see him hop down from the carriage and stop to pat Blitzi, the old mare, on her muzzle. What a gentle soul. He bounds up to the front door and knocks. Trudi answers and calls to me. "Lani dear, are you ready?"

"Coming!" I tuck a piece of hair behind my ear and emerge from the sitting room. Leopold smiles and bows a little. "Servus."

"Hallo."

He offers his arm to Aunt Trudi. She grasps it but admonishes him at the same time. "Don't act as though I'm some frail old woman, Junge."

"I wouldn't dream of it."

In spite of his words, he helps her into the carriage and then offers his hand to me. I accept. It is just as I would expect a young farmer's to be: warm and already cornered with leathery callouses.

He has no sooner clicked his tongue to get Blitzi in motion than Aunt Trudi breaks the ice and begins conversation. "Leo, dear, remind me again what year you were born."

"1902, Frau Schumacher."

"Richtig. I was out of practice by then, busy raising my own boys." She pats his knee. "You remind me so much of my Thomas."

He glances at me. "She tells me that at least once a week."

"She has told me all about him." I fix my eyes on my skirt and add, "I think it's lovely."

Leopold laughs. "Yes, well, I hope I live up to the expectations."

When we arrive in town, Leo slows Blitzi to a stop in front the church. It is an old medieval building, typical of Bavaria with its onion dome. Trudi pats my knee as Leo hops down and swings around to offer me his hand.

I hesitate.

"I want to get to the market, child. Run along," Trudi urges.

"Yes, of course." I accept the hand Leo has extended to me. When I turn to give one more look at Trudi, she nods. "Don't worry. The Pfarrer is a kind man. Much nicer than the man you've described back home."

That's comforting.

Leopold gives me a half-smile. "Should I meet you back here, or would you like to come find us at the market?"

"I'll meet you. The walk would be nice."

He dips his head and jaunts back around to the far side of the wagon. I will my heart not to skip a beat, though today he must have inadvertently put on his younger brother's Lederhosen, because they fit him a little too snugly.

I know what I must speak to the Pfarrer about. I march determinedly into the chapel, but there is someone ahead of me, already making their confession, so I settle into a pew and wait. *God, this is hard.* I'd almost rather be thinking about Gunter. My love for him was always innocent. Yes, I slept with him, but it was only after years of deep, intimate friendship.

My thoughts of him ran far deeper than a cute dimple and muscular legs.

Finally, I rise and make my way into the booth. Perhaps it too is more snug than I expected, or perhaps I am just getting bigger.

Perhaps I'm simply feeling claustrophobic.

I cross myself. "Bless me, Father, for I have sinned. It has been three weeks since my last confession. I am new here, unmarried, eighteen, and four months pregnant. I have been in confession back home for much of that time. I've been working through penance, examining myself, and have turned from my sins." I pause to catch my breath. "I admit that I still struggle. As soon as I arrived I noticed a young man in the district. He is charming and—well, I admit I find him desirable. I'm alone so much, yet I'm afraid that being around him might lead me back to the things that got me here in the first place." I hesitate, asking myself if there is anything else I need to tell him before closing my confession.

"It seems to me that you are doing all the right things, my child."

His voice is warm and gentle. I almost want him to keep talking. "I'm trying to."

"You know that Christ was made like us in every way, so that he could truly have mercy on us when we struggle." The priest pauses. "Furthermore, as we learn to love Christ more, we begin to see others through His eyes. We no longer see the opposite sex as an object of our lust—we see them as He sees them."

"How can this be?"

"It's a process of making the right decisions. If you have impure thoughts, you can indulge them, or you can push them away. The more you push them away, the easier it becomes to do so."

"I am trying."

"Then it sounds as though you are doing what you must."

"I'm trying." A third iteration of the same sentiment. Does it make me sound insincere? Because I'm not. Truly.

"Anyone can see that, my child. Our Savior is there to help us in our weakness. Are you ready to say your prayer of contrition?"

"Yes." I inhale deeply and begin to read aloud the words that are etched on a plaque in front of me. As I end my prayer, however, I realize I have only spoken the words, I have not thought about what I am saying.

"I absolve you from your sins in the name of the Father, and of the Son, and of the Holy Spirit." Unlike me, the Pfarrer seems to mean every word he says. *Forgive me, Father. I promise to take a moment to consider them next time.*

"Amen."

"You are free from your sins, my daughter. Go in peace."

I step out of the confessional feeling lighter than I did when I walked in. Sparing a moment, I examine the scenes around me. Stories from the Bible and Church history, which I know well after years of attending Mass. I feel loved, and comforted, but I do not yet feel worthy.

On the street, I make my way to the marketplace, which is bustling with the activity of late-morning shoppers. I spot Aunt Trudi talking to a few of the other townswomen at the far end of the square. Before she can spot me, I turn and busy myself, taking in the swath of colors in a flower stall nearby.

"Can I help you?"

"No thank you, just browsing." I wouldn't have any money to pay for these things anyway.

The woman eyes me suspiciously, as if she sees the same customers every week and I am not one of them. Pressured for speech, I venture, "Just passing through. The town is lovely."

"Where have you come from?"

"Close to the French border."

She nods and busies herself, attending to paying customers. I wander away, keeping Aunt Trudi out of my line of sight. Finally, Leopold appears and grabs my attention. "Frau Schumacher has been trying to get your attention for five minutes. You seemed lost in your own little world."

"I suppose I was."

He nods in her direction. "She caught up with a few friends. Nothing short of a hen party over there in the north corner, but now she says it's time to go."

"Very well." I follow him back to Aunt Trudi and our wagon, which is loaded with a few parcels and two bolts of fabric.

Leopold helps me up onto the bench, and Trudi follows. "You see what I've bought," she says, evidently pleased with her purchases. "You will need some new things to wear soon. I have a few things, but"—she clucks—"I'm afraid our proportions are far too disparate."

"That's very kind, Aunt Trudi."

"Oh, it gives me something to do in the evenings."

Leopold starts back in the direction of the farm. I keep my head turned away, intentionally avoiding looking at his legs, though I'm painfully aware of his presence.

"Isn't Pfarrer Balthasar wonderful?"

"Yes, I enjoyed talking with him."

"A devout and loving man. How blessed we are to have him."

"Indeed."

Leopold pulls up to Trudi's a few minutes later, stops Blitzi, and hops down.

"Really, Leopold, you fuss over us too much."

"Mutti would have me drawn and quartered if she thought I was anything less than a perfect gentleman."

"Well, save it for the ladies."

He dismisses her comment and helps us down from the wagon. "Is there anything else you need while I'm here?"

"Not today, I'm sure your mother is looking for you. However, the chicken coop is in need of some repair…and cleaning. I don't think we can wait another week."

"Understood." He tips his straw hat to her, and turns to me. "Shall I plan on taking you up to town again?"

"I can walk."

"I'm happy to ride up with you. There are usually errands I can do for my mother."

What a wonderful young man. With a nod, I force myself to accept his offer. "I would appreciate that, thank you."

He helps us collect our things and carry them into the house before mounting the wagon again and heading home. As he disappears down the road, Trudi comments, "He is such a nice young man. I really do think you two could grow to be friends."

I bite my lip. Yes, I suppose it is possible. In theory.

Chapter 13

Today's confession has evolved into a torrent of my most hidden feelings. I take a deep breath, twisting my fingers together to distract myself from the pain in my heart. Then I conclude, "I just feel so incomplete."

"In what way do you feel incomplete, child?"

"Something is just missing, as if there's a hole in my heart."

"And you believe this *hole* has been left by the young man with whom you had relations?"

"I don't know."

He pauses. "Young lady, you are not the first to come to me with such a confession. With these things, there is often a sense that something has been lost."

"Mother says if I could just settle down and get married…"

"Perhaps, but it is no guarantee." Again he pauses, as if he's thinking of the right words to say, rather than what a priest is *supposed* to say in these circumstances. "I could also tell you that all you need to do is allow God to fill the emptiness inside you, but that too seems like an oversimplification. I'm old enough to have observed that it often takes more than praying, coming to confession, attending Mass, and leading a devout life."

"I—I have not been attending Mass."

"Mmm. Why not?" There is no condemnation or judgement. It is a simple question.

"I am afraid of what people will think of me. They know I am staying at the midwife's. They will see my growing belly. They will know I am not married. Even married women are known to hide away during pregnancy."

"That is true." He pauses. "It is natural to be afraid of being the object of people's scorn, and as I said before, these outward things are not designed to heal the emptiness inside you anyway. It is regrettable that so many people refuse to step into a church building because doing so reinforces the unworthiness they already feel. It is easier to stay away."

"Yes."

He sighs. "I cannot change the hearts of those who cast shame and judgment on others who have stumbled, though I wish I could. What I can do is assure you that God does not see you the way others do."

I am silent.

"Fraulein."

"Yes?"

"You must allow the Lord to love you while you are broken and unworthy. Only then can He begin to mend what has been torn asunder."

"Thank you, Pfarrer."

"I do encourage you to begin to attend Mass, dear daughter."

"Yes, Pfarrer."

"All right. You may pray your prayer of contrition."

I place my hands together and bow my head. This time, I think about the words as I say them: "From the bottom of my heart, I abhor my sins. They have offended You. With the help of Your grace, I will avoid the opportunities for sin."

I receive my absolution and step weakly out of the confessional. Pfarrer Balthasar seems certain that God is willing to love me in spite of my condition. However, he did not free me from having to interact with people, feel their eyes, hear their whispers, and carry the weight of their scorn.

God does not see you the way others do.

I linger on my knees in the pew. Leo will be waiting outside. Perhaps Aunt Trudi is not being intentional about getting the two of us together. Perhaps she is being intentional about helping me work *through* this forced proximity, learning to deny my natural inclinations and be loved by God, so that I do not need to be loved by a man.

"Lord," I whisper, "help me learn to receive Leo's kindness without hoping for anything more. Perhaps in so doing, I will learn to receive Your kindness and love as well. I know I have deep, inner longings, but it's not Leo's job to fill them, just like it wasn't Gunter's. Forgive me that I can't yet trust you with them."

Wiping a few stray tears, I rise from the pew and make my way to the exit, glancing around until my eyes fall on the brown mare and Leo's straw hat. He waves and hops down from the carriage, meeting me halfway. "Would you like to grab a bite to eat before we go back to the farm?"

I've determined to accept his gestures of friendship— except now I fear what others will think of him if they see us together.

"No?"

I shake myself out of indecision. "Sure."

He gestures toward the bakery, and I follow. A few minutes later, with two pretzels in hand, we take a seat in the square near the fountain and enjoy the warm, perfectly browned, fresh-baked snack.

"You come from the *Pfalz*," he observes.

"Yes, right on the border with France, though I believe my father's family moved there from Bavaria."

He nods and chews. "I've never been farther than Munich."

"Never?"

"Never."

"I've only been to France. I lived there for a while during the war."

He's curious, so I elaborate. "I went to care for my grandparents. At least, that was foremost in my mind. I was struggling."

"How so?"

"Well, my mother is French..." I hesitate. "I guess I felt somewhat torn."

"Achso. I can understand that."

"I don't regret spending time there. I think it gave me the opportunity to figure out who I was and where I felt most comfortable."

"*Where* meaning Germany or France?"

"Yes."

Leo chuckles. "You are a wonderfully modern woman, Lani Schumacher."

"What do you mean?"

"I mean that you are not content to just sit at home and be told what to do. Most men probably run screaming."

"I have not had the opportunity to get to know many men."

Leo nods thoughtfully and enjoys another bite of his *Brezel*.

"I guess you know why I'm here."

He nods and continues chewing, looking casually around the square.

"Leo?"

"Ja."

"I'm not just here to help Aunt Trudi."

He shrugs, finishes chewing, and swallows before answering. "I know that, Lani."

"You do?"

"Natürlich."

I'm at a loss for how to respond to his casual response to what felt like a terrifying announcement. "I really appreciate this"—I hold up my half-eaten Brezel—"but I'm sure it's going to be awkward being seen with me. If not now, then soon. Don't feel like you have to do anything for me."

"I *don't* feel like I have to do anything for you. I just thought you'd be hungry."

"I know, and I appreciate it. I just want you to know, you know, for the future."

He shrugs, finishes his Brezel, and wipes his hands on his Lederhosen. "I'm not worried. As far as I'm concerned, you and I can be two peas in a pod."

He allows me to finish my Brezel and then rises to his feet and extends a hand. "I'm happy to run you into town any time you want. Weekly confession, market days, concerts, riots, whatever."

"Riots?"

"A joke."

I accept his hand and he pulls me to my feet. "Shall we?"

272

Chapter 14

August 1920

Dearest Lani,

Without a doubt, I owe you an apology. I could see the devastation in your eyes when Jochen and I left so abruptly. The letter I wrote you at the time was equally as abrupt, and probably nothing more than a way of purifying my own conscience for leaving you in the lurch.

You had asked me whether I was simply biding time by visiting you. Please do not look at it that way. You are one of the few people in the world whose company I enjoy. One of the few I trust with my soul. Even amongst my comrades, there were few who I could truly relate to. It took months of life in the trenches before I felt like part of the group.

If I pushed you past what you were comfortable with, know that I did it out of a sincere desire to grow closer to you, and not solely for a night's pleasure.

For what it's worth, I think of those nights often.

I promised myself this letter would not just be another pathetic attempt at excusing my behavior. There is no excuse, only the need for a genuine apology. I regret what I did to you. I feel as though I strung you along, and then when the time came to make good on what seemed like a promise, I simply couldn't deliver.

Ach, Lani. I hope you are finding great joy in your life, whether it is with François or whether you have gone on to find someone who is truly worthy of you. As for me, I am back in Hamburg for the time being. Perhaps I can finally finish my education and, if possible, find my way in this unstable, uncertain world.

Fondly,

Gunter

My heart crashes into my stomach and I crush the letter in my hands. Would things be different if I had remained in Germany during the war and maintained contact with him? Is this all my fault?

There is a knock at my door. Aunt Trudi appears and immediately observes the crumpled paper in my hand. "Bad news from home?"

Gunter's letter arrived tucked into a letter from Monika. I haven't touched hers yet. The moment his fell from inside, I grabbed it and read it with the foolish hope that he would tell me he'd changed his mind and was coming to make things right.

"Why am I so stupid, Aunt Trudi?"

She sits down beside me. "What on earth makes you say such a thing?"

"This is from Gunter."

She picks up the letter, straightens it out, and begins to read, nodding thoughtfully and ruminating over every word and paragraph. Then she hands it back to me.

"Well?"

"I don't know this young man, but it seems to me like an honest attempt at an apology."

I straighten the corners of the paper in my hand. "I just wonder how much of this is my fault."

"How so?"

"Running off to France. I left him in the lurch long before he left me."

"And?"

"There was a small stack of letters waiting for me when I returned home after the war."

"From Gunter."

"Yes."

She sighs and pats my knee. "I wish I had answers for you, Lani dear."

"And I wish I didn't love him so."

"It will fade."

"I thought it was, until this came along. It is like tearing the scab off a wound. Now I have to start the healing process all over again."

"Perhaps it is part of the healing process."

"As soon as I saw it, I got this stupid idea that he was going to tell me he loves me and ask if we can start again." From somewhere deep inside, a floodgate bursts. I crumble into a mess of tears, falling forward against Aunt Trudi's bosom. She puts an arm around me and waits out my pathetic tantrum.

Semi-composed, I push my hair out of my eyes a few minutes later and dab my tears with a handkerchief. "I really am a foolish, stupid girl, Aunt Trudi. Gunter rarely said it, but sometimes I could sense that it was what he was thinking."

"It doesn't sound to me like he feels that way."

"I don't know." I truly know nothing. I only know that I'm ripped with regret and devastated all over again. I was fine living under the assumption that Gunter would never be back. Even in his previous letter, in which he told me to go ahead and marry François, he gave me the impression that he was leaving the decision in my hands. I could marry François, or I could wait—if uncertainly—for Gunter.

Chapter 15

September, 1920

"Are you feeling all right?"

"Ja, why wouldn't I be?"

"You're not yourself."

I pull my jacket tighter around me. "Just didn't sleep well."

"*Schade*. That's too bad." Leopold snaps the reins to get Blitzi to pick up the pace. "Don't know what I'd do without a good night's sleep."

I rub a hand across the belly that now prevents me from sleeping comfortably. Leo reaches into the back of the wagon and pulls out a blanket that is worn but clean.

"Thank you."

"Anything you want to talk about?"

I bite my lip. After crying my eyes out last night, I dropped off into a heavy sleep, so heavy that I dreamed for the first time in months. One of those traumatized dreams in which you feel the person you lost vividly, as if they're right beside you. When the sun began to rise and the dream began to lift, I lingered in that in-between place as long as possible—that place between dream and reality, where you still feel as though you could reach out and touch the person you dreamt of.

"Lani?"

I shake myself. "Yes?"

Leo has turned to me, and he stares as if waiting for me to say something.

"What?"

"Do you want to talk?"

"Sure."

He chuckles and turns his attention back to Blitzi. I run my fingers along the old wooden bench of the wagon. "I got a letter."

"Achso. From the baby's father?"

"Ja."

"What did it say?"

"It was an apology."

"Really?"

"Yes. Strange, I know, but he and I were the best of friends for many years. Somewhere deep down inside, I guess he felt he owed it to me."

"That is rare."

"I don't know if it helped or hurt." I examine the plank that forms the seat. The wood is smooth and worn. No cushion to speak of. "I assumed I would never see him again. Then, for an instant, his stupid letter got my hopes up."

"I'm sure."

As we approach the church, Leo slows Blitzi to a stop and turns to me. "I hope it helps to talk to Pfarrer Balthasar."

"Always." I look into his deep brown eyes, grateful that I am learning to see him as a dear friend and not someone on whom to fix my longing. It would have made these trips to confession almost meaningless.

"I really appreciate you doing this, Leo."

"You say that every week."

"I mean it. I don't deserve a friend like you."

He huffs, and smiles as if I'm the one doing him a favor. "Na ja, I don't know how you'd get up here otherwise."

"I could walk."

"Not for much longer. Frau Schumacher would never allow it."

"Probably not."

He descends from the wagon and extends a hand to help me down.

My feet hit the ground. His eyes lock onto mine and he maintains his grip. "You know, Lani, my mother has taken in more than a few of the babies born at Waltraud Schumacher's."

"Really? Why has Aunt Trudi never said anything?"

"She doesn't advertise it. Frau Schumacher and my mother have an unspoken understanding."

I place a hand on my stomach. "Do you think—"

"I can't say, Lani, but I'm sure that your aunt will work hard to see that the baby is cared for."

"I'm afraid it might spend its life in an orphanage."

"I can understand that." He looks up at the church. "You'd better get in."

I brush off his urging, not wanting this conversation to end. "Do they ever talk about their birth mothers?"

"Not often. Heidi Jodl is their mother. That's all they know."

Again I touch my hand to my belly.

"As far as I know, a lot of the women go on to lead good, happy lives."

"Achso." I know he's saying this to comfort me, but the idea of my baby not knowing me is still too painful to consider.

"Are you going to go to confession?"

"Yes, of course—thank you for sharing with me."

He shrugs. "It was time you knew."

"How many other girls have you carted up to confession?"

"Not many, honestly."

"Well—" I curtsy as best as I can now that my center of balance has shifted. "I am grateful."

Leo stops me as I begin to move toward the church. "Lani, I'm here for you. Any time. All right?"

"Thank you, Leo. I am here for you, too."

He tips his hat. "Right now I'm more concerned with you, Lani Schumacher."

I turn and hustle into the church. What could I possibly do for him in my position, anyway?

Chapter 16

Aunt Trudi bustles in from the backyard. "I must fetch Leopold. We lost two chickens last night, and I've found a gaping hole in that henhouse. This can't wait until tomorrow."

I set aside my stitching. "I can go."

She eyes my expanding middle. "Are you sure?"

"Absolutely. Please, let me do it."

She turns to the sink and begins scrubbing the dirt from her fingers. "All right, if you're sure. I have so much to do around here, it really would help."

After washing, she follows me to the door. "You are a strong young woman, Lani dear."

"Me?" I laugh it off and pull on my boots and coat.

"Thank you, dear."

"Gern."

The Jodl farm is only two kilometers away, brisk but enjoyable in the crisp fall air. Far off in the distance, the hills rise to greet the mountains.

Leo sees me before I even make it to the yard. He waves a hand and comes running. "What are you doing here?"

"Aunt Trudi sent me. We lost two chickens last night. She says she found a hole in the henhouse."

He curses. "I'm sorry, I thought I fixed that."

"You did… maybe the critter found another weakness."

He runs a hand over his hair. "I'm tied up here for a little while—perhaps you could come inside and meet my mother? She'd be happy to talk over coffee and cake while I finish up."

"Bitte. I feel terrible that I've been here for three months and have yet to meet your mother."

"Well, if you'd come to church"—he nudges me—"Joking, Lani. If anyone understands, it's Mama."

Aside from her greying hair and other obvious differences, Heidi Jodl looks like Leo, with dimples and shining eyes. It answers a question I had not thought to ask; the resemblance is too great for him to be one of her adopted children.

"Mama, this is Lani, the girl who is staying at Frau Schumacher's."

"Ah, the elusive Lani. Welcome." She wipes her hands and gives me a hug. "I am glad to finally meet you. Leo has told me what a sweet girl you are."

"It's nice to meet you too."

"Mama, I will need to go back with Lani to do some work after I'm done outside. I told Lani she could wait here and I would drive her back."

"Of course." She waves Leo off and pulls out a chair. "Why don't you have a seat, and I'll get you something to eat."

"Thank you, ma'am."

"Don't bother with that ma'am business. You can call me Heidi."

"Thank you, Heidi."

She fixes me a sizable slice of cake and places some water to boil before settling into the chair across from me. "Leo says he told you a little about our story."

"Yes."

"Then you must know there is no judgment here."

"Yes… thank you."

"You have been seeing the priest."

"Yes."

"Trudi has always encouraged her young women to go to him. I am glad to hear that you have followed her advice. Pfarrer Michael Balthasar is a fine man."

"He is kind."

We sit in silence for a moment. Heidi observes me as I take a few bites of cake.

"Frau Jodl, this is delicious."

"Heidi, please."

"Heidi, I'm sorry."

"Kein problem."

I take another bite before asking her about herself. "How many children have you cared for?"

She sighs and purses her lips in thought. "There are two school-aged boys here now, plus Leo. The rest have grown and moved on."

"All boys?"

"We've had a few girls in the past, but as a rule"—she looks out the window thoughtfully—"the Lord just saw fit to give us boys."

"Us. Your husband?"

"Yes, yes, Karl-Heinz. I think he secretly loves having all these young men around, whipping them into shape. You know. Keeping them in line so they don't fall through the cracks of society." She laughs and places the tea before me. "I do hope Karl realizes that it is actually *me* he has to thank. After all, I whipped *Karl* into shape long before he became a father."

We share a laugh. She rises to fix my tea, but seems to continue running through a mental list as she works. "I believe we've cared for twenty-two children over the years. Karl was very hesitant when I first suggested caring for a child that was about to be born over at Trudi's, but I knew she would've kept that baby to her detriment."

Heidi sets two cups of tea on the table and resumes her place across from me. "It really does take a village, you know."

"How come you and Aunt Trudi don't see each other more often?"

She glances back out the window in the direction of Aunt Trudi's. "We don't get along as we once did."

"She seems to enjoy having Leo over."

"Yes, well, Leo was like my olive branch. I could tell she was struggling to keep the place up—a person could tell from the road. *Unordentlich.* Horribly disordered. One Sunday, when she actually showed up at church, I sidled up to her and offered to send him over to see if anything needed to be done. He's been going weekly ever since."

It's none of my business, but I truly wonder what separated these two godly women.

"I didn't mean to cut her out of my life."

"So, what happened?"

She traces the lines on the table. "I said a few things that she didn't like. Looking back, I can see that I should've chosen my words more carefully. Trudi chose to take offense rather than talk about it. The priest warned us of a root of bitterness, but I guess neither of us heeded his words. Leo goes over there weekly, but she and I rarely speak."

Leo appears in the doorway at that moment. "I'm going to wash up. Then we can go."

I nod. He disappears again. I pause a moment before rising from the table. "You know, I think Trudi would be happy to see you. You should come with Leo sometime."

She bites her lip, as if she knows I'm right, but finds a reason to protest anyway. "Not today. Leo might be the rest of the afternoon in fixing that hole in the henhouse."

I stand slowly. "I understand. Thank you so much for the cake. It was delicious."

In the yard, Leo has the wagon hitched up. Blitzi flicks her tail. Leo extends a hand and assists me into the seat. "I thought about going over on horseback, but thought you'd be more comfortable in this."

He thought right.

I give him a moment to slide in and get situated before feeling my way into a conversation I wasn't comfortable having with Heidi. "I am sad about what happened between your mother and Aunt Trudi."

He heaves a sigh. "I know. I've spoken to her myself."

"What happened between them?"

"The priest calls it a root of bitterness."

"She used those words too."

We continue towards Aunt Trudi's in a companionable silence, enjoying the changing colors and the crisp fall air. Upon our return, Trudi hurries Leo back to the henhouse.

I'm grateful for his steady presence. I whisper a prayer for Heidi and Aunt Trudi, and set about the chores I neglected earlier. Perhaps together, Leo and I can help the two women make amends.

Chapter 17

November 1920

Dear Monika,

In a little over a month, I will be home with you and Mama and Papa again. Only the Lord knows what will happen to this little one, and I must trust that He has the child's best interest at heart.

My pen stops. I place a hand on my belly. *Please God, I know it is asking a lot, but could Heidi find room in her heart and home for one more child?*

I breathe deep and continue the letter.

I do not know what I am going to do when I get home. Perhaps the inn will have need of another barmaid—although I don't feel well-suited to such work.

Am I a fool for not staying here? Perhaps seeing where things go with Leopold? No. I learned back in France that home is home, my little village nestled amongst the hills, beneath rocky outcroppings and ancient castles. French or German, occupied or not, my home is with you and Father and Mother. I cannot remain here.

I miss you all terribly, but I am grateful for the knowledge that I will finally be coming home.

Much love,
Lani

Chapter 18

December 1920

Monika must have packed her bags and headed for the train station the moment she received my letter. We both stare after the taxi that has driven her all the way out here, likely at great expense.

"What are you doing here?"

"I couldn't let you have that baby alone."

"Aunt Trudi's here."

"Yes well"—she heaves her luggage in and pushes past—"I'm here now too."

Trudi appears in the living room and gasps. "Monika?"

"Hallo, Aunt Trudi."

"Mein Gott, the last time I saw you, you were in diapers. Look at you now. As lovely as your sister."

My sister laughs. "Hardly."

Trudi bites her lip. "I will have to give you Thomas's room."

Monika eyes me, remembering my discussion of the untouched bedroom with all the *Tracht*. "Are you sure?"

"Yes, yes, it will be fine." She hurries Monika towards the bedroom. "Get your things put away and we'll have coffee and cake."

I follow Monika into the room while Trudi returns to the kitchen. "What made you decide to come?"

"I told you. I couldn't let you have that baby alone." She hefts her valise onto the bed. "I also couldn't bear the thought of you traveling back home on your own."

I suppose I should appreciate Monika's concern for me—something she never had in our youth. She sighs and paws through her things half-heartedly. "François has stopped by a few times."

François. One of the two names I never thought I'd hear again, and the one I was hoping I wouldn't. "What did he have to say for himself?"

"Well, to be honest, I think he's still hoping he'll change your mind."

"Change my mind about what?"

"He really likes you Lani."

"So?"

"I know it's not ideal. He knows you'll always carry a torch for Gunter, but I think we both have to admit that's a dream you need to let go of."

"I already have."

"Have you?"

I close my eyes and place a hand on my stomach. "Some days it's still hard."

"Have you decided what you're going to do?"

"I know what I *need* to do." My throat tightens as the tears well up. "I just don't know if I have the strength to do it."

Monika grasps my hand. Pride sparkles in her eyes. "You've gotten this far, Lani. Even when you knew it would be easier to end things, you chose to have this baby. I could never have done that."

"I'm so afraid I will regret it if I give him up. I've already lost Gunter. To lose him too…"

She reaches for my hand and gives it a squeeze. "I know. Now come, let's go have a bite of cake. Sweets always make things better."

I give her a little laugh. "They certainly seem to."

*****

Before retiring to Thomas's bedroom, Monika stops in my room and slips into bed beside me, pulling me into a sisterly embrace and running her fingers through my unplaited hair. Any façade I was still maintaining crumbles, and I press my head into her shoulder. "This wasn't supposed to happen."

She continues stroking my hair.

"It's my fault. *All* my fault."

"I think Gunter bears some responsibility."

"I never should've slept with him."

She huffs softly. "And I'm sure you've dealt with that."

"I've lost count how many times I've gone to confession."

"Then I'm sure you're abundantly forgiven. You can't let your past determine who you're going to be."

I shake my head.

"Are you sure there's no possibility of love between you and Leopold?"

"What?"

"He seems to care deeply for you."

I shudder against her. The desire for love has not completely gone away. "He is a dear friend."

"Of course." Another thoughtful pause hangs between us, and she cups my cheek in her hand. Though her touch will never replace the comfort of a man's solid, quiet strength, I want to treasure this moment. I lean into her palm. "What about you, Moni?"

"What about me?"

"I've never understood how you can be with so many young men and not grow attached."

She rolls onto her back, and I realize how my words must sound to her. "I'm sorry. I didn't mean it the way it came out."

"No, Lani, it's a fair question." There is a pain-filled pause. "I've been through a lot while you were gone, all right?"

"I wish you had said something."

"No. I'm here for *you*. We will have plenty of time to talk about that after we get home."

Perhaps whatever happened back home is part of the reason she came so quickly. "Please tell me. I'd like to get my mind *off* my problems for a few minutes."

She hesitates. A few sniffles work their way through her body. "Do you remember how François said he could have things…taken care of?"

"Ja."

"Well, he cares enough about you to take your sister to see his *friends* and have her mistakes taken care of."

"What?"

Monika begins crying in earnest. "I'm always careful with those stooges at the inn. I knew if I ever got pregnant by one of them my life would be over."

It is my turn to pull her into my arms, which is nearly impossible in my current state. I stroke her hair and lay my cheek against her head. "Does this have anything to do with Wilhelm?"

"Wil*rich*? Yes."

I sigh. She curses. "This is why I never wanted to fall in love. We got careless. I got pregnant. He was furious. Wouldn't you know François showed up two days later? I saw my opportunity. I could have it taken care of and tell Richi I miscarried. No harm done, right?"

"Except?"

"Except it was too late when I realized what I was doing."

I squeeze my sister, heedless of the discomfort my bulging stomach causes both of us. She erupts in tears she's probably been too ashamed to cry.

"No one knows except me, Richi, and François. Mein Gott, Lani, can you imagine if I told Mama and Papa? Not only were all three of their daughters deflowered before their wedding day, all three got pregnant."

"Mama and Papa never shamed me."

She pulls away and wipes her eyes. "Yes, but of *course* I would be the one to have my baby killed. I'm the only one who is home to see what all of this has done to them. Papa forgives you, yes, but he also blames himself. So does Mama. I hear them talking late at night. Agonizing over where they went wrong."

My heart shatters. "They can't possibly think this is their fault."

"Yes, well, they do."

I sigh and place a hand on my stomach. I was the good girl. My sister had her reputation, but me? The baby shifts, pressing his little foot into my palm and reminding me that there is still beauty somewhere in this awful situation. "I don't feel like sleeping, Mon. Do you want some tea?"

"Please."

I rise to my feet. Water splashes down my legs. I gasp.

"What?"

"I think—"

"It's time?"

"Ja."

"I'll get Trudi. Don't move—I'll be right back."

I stand in the room, staring at my dim reflection in the mirror. Next door, Trudi and Monika exchange a few muffled sentences. They bustle back in together with a pile of linens.

"Have you had any contractions yet?"

"A few, maybe. I couldn't tell if it was just the baby moving around."

"You'll know when you feel them." Monika lights a lamp and Trudi eyes the puddle at my feet. "Monika, be a dear and help your sister."

Chapter 19

"A boy!" Monica announces jubilantly. She whisks the wailing, bloody infant away from Trudi, snuggles it in a blanket and lays it on my chest. "Oh, Lani, he is incredible." She stares wide-eyed at the tiny creature in my arms. "A little boy. Just like you thought."

"Mother's intuition," Trudi says flatly.

Trudi's seen this a thousand times. Monika continues to stare in awe, her face brilliant with joy. She extends a finger, touching his little cheek. "He's perfect."

Yes. He is. I could love him so easily.

"You'll need to feed him," says Trudi from below, all business while she waits for the afterbirth.

"I should wash him up a little first, don't you think?" Monika has not taken her eyes off of him for a second.

I nod and release him into her arms, falling back against my pillow and sighing heavily.

"Ah ah," Trudi shakes her head. "You need to give me a few more pushes."

I breathe deep and summon the last of my strength.

"There it is."

Finally I can release myself into the comfort of the oversized pillow on Hans's bed. Beyond Trudi, the baby fusses, but Monika's cooing soothes him as she wipes him gently with a wet cloth and bundles him in fresh linens. "Oh, Lani, he is so special—can't you feel it?" She swings back over to me and places him gently in my arms.

"He needs to eat," Trudi nags.

"Ja…" I loosen the top of my nightgown and press his little mouth to my breast.

"If he doesn't get it at first, give him some time."

I try again to connect his little mouth to my nipple. This time, he accepts it, his eyes closing in contentment. Again I look away for fear of developing feelings for this tiny person that needs me so desperately.

"Have you picked out a name?" Trudi's voice has softened.

I hesitate. Trudi raises an eyebrow.

"I thought maybe if I didn't name him, it wouldn't be so hard to—" I choke on the lump in my throat.

"You have made your decision, then?"

I nod. There's no going back now.

"You can still give the poor child a name."

"Ja." Cautiously, I gaze down at him, taking in his features for the first time. Blue eyes. *Na ja, all infants have blue eyes.* Fuzzy brown hair. Plump little face. I see myself in him, yet I also see Gunter.

"I've always liked the name Thomas," Monika offers.

"Thomas." There is a hint of longing in Trudi's voice.

I look at her silently, though she senses my question: *Would it be all right?*

Yes, Lani dear. I would be honored.

With a smile, I turn to my baby once again, and stroke his temple. "Thomas." *May you be loyal and honorable… all the qualities your father wanted to claim, but did not manage to.*

*****

A knock at the door wakes me from my slumber. Disoriented, I grapple for Thomas.

"I've got him, Lani," my sister whispers. I turn to see her, rocking contentedly, Thomas the picture of perfect peace in her arms.

Trudi gasps from downstairs. "Mein Gott, Leopold. I had almost forgotten you were coming. The baby came last night. I didn't have time to get word."

There is some muffled conversation, then footsteps mount the stairs. Trudi appears. "Leopold is here."

"Send him in!" Monika squeals before I have a chance to answer.

Trudi looks at me. "Are you sure that is all right? He will certainly understand if you are not ready to receive visitors."

"It's fine."

"Monika, dear, why don't you go down and get him. I don't think these old legs can take one more trip up and down those stairs."

"I'd be happy to, Aunt Trudi. I've been looking forward to meeting him." She rises and places Thomas in my arms while Trudi slumps into the rocking chair.

As Monika reaches the bottom of the stairs, there is the unmistakable sound of an introduction, followed by Leopold's laughter and Monika's giggles. He bounds up the stairs and arrives in the room. "Good morning, Lani."

"Hallo, Leo."

"Wow. He came quick."

"He certainly did." Trudi finally has a moment to sit down, and her voice reflects her exhaustion.

Leo approaches the bedside and looks at the tiny human in my arms. "A boy, just like you thought."

"Yes."

"Monika wouldn't tell me his name."

"Thomas."

His mouth turns up in a smile and he looks at Aunt Trudi. "Before I get to work, I'd like to return home and tell my mother."

"Is it that urgent, young man?"

Leo glances at me and winks, but directs his words back to Trudi. "Yes, ma'am, it is that urgent. I'm sure she'll want to meet Thomas."

Trudi stiffens, closes her eyes, and breathes deep. "Yes, I suppose. Please give us some time to freshen up or eat breakfast first, though, would you please?"

"I'm sure Mother would be happy to bring along some breakfast."

"I hardly expect her to do that. Monika, dear, why don't you go out to the henhouse and see what the girls have left us."

"Yes, ma'am."

Trudi looks again at Leo. "Well then, go on young man."

She waves him off and looks at me. "You two have had this up your sleeves all along, haven't you?"

I give her an innocent look.

"Na ja, I suppose it will be good to see Heidi."

"Of course it will."

Thomas begins to stir.

"You will need to feed him again. I am going to get cleaned up a bit."

"Thank you, Aunt Trudi."

She gives me a look that hints at consternation over the plot she believes Leo and I have hatched. "I will bring you your breakfast when it's ready."

Chapter 20

I'm just beginning to settle back into a light sleep when there is a commotion downstairs, a bit of a clattering and some tear-filled laughter.

Heidi must have arrived.

"Mein Gott, how long has it been?"

"Two years, three months—"

"Na ja, water under the bridge."

"You look like you haven't slept in two days."

"I haven't."

Heidi tsks. "I brought breakfast. Why don't we sit down to eat and then I want you to go take a long nap."

"I was fixing breakfast when you arrived."

"All the better. With the slim pickings around these days, two breakfasts should almost feel like one."

Their voices disappear into the kitchen, and I can no longer hear the conversation. I settle back into my pillow, but within a few minutes there is a determined mounting of the stairs. The door swings open to reveal Trudi and Heidi, together at last.

"Hallo, Lani dear." Heidi comes to sit on the edge of the bed. "I could hardly believe it when Leo told me. An eager little fellow, isn't he?"

"A bit too eager, I'd say." Trudi exhales as if she'd given birth herself.

"Still a sourpuss, Waltraud?" Heidi lifts Thomas from my arms and gasps. "He's a big one, too."

I shrug. Trudi crows again from the doorway, "He's a big one all right. Over 4 kilograms."

"A survivor, I can see it already." Heidi inhales and makes a face. "Ach, you're going to have to clean him up now, Trudi dear."

"What about my nap?"

Heidi looks at Thomas with feigned reluctance. "Na ja, I suppose I could bathe him. Heaven knows he's going to need it now."

Monika arrives behind Trudi with a loaded tray of food. Anything looks like a delicacy after what I've been through.

"You left that poor boy alone downstairs?"

"Leopold said he already ate. He's in the backyard mucking the chicken coop."

Heidi smiles as Monika slides the tray onto my lap. "Go ahead and eat. I will get this fellow cleaned up and then you can nurse him. He'll go down for another nap, and we'll help you get out of those filthy rags. I'm sure you are quite uncomfortable."

She bundles Thomas in one arm and rises from the bed. "Trudi dear, why don't you go take that nap."

The two exit, and I'm alone with my sister.

"Well, go on. Eat!"

I pinch apart a bread roll.

"There's plum jam there. Heidi made it. It's delicious."

"Is there anything that woman can't do?"

"Some women are just like that."

"Well, I'll never be."

"Don't say that. You will be a fine Mama someday."

"Yes, well…" I press the soft bread into my mouth. I am certainly not ready to think about such things.

*****

Heidi swings into the room, clutching Thomas tight against her chest. "He is sparkling clean and smells wonderful," she announces. "I hardly want to give him back."

I give her a tired laugh. She lifts him carefully to her nose and inhales deeply. "Ach, this scent never gets old."

"I forgot how old your youngest is. I know Leo told me."

"Seven."

"That's right."

She approaches and lays Thomas against my chest. "I added lavender to the water. Once you put his mouth to your breast he is going to fall right asleep."

I inhale deeply. Yes, the scent of lavender clings to his skin and the linens she has swaddled him in. "It might put me to sleep too."

"You can't sleep too much in these first few months, I assure you of that."

I unbutton my gown and give him a breast. Heidi settles into the rocking chair.

"How did you do it with so many children? I can't imagine taking in multiple children who were not my own."

"One person has one gift, someone else has another."

"Your gift is caring for children."

Heidi smiles, a little laugh coursing through her. "Yes, and being able to function on three or four hours of sleep."

"From what I understand, that's why my mother stopped with me. She was desperate for a good night's sleep."

Heidi waves a hand. "I'll sleep when I'm dead."

We fall silent, with only Thomas's contented sucking and the ticking of the cuckoo clock downstairs livening the room.

If only I felt closer to this woman. I would gather my courage and ask her, if she truly feels that way, would she consider one more?

Leopold appears in the doorway. "Frau Schumacher is out like a light." He glances at me. "Monika too. I took the liberty of cleaning up from breakfast."

"*You* did the dishes?"

He laughs. "No. I ate the leftovers."

Heidi looks at me and gestures to Leopold. "Has a hollow leg, that one."

"Hey, I work hard."

"You certainly do."

As predicted, Thomas's head rolls back, a contented expression on his now-sleeping face.

"We'll sit a few more minutes and then you can move him to the cradle. Then I'll help you clean up," Heidi whispers. "Leopold, if there is any more work to be done—"

"I can ask Frau Schumacher—"

"Don't you dare wake that poor woman up."

He nods.

"Maybe you can find a book in the room next door." I glance around the room. "Thomas was a reader. Hans not so much."

He wanders off. I look again at Heidi. *Dear God, if this is meant to be, you're going to have to make it happen. I could never impose on this dear, dear woman.*

Chapter 21

Trudi sits in the rocker, observing me as I struggle to pull myself from the deepest sleep I've had in months. As I come to, my eyes immediately search the room for Thomas.

"He's fine, Lani dear. Heidi's got him."

"Ach." I pull myself into a sitting position. Trudi observes me with concern. If Thomas is fine, what could be wrong?

"I don't have to tell you, this won't be easy."

"What won't be easy?"

"Letting him go." She folds her lips into a line and stares out the window. "Things have been a little different because you're family. My nephew Ferdinand entrusted me with his little girl's heart." She shifts in the chair. Her posture becomes more official. "This will only get harder the longer you wait."

"I know." I run my fingers over the wrinkled sheet. "Where will he go?"

"You mustn't know that, dear."

"I was hoping maybe Heidi would take him."

Trudi holds up a hand. "Even if she were willing, I wouldn't be able to tell you that. It would make it harder on everyone involved."

My stomach seizes. Trudi senses my pain. "God's got this little one, Lani. Do you believe that?"

"Of course I do."

"No. I mean, do you *truly* believe that?"

I hesitate. *Do I?*

Trudi continues, "Wherever Thomas ends up, he'll be there because God has a purpose for him."

"I would trust Heidi with him."

Again Trudi silences me. "Do you trust me?"

I look sadly at the aging woman in the rocking chair. What makes me trust Heidi more than her—and more than God? A rush of resignation passes through me. "Yes."

"Good." Aunt Trudi rises from the rocker and calls for Heidi, who enters the room carrying Thomas. Leo follows and takes a place beside the bed, opposite his mother.

"We're going to take him for now, until he can be placed." For the last time, Heidi hands Thomas to me. Suddenly, I wish they *had* sent him away without giving me the chance to say goodbye. I can't bear to look into his baby-blue eyes, so I close mine and squeeze him to myself. A tear trickles into his soft brown hair. "Goodbye, Thomas. *Ich liebe dich.*"

A deep sigh shakes my body as I hand him back to Heidi. She departs. Leo gives me a half-smile.

"Will I see you again, Leo?"

"I guess it depends on when you plan to leave."

I look to Monika, who now stands in the door, twisting a dishtowel nervously in her hands. She shrugs. "I'm sure Mother and Father won't expect you until you're well enough to travel."

"I feel all right. I'd like to be home for Christmas."

"I nearly forgot," Trudi comments, offhand.

"Well, then"—Leo leans down and kisses the top of my head—"Merry Christmas, Lani Schumacher."

"Merry Christmas, Leopold Jodl."

He bows to Monika. Aunt Trudi follows him out of the room and sees him and his mother to the door. Monika approaches my bedside and whispers, "I hope you aren't going to regret letting that one slip through your fingers."

I shake my head. "I'm not ready, Monika."

"Well, I wouldn't wait too long. That boy is a treasure just waiting to be discovered."

With a deep breath, I make my confession. "I know. I wish we had met under different circumstances."

"I have seen the way he looks at you. Your circumstances don't seem to bother him one bit."

I turn my gaze out the window. I wish I could say the same.

*****

Monika and I enter our Mama's house on Christmas Eve. Father follows, carrying our luggage without a word of complaint. Soft music plays on the gramophone, and the scent of Stollen precedes Mother as she bustles out of the kitchen. "Oh my girls."

"Mama." My eyes fall on the sitting room as I open my arms to embrace her. The fireplace, where Gunter first greeted me after he and his brother returned from their battles in the Baltics. The sofa, where he and I sat to catch up and discovered that we were no longer content to stare into each other's eyes.

I press my face into Mama's shoulder and try to ignore the too-familiar ache that still arises in my heart when I think about living a life without the young man I always planned on marrying.

Mama releases me from her embrace just in time for us to catch a glimpse of Papa slipping a postcard into Monika's hands. She tucks the letter into her pocket and straightens her shoulders. "That bread smells wonderful, Mama. Is it ready?"

"It should be, Monika dear."

My sister darts into the kitchen. I open my mouth to speak, but Father silences me and extends an arm toward the kitchen.

Monika is already cutting into the powder-dusted loaf as I arrive. A twinkle lights her eyes and she is working hard to swallow the smile that tugs at her mouth. Again I open my mouth to speak but Papa silences me. I settle discontentedly down at the table, and Monika places an extra-large slice of Stollen in front of me. Mama pours me a cup of tea. It is obvious that the postcard is none of my business, so I content myself with the nearness of my family, the sweetness of the Stollen, and the tender sound of a choir singing *Stille Nacht, Heilige Nacht* on the gramophone.

My baby was certainly not born to save the world, but I believe God has a purpose for him as well. I was faithful to give him life. God will be faithful to show him the rest.

I pray he listens.

Epilogue

Bavaria
May 1939

Thomas Jodl

I arrive home only hours before the festival is supposed to begin. Tonight, there will be music and dancing and all the trappings of Bavarian tradition–then a few days at home with my family before I take up my new position in Berlin, where I will be driving for an officer who insists he needs *me*, specifically.

Two of the littlest boys leap onto me. One hugs my ankle, another hangs from my suspenders. Heidi–I've always just known her as Mama–snuggles a baby in her arms. "You are looking sharp, young man."

My cheeks flush.

"The girls won't know what to do with you in that uniform."

"I don't intend to wear the uniform, Mama."

"Don't you?"

I try to lift a leg but two-year-old Anton is still firmly attached to my ankle. "Do us a favor, will you?" With my eyes, I direct nine-year-old Johann to my ankle. He shakes his head and scoops up the toddler. I swing around and reach for the five-year-old who is determined to climb up my back. "Six boys, Mama. It's a lot."

Mama pats my cheek. "It's nothing."

Jakob wiggles out of my grip and scampers off into the backyard, chased by Adi and Friedrich.

"You are sure you'll be all right?"

"You've been offered an excellent opportunity. I'll never forgive you if you don't take it."

With the boys causing trouble in the backyard, Mama and I proceed into the house, to my old bedroom, where I throw open the doors to my wardrobe. "Oh no."

Mama chortles. "Is there a problem, Thomas?"

I pull out the leather shorts that used to fit me like a glove. "I can't wear these."

"And that is why I asked you if you intended to wear your uniform to the dance tonight."

"You know I can't dance in anything but *Plattlerhosen.*"

She bites her lip. "Yes, well, that seems to be a problem." She feigns disapproval as she estimates my height. "Two meters?"

"Not quite, 1.9."

"They're feeding you too much."

"I'm sorry." I chuckle and place the old Lederhosen back in the closet. Silence descends between us. We both know why I'm so darned tall. "What was he like, Mama?"

"What was who like, dear?"

"My biological father."

Mama sighs and takes a seat at the end of the bed. "You know the rules, Thomas dear."

"Yes, I do, and I'm an adult now. I'd like to know the truth."

"Young man, I don't even know the truth."

“Doch. You know something.”

She laughs and pats my hand. Her eyes are warm with love. “Well, I do know he was tall, if that is what you are asking.”

I stiffen my jaw and distract myself by examining the intricate embroidery on my Plattlerhosen.

Mama rests a hand on my knee. “I also know that I loved you so much, I couldn’t give you up, Thomas Augustin.” After a brief pause, she adds, “Besides, Leo would never have forgiven me.”

Leo was nineteen when I was born. I barely remember him. “Whatever happened to him?”

She folds her mouth into a line and shakes her head. “He spent a year or two in Lorraine before leaving for America, that is all I know. He would’ve stayed here forever, just like you, if I had not insisted he go.”

“Sounds familiar.”

“Well, what kind of mother would I be if I didn’t allow you boys to spread your wings and fly?”

I shake my head. “At least he’s safe in America. Everyone here is worried about war.”

Mama gives a rueful laugh. “We Germans weren’t born to ease, Thomas. On the contrary, I think we were born to trouble, so they say, as the sparks fly upward. War and adversity may be the thing you fly into—but it may also be what causes you to soar.”

I pat her knee and reach for the linen shirt that once belonged to Leo. “This isn’t going to fit either, Mama.”

She shakes her head. “Na ja. It has had a good life. Belonged to another Thomas before it belonged to Leo.”

"Did it now?"

"Yes, your namesake. Thomas Augustin Schumacher. A very fine dancer. Now"—she rises and pats my cheek—"Herr Schwarzmüller is about your height. He used to dance before his knee started giving him trouble. Perhaps he has something you can wear. The thought of you not being able to dance is bad enough. I would also hate for you to stand there looking so official when you are supposed to be enjoying yourself."

I follow her out of the bedroom and into the backyard. Johann and the older boys kick a football around. Anton sits in the yard stuffing dandelions and grass in his mouth.

"Anton!" Mama rushes to the toddler and shoots a death glare at my brother Freddi. "You were supposed to be watching him, Friedrich!"

"Eating grass hasn't killed him yet."

She scowls, hands Benni off to me, and lifts Anton from the grass.

"Are you sure you're going to be all right with me way up north, Mama?"

"I was doing just fine until you distracted me, Thomas. I'll be just fine once you leave."

I chuckle and shake my head. "So while adversity might cause me to soar, I'm also the dead weight that causes you to sink."

"I didn't say that."

"I'm afraid you did."

She gives me a look of admonishment. *"Na dann."* Balancing the two-year-old on her hip, she reaches for Benni again. "Get on your way to Herr Schwarzmüller's, or you'll never be ready for tonight's dance in time."

"Yes, ma'am." I turn to go.

"And Thomas?"

"Ja?"

"It is good to have you home."

Author's Note

I wrote *Born for Adversity* almost immediately after finishing my novel *Dearest Gunter,* and it is there that readers can discover the story of Lani and her lost love, Gunter Schrader. Knowing a little more about the history explored in *Dearest Gunter* will also shed light on the circumstances we find Lani in when we meet her in *Born for Adversity*.

Dearest Gunter begins in the summer of 1914, before the onset of the Great War. Gunter and his brothers are spending their summer holiday with their grandparents in Lothringen, on the border between Germany and France. Coupled with its adjacent province, Elsass, today we know this region as Alsace-Lorraine, and after changing hands four times in 80 years, it has remained French since 1945 (the end of the Second World War).

Lani herself is half French and half German, so she feels her divided loyalty intensely as the Great War drags on. She even goes so far as to spend some time living in her grandparents' home, which is farther into France, away from the border region. There, she meets a wounded soldier named François, who falls in love with her.

When the war is over, Elsass-Lothringen, including Lani's village, is reclaimed by France. For those who are unfamiliar with my writing, I write almost exclusively from the German perspective, and therefore, in the eyes of my characters, Lothringen is a German province that has come under French occupation.

Gunter Schrader represents many German men who returned from the First World War. Combat veterans of every age find it difficult to adjust to civilian life, but we don't often take into account the difference between returning to a victorious nation, and returning to one that has been defeated.

By late 1918, Europe was in the throes of an ideological battle between the democratic, capitalist West and the communist East. Germany was a hotbed for this political unrest. The wounds of the war had so seared the young men of Germany that they saw little else beyond another opportunity to fight. In their minds, they were protecting Germany's borders, which had already been compromised by Versailles.

Like so many other young men, Gunter was wounded both internally and externally. Lani hoped that by sleeping with him, he might be convinced to stay, but he was unwilling—or unable—to love her the way she needed.

For Lani, the choice became whether to endure the shame of remaining in her small village as her pregnancy became more obvious, escape to Bavaria to stay with her father's aunt, or terminate the pregnancy.

Abortions would become commonplace a few years later, in the unhinged culture of the Weimar Republic, but already in 1920 her communist-leaning suitor François insists she have it *taken care of.* Yet faithful Lani does not want to do the *easy* thing; she wants to do the *right* thing.

A word here is needed about my choice to write from a Catholic perspective instead of my own protestant, non-denominational background. The milieu of the story was best served by respecting the religious setting of both Lani's hometown and Bavaria. I myself have walked through the streets of Germany, observed the statues of saints on street corners, and visited the tiny village churches. I know that in

Germany, for many hundreds of years, you were Lutheran or Catholic, not due to your own choice, but your birthplace and your mother's religion.

Although I spent a few years attending a Catholic church as a teenager, it was a bit of a challenge to write within a religious framework I am not entirely accustomed to. I actually enjoyed getting to know the process of confession and see its value, specifically in the area of accountability, which is an area in which modern evangelicals are often lacking. I also tried to portray the priests fairly—one as cold as stone, the other fatherly and comforting.

Readers have Hannah Hood Lucero to thank for the fact that I did not completely close the door on Lani's future with Leopold Jodl. I liked him too, but because this novella directly relates to my Separate Ways Series, I had to work within the constructs of what I have planned. However, Hannah is right— there is a potential love story there that I could not let go of.

The Separate Ways Series is also the reason I opted to include an epilogue from Thomas's perspective, 19 years later, when he is a young adult. He will become important in other books, not the least of which is my novella *Schneewittchen,* which is available in the collection A Worthy Love from Beyond the Bookery.

It has been a joy working with Hannah, Jennifer Q. Hunt, our editor Sarah Everest, cover designer Kelsey Gietl, Samantha Fury who worked wonders on the formatting, and Sarah Hanks who initiated and planned this project! I also want to thank all the members of Brave Authors, Christian Mommy Writers, Optimistic Writers, Joy CC, and FGAS—

especially our Bavarian Dancers, who get an enthusiastic nod in this story.

I would also like to thank my husband Brian and our three children, my extended family and friends, and most of all, my Lord Jesus Christ.

Other Books

OTHER BOOKS FROM BRAVE AUTHOR BOOKS
Every Captive Freed
Every Voice Heard

OTHER BOOKS BY JENNIFER Q. HUNT
Wisteria House Series
Song and Sorrow Series

OTHER BOOKS BY HANNAH HOOD LUCERO
Sons of Vigilance Series
The Glory of Light

OTHER BOOKS BY AUBREY REISS TAYLOR
Dearest Gunter
Gott Mit Uns Series